SEASON OF THE WITCH

BOOKS BY CHRISTOPHER KNIGHT

ST. HELENA
FEROCITY
THE LAURENTIAN CHANNEL
BESTSELLER
SEASON OF THE WITCH

Season of the Witch

Christopher Knight

AudioCraft Publishing, Inc.

Topinabee Island, MI

SOME THANKS

Diane Gurnee, Sheri Kelley, Jevona Livingston,
Cindee Rocheleau-your help is necessary and appreciated.

The gang at *Foggy's,* Christmas, Michigan.

And my wife. I'm your biggest fan.

-Christopher Knight
June 2003

MISSED
APPOINTMENT

ONE

D eath, in a shockingly literal sense, paid me a visit on a warm, sunny, July afternoon.

I was in the living room working on my old Pioneer cassette player. The unit had been acting up and recording over my precious collection of tapes that I'd assembled since high school. Fleetwood Mac, Boston, The Cars, Journey, Styx, The Allman Brothers, The Eagles, Lynyrd Skynyrd, and everything in between. The good stuff. Of course, tapes are nearly a thing of the past these days, with newer technology in compact discs, MP3's and the like, but I don't feel the need to replace my favorite tapes with more modern media of the day. Not yet, anyway. A cassette tape in your hand just *feels* good. Solid. CDs? Sure, they *sound* good. But they're just too damned *dainty*. Drop'em on the ground and a single grain of sand will do them in. Cassettes, on the other hand, are tougher. Bruce Springsteen's *Darkness on the Edge of Town* bounced around under the front seat of my Chevy Impala for months during my senior year in high school, getting stepped on and muddied and beat up. Twenty years later Bruce still sounds great. A little bit of tape hiss, but all in all, the Boss is still kicking butt.

So when my cassette player began spontaneously *recording* over my precious tapes instead of *playing* them, you can imagine my distress.

My wife Joyce had taken our two children, Justin, who turned eight last week, and Molly, who is ten, to swimming lessons at the state park. I decided to use the time to try and fix the old Pioneer.

I don't have much of a workshop (read: *any workshop*) so when something around the house needs a little TLC, it's easy enough to spread things out in the living room and give'er the old best shot.

The back and top of the unit came off with a few twists of a screwdriver. I put in a blank tape and hit the play button, watching the wheels turn through the plastic window. Everything seemed fine.

I stopped the tape, flipped it over, pressed play again. Stopped it once more, turned it back over, and pressed play once again, watching to see if both the record head and the playback head were activated. The little wagon-like wheels turned, but I couldn't tell if it was recording or playing. The prospect of a new unit loomed.

There was a knock on the door, a heavy, solid rapping, and I wondered who it might be. Certainly not a neighbor; hell, they'd just poke their head in the door and yell. A salesman? No, we don't get any of those here. Not in Courville, Michigan, anyway. There'd be slim pickings for any traveling salesman in Courville. And it wasn't Saturday, so that nixed the Jehovah's Witnesses, who were about due. A couple of houses down lives a crotchety old woman by the name of Eleanor Finch who used to stop by and hand out Bible tracts, but I think I scared her off a few months ago. I still see her once in a while, hobbling up the street and pestering the kids, but, for the most part, she's harmless, and she hasn't been knocking lately.

I stood up, walked to the door, and opened it. People in Courville, myself included, don't peer around a curtain to see who's knocking. That's for city people who have good reason to wonder just who is coming to their home and why. Here in Courville, when someone knocks on your door, no matter how rare it may be, you just get yourself up off the couch and greet whoever it is.

Which makes me wonder: would things have been different had I not opened the door?

Perhaps.

But I doubt it. I've since learned that when Death pays you a visit, he means business.

TWO

He stood on the porch, arms at his sides, dressed entirely in black. I swear to God he looked like something out of the movies, and I couldn't help but wonder if he was some special agent working for the CIA or FBI or something. Perhaps he was an actor. Or one of Satan's own henchmen. I had no idea how close I had come with the latter guess.

He wore a black hat, dark sunglasses that concealed his eyes, and a suit that was stolen from night itself. Dark shoes gleamed like obsidian glass. The visible skin of his face and hands was a jaundiced, yellow-brown, with a chrome-like glaze, almost silvery, perfectly smooth and completely unblemished: a thin laminate of skin over bone. The man appeared to be in his forties, but I couldn't be sure.

And that *smile*.

His teeth were perfect and he had the steely grin of a snake. It reminded me instantly of my son's favorite Christmas cartoon: Dr. Suess's *How the Grinch Stole Christmas*. The part when Grinch gets that really shitty smirk as he hatches his plan to screw with the Whos' holiday.

You're a mean one . . . .

There was a distinct odor about him, too, although this wasn't something I was conscious of at the time. It was the stench of burnt almonds, all smelly and dry and noxious. This was something I would notice later, during our next meeting.

He took a quick breath and nodded slightly. He paused for only a moment, and then an engaged, fatherly look came over his face, like a TV newscaster that was just about to say something that, he would tell you, was of great importance to us all. I see that Stone guy (I can never remember his last name) do that right before he begins talking.

And then he spoke. His voice was polished and satiny-smooth, and his television-perfect teeth flashed.

"Mr. Ryker."

He spoke my name without question, as if we were old friends that hadn't seen one another in a long time. He knew who I was, for sure. I, however, was certain that I had *never* seen him before in my life.

"Yes," I replied, a bit surprised at how the word came out. There was no question in my voice, but rather a subtle commitment, as if to say, *yes, it's me, you've got me. Shucks.*

And then I *did* wonder if he was some sort of special agent, or someone from the IRS conducting a surprise on-the-spot audit. I don't know if they even do those kinds of things or not, but I shot a nervous glance behind him, anyway. I saw no car in the drive or in the street. No suspicious looking black sedan that would have given him away.

"We have some business to discuss," the dark man said icily. I tried to see behind his glasses, but it was impossible to read his eyes beyond those black lenses.

Without extending a hand in greeting, without introducing himself, without even *asking* . . . the man took a step toward me and allowed himself into my house. I have a vague memory of actually letting him by, allowing him, a *stranger,* to come walking into our home without invitation. Maybe I stepped aside, I don't know. What I *do* know is that he strode straight into the living room, turned, and sat down in the brown leather La-Z-Boy that Joyce gave me for Father's Day several years ago. He slapped his palms on the armrests as the chair enveloped around him.

"Sit, Mr. Ryker, sit," he said, gesturing with a casual wave of his hand. "We have much to discuss, my boy. I'm here to see you about your illegal cable hook-up." All the while, his perfect white teeth glistened back at me with that reptilian smile.

"Illegal cable hook-up?!?!" I protested in confusion. *"We don't have an illegal cable hook-up!"*

At this, the dark man threw back his head and roared with arrogant laughter.

"Quite right, Mr. Ryker," he said, tipping his head forward and adjusting his hat. His smile gleamed. "Your cable television is perfectly legitimate." He tipped his head forward and, although all I could see when I looked at him was my own reflection in those cold, dark lenses, I knew he was looking right at me. "Your bill is forty-one dollars and thirty-six cents a month, consistently, and the last time you were late was last November . . . when you were on vacation."

My brain went into rewind, and there was a moment of suspended animation when I realized—

Holy shit. He was right. I had spaced-out that bill before we left for vacation, and I received an overdue notice by the time we got back.

"And you did, however, *have* illegal cable at your apartment on Maple Street in Mt. Pleasant when you were in college," the man said, nodding curtly. He looked up, appearing to be deep in thought. "Your friend Jerry Simmons did the handiwork, if I am not mistaken." Then he lowered his gaze and looked directly into my eyes. "And Mr. Ryker, I assure you: I am *never* mistaken."

Who in the hell is this guy?

"Who . . . who are you?" I demanded, still amazed that I had just allowed a complete stranger to walk into my house and make himself at home. I didn't care how or why he had information regarding my cable bill. Lots of people probably have access to that kind of information, I suppose. How he knew about the free cable at the old place on Maple Street—now *that* was strange. Nevertheless, now I was getting annoyed.

Sensing my anger, the dark man leaned forward on the chair and spoke. His voice was calm, but cold and commanding.

"I apologize," he said. "Sometimes I get so busy that I act a bit hastily. My job, however, does get a bit mundane at times, Mr. Ryker." He rose to his feet. "Please excuse my sudden intrusion. I have come to make arrangements for your . . . *departure* . . . into the next world."

THREE

He extended his hand and I took it in slow-motion, a zombie performing a menial task. His palm was hot and greasy, like a slab of steak just removed from the oven. When grips released, I had to fight off the urge to wipe my hand on my pants.

His grin never wavered, never changed one hundredth of an inch, as he removed his dark glasses, revealing two empty sockets. His eyes—or, where his eyes *should* have been—were nothing but cavernous holes. Grotesque, keloid scars—torn portions of pinkish-red flesh—bubbled beneath his brow and above his high, arched cheekbones. I blanched and the gorge rose in my throat. It felt as if I was about to throw up or faint, but I couldn't look away from the hideous sight. His eye sockets had the appearance of being carved out by an animal or hollowed by a razor-sharp ice-cream scoop. For a few moments I stood frozen in horror, unable to speak or even move. Then my natural reflexes returned and I recoiled, quickly withdrawing my hand from his.

"Sorry," the dark man apologized. He shrugged. "That gets everyone the first time. You'll get used to it." He returned his glasses to his face.

My heart pounded like thunder and I backed away, trying to distance myself from this apparition from hell. Somehow, a supernatural door had opened, a spectral veil had lifted, blurring the line between fantasy and reality.

"Who *are* you?" I gasped. My mouth was dry, and I swallowed hard.

At this, the man returned to the chair. His smile regressed to a knowing smirk, and he nodded. "My name," he said calmly, "is Rimmon Diabolus. I am an angel of death."

FOUR

My emotional state swayed, darting from one end of the scale to the other. The unfolding episode seemed both surreal and seriocomic. One moment I was scared shitless; the next moment I was laughing inside. I went to college with a guy who was always joking around, donning stupid costumes and fake scars to garner a few laughs. It worked; we all gave him the attention he so desperately craved. I kept waiting for the dark man before me to shed his costume, tear off his gruesome mask, and resume the role of one of my old school buddies.

Ha! Fooled ya, pal! Hey . . . got any beer?

But I somehow knew *that* wasn't going to happen. Not this time. The man that entered my living room wasn't playing a prank. Somehow I knew that the dark figure in my living room was the Real McCoy. With this startling realization, a roaring sound filled my ears. My heart thumped harder and faster, my mouth went dry again, and the urge to run seized me, but the tide of terror was too strong, and I couldn't escape from its grasp.

"Don't be alarmed," the man said smoothly, and suddenly a clipboard appeared in his hand. The item emerged from nowhere: he hadn't had it when he walked into the house, and it certainly wasn't a clipboard that I had left laying around. Nevertheless, Rimmon Diabolus was now holding a clipboard, looking very official, like a doctor making his rounds at a hospital.

"This is how it is," he continued plainly. "How it *always* has been, and how it always *will* be."

Run. Just turn around, and run out of the house. The guy is a freak. He's a nutcase, and I need to get out of here and call the cops.

"There's nowhere to run, I'm afraid."

Mr. Creepshow wasn't smiling anymore.

"Oh, yes, I know what you're thinking," he continued. "I can *hear* you think, Mr. Ryker. But as I mentioned, there is no need to be alarmed. I'm not here to hurt you, and in a few minutes, I'll be on my way. I'm a very busy man, as you must know."

I eased up, but not much. Surely, if he wanted to hurt me (or worse) he could have done so by now.

"What . . . what do you want?" I asked. My words were jerky, awkward.

"I am here to make arrangements for your departure into the hereafter, Mr. Ryker. It will only take a few minutes of your time, and then I will be on my way."

His words were driving me crazy. Here he was, talking about my death like he was setting a tee-time at the local golf course.

"Hereafter?" I echoed, not without more than a hint of confused disbelief.

The dark man nodded. "Precisely," he said, glancing down at his clipboard. "Marcus R. Ryker, 2242 Johnson Court, Courville, Michigan."

The supernatural door opened wider. I could almost hear the hinges creak as reality slipped further and further away.

He tapped the clipboard, which now rested on his knee, then he looked up. I'll never forget the expression on his face or the tone of his voice. The man had no eyes, but there was something behind those dark glasses that was burning.

He continued speaking, those empty sockets boring into my skull, and his voice chilled me to the marrow.

"Mr. Ryker, you are scheduled to depart—to leave this world—two weeks from now, on July 17th, at exactly five fourteen in the afternoon. I am here to make a few arrangements to prepare for your departure."

FIVE

My face flushed and my skin tightened. My whole body went rigid, and my head felt suddenly hot and feverish. I blinked uncontrollably as his words ricocheted inside my head.

Mr. Ryker, you are scheduled to depart two weeks from now.

No.

Mr. Ryker, you are scheduled to depart two weeks from now.

No!

I am here to make a few arrangements to prepare for your departure.

Insane. I had gone completely mad. The days of my recreational college experimentation had finally caught up with me, and the neurons in my brain had, indeed, fused together. I'd had a bad experience with hallucinogenic mushrooms when I was twenty; for years I waited for a recurring flashback—and here it was. I closed my eyes.

Okay. It's okay. It's just a flashback. Or a nightmare. Or something. I'm going to wake up. I'm going to wake up. I'm going to—

I opened my eyes, only to find *him* still sitting there in front of me.

The dark man studied my face. He shook his head.

And that goddamn smile of his. Shit. Stop it. Stop smiling like that. Like you own the fucking planet.

"No, Mr. Ryker," he said, as his head rotated from side to side. "You are not going mad, nor are you having a nightmare or a flashback. Psilocybin mushrooms won't do that for you, although the toxic high is quite . . . unearthly. And I'm sorry you don't appreciate my—*features*. But, I assure you, I am not here to hurt you. I don't own the 'fucking planet'. I simply want to—"

"What do you mean I'm scheduled to . . . to—"

"Pass on," he said, nodding like a real estate agent telling me that *of course the septic works well, and the roof was repaired several years ago. Of course everything is in order, Mr. Ryker. Sign here.*

Mr. Creepshow continued. "Give up the ghost," he said. "Kick the bucket. Croak." He leaned forward a bit, cocked his head, adjusted his hat again, and said in what could only be his best Robert DeNiro: *"Swimmin' wid da fishes."* He sniggered and tilted his head back. "And my all-time favorite? *Bite the Big One.*" He let out with a chuckle and shook his head. "I'm not sure where *that* one came from, but I do find it so *very* entertaining, don't you, Mr. Ryker?"

With his right hand he tapped his fingertips on the clipboard, rolling them like a drum cadence.

Brrrrrump. Brrrrump. Brrrrrrump-bum-bump.

The sound drilled at my temples, driving me mad with its tortuous repetition.

Brrrrrump. Brrrrump. Brrrrrrump-bum-bump.

"Mr. Ryker?"

I think it was at this moment that my own mortality must have kicked me in the face. I no longer believed that this was some sort of prank, some stupid joke that one of my friends was playing on me. It was real. It was *real,* and it was *now,* and it was happening in my very own living room. That much was certain.

Death himself had called on Marcus Ryker.

Me.

I was shitting bricks, churning out those eight-inchers like a cement machine gun. Horror exploded within every cell in my body. All control of my body fled, and I felt like nothing more than a puppet in a suit of cold flesh. My shoulders were as heavy as granite, my arms like lead. A muscle in my jaw twitched, and the more I tried to make it stop, the more it quivered. All the while, Rimmon Diabolus—the dark man—watched.

And then, in the split of an instant, it was all gone.

All of it.

All of the terror, all of the confusions, all of the sorrow and the strangeness of it all. I felt a cogent resignation, like I knew that there was nothing I could do, that I wasn't going to get out of this one. That it wouldn't be as bad as I had expected.

Suddenly, it all made sense. Somehow, everything seemed to fit *perfectly.* It was like straining to remember something from long ago, having it on the tip of your tongue, and then: *whamo!* There it was.

Of course. I'll be dying in a few days, and Death was kind enough to send a welcome wagon. How thoughtful.

And he could read my thoughts. I knew it now. He'd already picked up on more than a few of my unspoken words, yet, I was certain, I hadn't uttered them.

He could read my mind. He knew what I was thinking.

"Yes, I can," the dark man said, nodding. "You need to understand, Mr. Ryker, that I am not here to harm you. I hope you have concluded that by now."

Holy shit.

"Oh, there's nothing holy about shit, nothing holy about it at all," he replied in response to my thought. "You're one of the skeptical ones. The analytical ones. I imagine I'll have to explain all of this to you."

And with that, Rimmon Diabolus explained the hows and whys of what would be happening to me in the very near future.

A future that was closer than I'd ever imagined.

SIX

W hen it is time for an earthly one's transfer, someone such as myself is disbursed."

The dark man spoke with a calm easy intonation, like he was explaining the details of an auto loan to someone who didn't understand how interest was compounded. And there was a certain matter-of-fact-ness to his voice, too, despite the rather bleak circumstances.

"You see, Mr. Ryker, death is not something that people are comfortable discussing. Oh, wills are drawn up and minimal plans are made for one's passing, but the real details—the real 'nitty gritty,' as you like to call it in this realm—are things that most are uncertain about. Are you uncertain about where *you* will go when you die, Mr. Ryker?"

I had a sudden recollection of a preacher that I'd encountered years ago, as a boy. The preacher had been wielding some heavy evangelizing beneath a tent at the Courville fair. I watched from the cotton candy stand as he went on about Jesus coming back, maybe tonight, maybe *this minute,* and that we all needed to repent or burn in hell forever. As an eight-year-old boy, this wasn't something that I understood fully.

Later that day, as I was leaving the fair, I just about walked into the preacher as I came around the corner of a big red and white tent. I'll never forget those burning, feverish eyes and the way his puffy jowls shook as he spoke to me.

"Boy," he said, pointing a chubby finger at me. *"Boy, are you eternally secure?"*

I have to admit, I was a bit frightened by his overwhelming presence. I had no idea what 'eternally secure' meant, so I just nodded.

"Are you sure, boy?" he pried.

I nodded again, and took a step backward. Immediately, his disposition changed. A smile grew, and perhaps he had realized that he had inadvertently frightened me.

"How do you know, my young friend?" he asked pleasantly.

I had no answer to a question I didn't understand.

Suddenly, the man reached into his powder-blue suit and brandished a small black Bible, just larger than a pack of cigarettes. He handed it to me, and I took it.

"There's your answer, young man," he said quietly and with a confident nod. *"Everything you need to know about anything is in that book. You may keep it."*

I edged away, and without another word, the preacher turned and walked off.

I looked at the book in my hand. *HOLY BIBLE* was embossed in gold on the front cover. *KJV* was inscribed at the bottom. I figured that *KJV* was probably the initials of the preacher, or maybe the guy who wrote the book.

Years later, I came across that Bible when Joyce and I were going through items to sell in a garage sale. At first, I put the book with other things to sell. Then, after a moment, I picked up the bible and put it in a box to save. I don't know why, for sure. I know it's silly, but I think I felt a tinge of fear at the thought of losing that book. I had never given it more than a casual reading, and my knowledge of spiritual matters was a bit limited. Perhaps I felt, somehow, that if I lost that book, something would happen to me. Something *bad*.

Two weeks ago, that Bible had been in a box of books that Joyce dropped off at the Cheboygan Salvation Army. Had I known it was in that box, I would have taken it out. My superstitious side felt a stab of trepidation, but I quickly shrugged it off. The Bible was gone, and nothing more could be done about it.

Now, Death was in my living room, staring me in the face, telling me how things really operate. I couldn't help but wonder if it had anything to do with the discarded Bible.

And I had no answer to Diabolus's question. I had no idea where I would go when I die. Heaven, perhaps. But there had always been a sneaking suspicion that when the ride was over, the carnival was closed, folks—and I would be placed in the ground to rot and fertilize the earth. When the wheel stopped turning, the show had ended. Time to go home, everybody.

Now, of course, it appeared that I was about to learn differently.

"I . . . I don't know," I finally stammered, answering the dark man's question.

"Ah."

He sighed, folded his hands, and placed them on his knee. It reminded me of my college dean when he had warned me that I'd better get my grades up, or else.

"I hear that a lot," he said. "Many people that were so sure at one time take one look at me and their years of certainty go out the window. I've even had people try to bribe me, of all things. Can you believe that, Mr. Ryker?"

I shook my head in disbelief. Not because I found it incredible that someone would try and pay off Death, but because I still couldn't believe I was sitting here having this conversation.

The dark man shook his head. "I suppose it *is* quite a shock to most when they find out that their existence here in this world is coming to an end. Yourself included. I can tell that you, Mr. Ryker, are still a bit confused. Nonetheless, I think I can shed a little light on the subject.

"The ending of life on this earth could be very bewildering. Were it not for someone like myself, most people would be terrified during the moments after their death. As you will find, Mr. Ryker, the transitional process will not be a fearful one.

"You see, no one ever truly *dies,* Mr. Ryker. No one. You are simply relocated to another place. In the moments after your death, you will be conscious and aware of your surroundings." He spread his arms out slowly, his hands palms up. "You will be able to look around, to hear and see things . . . even your own self. It is, as some have written, an 'out of body' experience."

When he said those words, an arsenal of book titles skipped across my mind. Joyce has several books on the subject of near-death experiences, and, although I'm a bit skeptical regarding the matter, I found one of the books quite fascinating. A bit far-fetched, yes, but fascinating. Now I realized that the books were probably more truthful than I had imagined.

"Which is," the dark man continued, "where I come in. In the moments following your earthly demise, I will be a recognizable face to you. I will be there to assist you on your journey. No, not a tour guide, but more of a . . . *valet.* A mere shuttle from this world to the next."

"Where am I going?" I asked in a trembling whisper.

The man smiled widely and shook his head. The movement was robotic, and it reminded me of the way a yellow jacket or a praying mantis swivelled its head from side to side in precise, automatic rotation.

"Can't tell you," the dark man said, showing his yellowed palms. "Can't tell you. I would if I knew myself, but I don't. It's not for me to decide. As I said . . . I am merely there to assist in your transition."

"Well, then . . . just who decides?"

He raised his hands in another gesture of supplication. "Another one I can't answer. I would if I could, but I can't."

I suddenly felt very foolish, like this whole thing really *was* a prank, after all. And, had circumstances been a bit different, I would have probably stood up and looked for a hidden camera somewhere in the wall. I would have been certain that someone was filming this for one of those television gag shows. This would have been a good one, and I'm sure that a lot of people would have had a pretty good laugh.

But the man sitting in my living room wasn't some made-up actor. He was real, and he was alive . . . sort of.

And so I asked the question that had been burning beneath my skin. I wasn't really aware of it, but it was there, all right, simmering just below the surface.

"Just how am I going to die?"

"Ah, the question everyone gets to sooner or later," the dark man said.

I nodded, and unconsciously allowed my jaw to slack. My mouth hung open.

"Nothing glamorous, I'm afraid." Diabolus said. He consulted the clipboard on his knee. "A simple car crash. I wish I could tell you that you were going to die doing something heroic like saving children from a burning building. Or perhaps trying to help land a crippled airplane. But if it is any comfort, you won't feel a thing. Sometimes, people die horrible deaths. You should feel fortunate that you're not going to die by fire. I've seen a few of those. Or the way some of those folks were killed in the lake last summer."

God . . . last year *had* been awful. Courville is a small town on Mullett Lake, in northern lower Michigan. Last summer an enormous muskellunge—over twelve feet long with razor-sharp teeth—had killed several people. The damned thing was big enough to eat people . . . and it did, too, shredding flesh, crushing bones and bloodying the waters of Mullett Lake until the beast was finally caught and killed.

The dark man shook his head. "Painful for *me* to watch, and I've seen it all. Chewed by a fish. Ugghh. In fact—"

"A car crash?" I asked, interrupting.

Holy shit, I thought. *I just interrupted Death while he was speaking to me.*

"Yes," he nodded. "Nothing big. Happens every day." Again, he surveyed his clipboard, only this time he ran a bony, yellow finger down what appeared to be a piece of paper. I couldn't tell what was written on it, and when I leaned closer to get a look, he tilted it away.

"Here we are," he continued. "Marcus R. Ryker, 2242 Johnson Court. Courville, Michigan. You're scheduled for an accident at the corner of M-33 and US-27 at . . . " He stopped speaking as he surveyed the clipboard. "Ah. Yes. Five fourteen in the afternoon. Friday, the seventeenth of July. A semi truck is going to lose control. You'll be at the intersection, and the truck will broadside you. You won't feel a thing, and from what I can gather here," he tapped his fingers on the clipboard, "is that you'll be looking the other way and not even know what hit you. All in all, a rather simple way to go. A bit messy, certainly. But simple."

"But I can't . . . I mean, I *won't*—"

He raised one hand and I stopped speaking

immediately. I was amazed at how much control he had over me.

"Mr. Ryker, I have been through this millions of times, and that's not an exaggeration. Naturally, you have many questions, but I am afraid I can't answer all of them. Even if I could, I don't have the time. Matter of fact, I'm running a bit behind as it is. There is a gentleman across town that I need to see about a heart attack."

He stood up, smiled that perfect game-show-host smile, and extended his hand. "And that, I'm afraid, is about all I can tell you. I will see you again immediately after your death, and I will accompany you for a brief period of time until you are to depart to places unknown."

I took his hand absently. It was waxy and warm, like a greasy candle.

Suddenly, his smile faded, and his hand gripped tighter. His skin felt hot, almost burning. I tried to pull away, but his grip grew firmer and his skin grew hotter. His head nodded forward.

"I know what you're thinking, and I must impress upon you: it won't work. I want you to listen to me carefully, Mr. Ryker."

At this, he reached up with his free hand and pulled away his dark sunglasses. I cringed once again at the sight of those horrific, empty sockets and the bubbled, crumpled flesh that surrounded them. With his glasses on, he could have been a movie star. A slightly *discolored* movie star, yes. But he could have passed for a *human,* anyway.

But with his glasses off, it was easy to see exactly what he was ... and, once again, I had no doubt that I was staring Death square in the face.

"No one," he continued in a serious tone, "ever, *ever* cheats death, Mr. Ryker. *No one.*"

"But if I know where and when I'm going to die, I can

avoid it by not being there. I just won't show up, now that I know."

"You *won't* know, Mr. Ryker. I can assure you of that." He returned his sunglasses to his face. "When I leave here in a few moments, you will have no recollection of our conversation. Not at all. Your life—and death—will continue along, just as planned, and you will have no memory whatsoever of our meeting."

Bullshit.

"No, it's not 'bullshit' Mr. Ryker," he said coldly, responding to my thoughts, "no matter what you think. No one—not you, not *anyone*—ever cheats death."

And with that, the dark man released his grip, turned, and strode across the living room. He opened the door, then turned back to me. His leering smile returned, and he reached up and tipped his hat.

"Do have a good day, Mr. Ryker."

Death stepped onto the porch and closed the door behind him.

SEVEN

I didn't have much luck with the cassette player. Joyce came home with the kids a little earlier than expected, and I bagged the project until later. The lawn needed to be mowed, and that was something that I'd told her I'd have done before dark. I'd also promised her that I would replace the tail light in her Caravan; it had burned out a couple of days ago.

I put the disassembled unit in a box, placed it in the garage, and vowed to give it one more shot in a few days.

On Thursday morning, July 16th, I made one final attempt at fixing the old Pioneer cassette deck before heading off to work.

In the garage. Both of the cars were parked, my silver Buick Regal and Joyce's green Dodge Caravan, and they took up the majority of the space. I removed the dismantled Pioneer and its parts from the cardboard box, along with several cassettes, and placed them carefully on the cement floor next to the Regal.

I plugged the unit into an orange extension cord and turned the power on, ignoring the small warning on the back of the unit. A cassette was loaded. I pressed the *rewind* button and the little wheels blurred.

When the tape was completely rewound I pressed play, once again trying to see if both the record head and the playback head had been activated.

I had just turned the unit on its side when I heard a noise. Something coming from the speaker.

Well, at least it's not recording this time, I thought in disgust, wondering how many tapes had been ruined. I turned the volume up a notch.

Rap rap rap.

Knocking. Then: shuffling noises.

I turned up the volume further and listened to the muffled sounds that simmered from the speakers. I could hear tape hiss, and the sound of someone moving away, then a door opening.

Then—

A voice. A man spoke my name.

For the next five minutes I sat on the garage floor, spellbound, listening in disbelief to a conversation I never had, with someone I had never met before.

Impossible.

No. It *was* possible. Had to be possible. The voice on the tape was mine . . . *but who did the other voice belong to?*

When the conversation on the tape ended, I immediately rewound the tape and played it again. And again. And again. For the next hour I sat there, robotically playing the tape over and over again. Listen, rewind, play, listen, rewind, play. The thought never occurred to me that at any moment, the tape player could malfunction and record over the tape. Regardless, it worked fine.

But the more I listened to this macabre conversation, the more I began to recall things. I could actually *see* the man speaking. I could see him in my head, could see what he was wearing. My memory was hazy, but there was something there, all right.

And a *smell.* The man had a foul, mephitic odor that reeked of burnt almonds, I was sure. Even as I sat in the garage, the repulsive smell licked at my nostrils.

Had this really happened? Had Death really paid a visit to my home? And was it possible that my memory had been erased so that I would have no recollection of the event? If so, then at least *that* part of the conversation was true. I certainly had no memory of the episode.

At least not until I heard the tape.

That's what happened, I thought, trying to weave together the impossible, the improbable, and the actual. *When I had been trying to fix the cassette unit a couple of weeks ago, the span of time had been recorded on tape.*

Listen, rewind, play. Listen, rewind, play. I was completely engrossed in this strange banter between myself and some strange being that claimed to be an Angel of Death.

And his *voice.*

He spoke smoothly with perfect intonation, his tone hypnotic and mesmerizing.

Five fourteen in the afternoon. Friday, the seventeenth of July. A semi truck is going to lose control. You'll be in the intersection, and the truck will broadside you. All in all, a rather simple way to go. A bit messy, certainly. But simple.

Jesus, I thought. *This can't be real. This can't be—*

The door to the house suddenly exploded open, startling me. I quickly stopped the tape and turned. Molly stood on the step, one hand on the doorknob, the other on her hip, her face imbued with youthful defiance.

"Daddy, Justin keeps stomping on my Barbie!"

"Am not!" Justin called from somewhere in the house.

"Are too!" Molly shot back with a snap of her head.

"Justin," I called out. I tried to speak sternly, but the

best I could do was just kind of an absent, lost tone. "Leave your sister alone."

Satisfied, Molly turned, sauntered back into the house, and closed the door behind her.

Listen, rewind, play. Listen, rewind, play. Listen, rewind, play.

Holy shit.

Listen, rewind, play. Listen, rewind, play. A cloak of terror wrapped around my body. My skin tingled, and my muscles tensed. And—

I remembered our meeting.

I could see him now, his dark suit and his dark hat. Dark sunglasses that hid empty sockets and torn, scarred flesh. An Angel of Death had indeed paid me a visit. And, according to our conversation on the tape, we would be meeting again.

Five fourteen in the afternoon. Friday, the seventeenth of July.

Tomorrow.

My death was scheduled for tomorrow.

EIGHT

Your own death haunts you from the moment you begin to conclude that, by golly, *the world doesn't revolve around me, after all.* I think for most people this begins somewhere during childhood, before the age of ten. But then come the teen years, and sometimes up into the twenties, where death is rarely thought of. Mortality is something that is kind of swept beneath the rug. Life is limitless, and we're all bullet-proof. Have another drink, and all that.

Soon, however, you begin to realize the seriousness of the matter. Death is simply unavoidable and non-negotiable. You can't buy more time. When your number is up, it's time to go.

It's so goddamned . . . *final.*

And for all of the plastic surgery and facial creams and youth elixirs sold on the market, there's still that one appointment that we all have to face. In the end, it doesn't matter how youthful you looked or whether your hair fell out or what. If you're lucky, you are granted the *benefit* of earning a long life, the *honor* of gray hair and wrinkled skin and aching joints and bones. The *privilege* of seeing your own children—and their children—and knowing that, yes, indeed, that appointment is drawing nearer and nearer . . . but you were able to leave a little something of yourself behind, and know that, in a small way, perhaps you were able to contribute a little something to the goodness of humanity.

Often—far too often—the appointment comes too soon. Or, far sooner than expected, anyway. For over a year now a serial killer has been on the loose in Michigan, killing victims by slicing their skin into tiny strips, then decapitating the corpse and depositing the head in the toilet in some kind of sadistic symbolism. The killer has struck over and over again throughout the state, leaving notes, taunting the police. Each victim was still alive as the killer slowly ran a razor up and down, always longways in thin striations over their bodies, spoiling the skin with narrow, bloody bands. The pain the victim felt must have been unimaginable. The unfortunate prey finally succumbed to unconsciousness either from the intense pain or loss of blood.

Although I didn't feel their pain, I certainly could sympathize with the innocent victims, knowing that it was a definite matter of time—moments, perhaps, in their case—that death would come. When that first slice pierced the skin, they had to *know*. They knew that Death was on his way.

Or perhaps a fair warning is given, like the heads up you get when the doctor walks in with a grim face and tells you that it's cancer, and it's terminal. Get your shit in order now, pal. You've got an appointment to keep.

And, according to the man that visited me on that hot afternoon, my appointment was just over twenty-four hours away.

Work was a blur. I didn't have any sales calls to make that day, which was a good thing, because I couldn't focus on anything . . . except the atrocity of what was to come. I tried to immerse myself in paperwork, but every few seconds, the haunting voice of the dark man echoed through my head.

No one ever, ever cheats death, Mr. Ryker.

No one?

No one.

I can, and I will.

No one.

I will. Now that I knew where my death was supposedly going to take place, I wasn't going to show up there. I wouldn't be on the highway when the semi truck lost control and slammed into the side of my car. No way. How could I? Now that I knew how I was going to die and when, how could I put myself in that position? That wouldn't be an accident . . . it would be *suicide*.

No one ever, ever cheats death, Mr. Ryker.

I will. At five fourteen on July seventeenth, there was an appointment I wouldn't be keeping.

At least, that is what I told myself. I told myself that all day long. Whenever Death spoke to me, telling me that tomorrow was the day, I pushed him away.

I was *not* going to die tomorrow. I might have a stroke next week, or perhaps I'd die from a killer bee attack. Maybe it would be a car crash, after all.

But there was one thing for sure: I was *not* going to be in a car accident on Friday afternoon, the seventeenth of July. That was *not* how I was going to die.

I told myself this on the way home from work. As you can imagine, I was more than just a little bit cautious. What if Death knew of my plan and decided to come for me early? What if he bumped up the appointment?

As a precaution, I didn't even go *near* the intersection of M-33 and Old US 27. I was nervous all the way home, right up until I turned the car down our street and pulled into the driveway.

Jesus. I made it. I'm here.

A white *FedEx Ground* truck was parked in front of our house, and the blue uniformed carrier was just leaving the porch. He carried a small package under his arm. This is an every-other-day occurrence at our house, as Joyce is always buying and returning shit from magazines and home shopping television channels.

As I parked the car I glanced over and caught a glimpse of the driver as he hopped into the truck, and I heard the engine roar to life.

I turned my head away and was about to get out of my car when I did one of those neck-snapping double-takes. A horrific beast opened its mouth and swallowed me whole.

It was *him.*

The dark man.

The man that had visited me last week, the man on the tape. Mr. Creepshow. There was no mistake. He was dressed differently, though. Today he wore the blue uniform of a *FedEx Ground* carrier, complete with baseball cap.

But he did wear those same, concealing sunglasses. Hardly business-issue glasses from *FedEx*, but they were, I knew, the same pair of glasses that he had worn on his first visit.

And I knew what was behind those glasses.

A chill suffused over my skin. The sun was hot, but I felt cold and clammy.

And he *smiled.*

"Good day, Mr. Ryker," he said, tipping the bill of his hat respectfully.

He'd come early! Death was coming to get me early!

I shot a panicky glance around the yard, expecting to see a truck jumping the curb and barreling over the lawn. Expecting to see something *unexpected* coming at me, something that would take my life. Something that was going to kill me, right here, right now.

The man in the truck let out a sudden laugh, flashed a ringmaster's vaudevillian smile, and spoke.

"No, Mr. Ryker, I have not come early for you. I came to *remind* you. I want you to remember. This time, I *want* you to remember what we've discussed."

I was too dumbfounded, too aghast to speak.

"You *do* remember, don't you, Mr. Ryker? Of course you do. Yes, it has happened before. It is rare, but sometimes, after I visit a client, sometimes . . . they *do* remember."

His grin faded, and his face became stony and rigid.

"Mr Ryker, no one . . . not you, not anyone . . . will ever, ever cheat death. Remember that, Mr. Ryker. Remember that."

He put the truck in gear, backed out of the driveway, and sped away, leaving me standing alone in the late afternoon sun.

NINE

I don't know how long I stood there, my mind in a frenzy, my thoughts spinning and churning out of control.

Death had visited me again. Twice, now. He had come to my door for the *second* time, only this time I *had* remembered his visit. He had been here only moments ago. I swore I could still smell the noxious odor of burnt almonds mingling with the fresh scent of flowers from our neighbor's small garden.

I turned and looked down the block.

At the cul-de-sac at the end of the street, a group of children were playing dodgeball across two yards. Their shrieks and shouts were distant, drowned out by the wind chanting through the trees. A beagle appeared from behind a bush, lifted his leg for a moment, then bobbled across the grass, across the street, and behind another house.

As I turned my head, I caught the flicker of a curtain. Eleanor Finch, the irritable old biddy across the street and a few houses down, had been watching—and why not? She had nothing better to do.

But I wondered what she saw . . . if she saw anything at

all.

A call from my wife startled me.

"Marc?"

I turned to see her standing at the screen door, wiping her hands with a dish towel. "Dinner, honey," she said sweetly. Then she turned and disappeared.

I pulled my briefcase from the passenger seat of the car and walked up the porch, glancing several times over my shoulder to see where the *FedEx* truck had been parked. Then I looked back at the empty street.

He had been here. Again.

I walked into the house and performed the ritual that I love. Hugs were dispersed, kisses on foreheads. First the kids, then two tight arms around Joyce.

"What's for dinner?" I asked, after a quick kiss. My voice trembled a little, but Joyce didn't pick up on it.

"Pork chops and corn on the cob. Fresh from the market, too." She slipped out of my grasp and drew back, staring hesitantly into my eyes. Her pupils darted back and forth. "You're tense. Long day?"

"Yeah, kind of," I said, managing a sigh. My voice was smooth and more controlled this time.

"You look exhausted." She searched my eyes again, scanned my face. "Are you all right?"

I forced a weak smile. I don't know how, but I did. And it must have worked, because she smiled back, then turned and began assembling plates on the counter.

"Just tired, I guess," I replied, and helped her set the table. "What did the guy from *FedEx Ground* pick up?"

Joyce turned. She had a puzzled look on her face. "What *FedEx Ground* guy?"

"The one that was here when I pulled in the driveway."

Joyce shook her head and raised a puzzled eyebrow. "I didn't know he was here. Did he leave anything on the porch?"

"No," I replied absently. "Wrong house, probably." I dropped the matter, and Joyce didn't say anything more about it.

"Dad! I caught a toad today!" Justin shouted as he came running into the kitchen.

Five fourteen in the afternoon. Friday, the seventeenth of July.

Joyce: "Slow down, Justin. Get your sister, and both of you wash your hands."

A semi truck is going to lose control. You'll be in the intersection, and the truck will broadside you.

Molly, from her bedroom: "Mom! After dinner can I go to P.J.'s?"

Justin, from the bathroom: "There's no soap!"

All in all, a rather simple way to go. A bit messy, certainly. But simple.

Joyce, picking up a pot: "It's under the sink, Justin." To me: "Honey, here's the corn."

I stood up and took the pot of steaming ears from her hands and placed it on a pad on the table.

"Can I, Mommy? Can I go to P.J.'s after dinner?"

"Where under the sink?"

Mr Ryker, no one . . . not you, not anyone . . . will ever, ever cheat death. Remember that, Mr. Ryker. Remember that.

TEN

I was quiet throughout dinner, my thoughts shocked into a numb disbelief, silenced by the ghastliness of my situation. Joyce took notice, but she let me alone about it. Sometimes I can be a bit moody, and it has nothing to do with her. Instead of prodding, she just sort of lets me be, until I want to discuss it or I simply get over it. I have to believe that this is a skill that some women just instinctively learn. Or maybe she's just learned to tolerate me—for which I am grateful.

"Don't forget tonight is the going away party for the Stanton's," Joyce reminded me.

"Oh sh—*shoot,*" I said, correcting myself before I could utter the first vowel of a word I don't want to teach my kids. "Almost forgot."

"Are we going, Daddy?" Justin asked with hopeful anticipation. His eyebrows were raised, his eyes wide in an expression that I've always loved. Optimistic, child-like wonder. I was that same boy thirty years ago.

"Not tonight, bud," I said, and hope drained from his face. Normally, seeing that reaction in him wouldn't have caused me an overt amount of stress; tonight, however, it killed me . . . but I didn't let it show. Instead: "Crystal is coming over to watch you guys."

"Awww!" Molly protested. "I want to go to P.J's!"

"That sucks!" Justin complained.

"Justin," Joyce scolded mildly with that slight dip of her forehead that says *you are just about to go over the line, buster.*

"Where are Mr. and Mrs. Stanton moving to, Dad?" Molly asked.

"Near Traverse City," I replied. "Remember last year when we took a trip and drove up the Old Mission peninsula?"

"Yeah?"

"That's where."

Curtis and Lauren Stanton have been our neighbors since we moved to Courville. They are in their mid-thirties, like Joyce and I. They don't, however, have children. And their marriage has been a rocky road, to say the least, and had been on the brink of divorce a number of times. Curtis had a drinking problem that he'd finally gotten under control. Lauren had several affairs early in their marriage. For a while, they certainly provided their share of entertainment for our small town. Their screaming matches were legendary. We thought it was about over for both of them a couple of months ago, until Curtis told me one day that they were going to give it a last-ditch effort. They had bought a home in the country and were moving out of town to begin again, fresh and new. He meant it. Lauren did, too. I know that because she and Joyce were good friends, and they shared quite a bit. We were sad to hear the news that they were moving, but happy just the same for their future, especially if they could get their relationship back on an even keel.

My future, however, was in serious doubt. An ominous, dark cloud shadowed my thoughts, and I could do nothing to dislodge the feeling of impending doom.

But I knew one thing for sure: come five-fourteen tomorrow afternoon, I was *not* going to be behind the wheel of my car at that intersection. I don't care what Mr. Creepshow said: I *was* going to cheat him. If he got me with a cement truck a week later—well, all the better. At least I wouldn't know it was coming. But I was *not* going to deliberately put myself in the place where my own death had been—dear God—*scheduled.*

ELEVEN

The party was a mix of melancholy and joy, as you could imagine such an occasion would be. Curtis and Lauren were well-liked, and quite a few neighbors came by their home to hang out for a while and wish them the best.

Me? I was completely and totally preoccupied with other matters. I feigned interest in conversations that ignited sporadically around the house, laughing politely here and there when necessary. I was there . . . but I wasn't.

What if I did die? What if Rimmon Diabolus is right? What if I really can't cheat death?

Perhaps other arrangements had been made. Perhaps, if Death came and found that I was not at my proper place, he would immediately find me and arrange for my demise through entirely different methods.

And what about Joyce and the kids? What about—

My emotions churned like clothes in a washing machine. There were several times during the party when I was looking at Joyce and I almost started crying. Thinking how much I loved her, how much we'd shared. How much we'd *planned* to share. The thought of not being able to kiss her again, or to see her beautiful smile was bad enough, but the thought of leaving her and the two kids to fend for themselves was simply unbearable.

I thought about my life insurance policy. I'd paid the bills, but really hadn't given the policy more than a cursory glance. That was something that I'd set up just before the kids were born. I'm not sure what the benefit would pay, but two hundred fifty thousand dollars seemed to ring a bell. I made a mental note to check the policy disclosure when I got home that night.

I chatted with Curtis for a while, and he noticed my distraction. I told him that I was tired, a long week at work, told him that I was sorry to see him leave, that I really wished he and Lauren the best. When we were alone in the kitchen he turned to me and extended his hand.

"Thanks for being there for me, Marc," he told me. "For *us*. I think we can *really* put all of this in the past." He looked over at his wife, who was chatting with Joyce and a few other women. Curtis raised his glass of Pepsi. "Tomorrow is a brand new day."

He was certainly right about that, in a strangely prescient way.

I didn't sleep well at all that night. There must be some kind of chemical that goes off in your brain when you realize that your death is potentially right around the corner. I felt wired, like I'd drank three pots of coffee and followed it up with a box of sugar doughnuts.

I had been right about the life insurance, though. If the unthinkable *did* happen and my body was turned to liquid shit by a semi truck, Joyce would receive two hundred fifty thousand dollars. There was also an added benefit of ten thousand dollars for both Justin and Molly, to be used for college.

It was a comfort, but not much.

I went to work Friday morning, but again I took the long way and bypassed the M-33/Old US 27 junction completely, just to be safe.

When I got to the office, I canceled all of my sales calls. I had plenty of paperwork to do, anyway, and besides . . . I felt safer at the office. I had considered not coming to work at all, but decided against it. There was still a part inside of me, however small, that told me that this was just a bunch of bullshit. Some kind of weird fantasy or hallucination I'd been having. Regardless, I was going to play it safe.

Until an idea came to me during the lunch hour.

TWELVE

If this isn't a crock of BS, I mused, *then there will be a truck that goes out of control at that intersection. That's a given. But if there's no truck . . . .*

That would mean that, yes indeed, the whole Death thing was just some bizarre delusion, an abhorrent creation of my imagination. Mr. Creepshow would have existed only to me, and only in my head.

If there's no truck at that intersection, there is no dark man.

And so, I would see for myself. I would go to the intersection of the two highways to see what happened at exactly five fourteen. If there was no truck, I would have a good laugh at myself and go home and have a beer. My worrying would have all been in vain.

And if there was a truck? If there really *was* a semi that lost control and swerved into another lane?

Well, I was going to make damned good and sure that I was a long ways away, pal. I wouldn't go near the highway. Hell, I wouldn't even be in a *car.* I could watch from a safe distance and be away from the action; if, of course, there *was* any action.

The day flew by. Time rocketed like an F-16. Seconds

ticked past in machine gun bursts, and there was nothing I could do to slow it down. It was a normal day at the office; I chatted, I laughed, I returned phone calls . . . all with an actor's professional determination of remaining immersed in a character, of hiding a true identity. It was like I was wearing a Halloween mask, hiding my face, concealing what was really going on inside.

At three o'clock I called Joyce at home, but got the answering machine. I left her a message saying that I might . . . *might* . . . be a few minutes late, that I had a couple of things to wrap up. I told her that I loved her, and I hung up.

Then:

Five o'clock. Time to go home.

THIRTEEN

I drove to a gas station that is down a ways from where the two highways meet. Too risky getting any closer, I told myself.

It was eight minutes after five.

I got out of the car and walked through the gravel parking lot, stopping where the hard-packed dirt ended and grass began. From there, I was still several blocks from the intersection. In my mind's eye, I tried to imagine from what direction the semi would be coming from.

Probably Old US 27. I'd normally be coming off of 33, turning onto 27 to head south. The semi will probably be heading north or south on Old US 27.

I walked through a field of tall, sinewy grass, the color of beach sand. At the far end of the field stood a clump of maple trees; some of them quite large. If, for any reason, the semi went so out of control that it came my direction, it would still have to get through the trees to get to me.

Mr Ryker, no one . . . not you, not anyone . . . will ever, ever cheat death. Remember that, Mr. Ryker. Remember that.

The voice startled me, until I realized that it hadn't been a voice at all. It was in my head.

Mr Ryker, no one . . . not you, not anyone . . . will ever, ever cheat death. Remember that, Mr. Ryker. Remember that.

I remembered. But I was going to cheat death, anyway. I knew I would.

Five twelve.

Several cars sped by on Old US 27, and the usual stop and goes from merging M-33. No sign of any semi truck.

Five thirteen.

I reached the clustered trunks of maples, stopped, and turned.

I heard the low throbs of a rap song coming from a car that slowed and turned onto M-33. A white van pulled out and headed south onto 27. A car honk blasted from the gas station on the other side of the field, followed by boisterous laughter.

Five fourteen.

Traffic seemed to stop. No vehicles were visible on Old US 27. On M-33, a small Datsun rolled up to the flashing red light, almost came to a stop, then accelerated and headed north on 27, belching a plume of blue fog from its exhaust pipe.

And to the south—

A semi truck! A semi truck is coming!

My heart began to pound. My breathing grew shallow and quick. Frantic, I glanced around, looking at the tree trunks. Was I far enough away? Sure, the semi wouldn't be coming in my direction—it would pass me by several hundred yards—but could it *somehow* make it through the field and into the clump of trees?

No. Impossible.

And even if it did, there was no way it could plow through a dozen huge trunks.

My attention was now riveted to the coming semi. It was approaching from the south, heading north, and would pass through the intersection in seconds. He would have the right-of-way; it was the traffic from M-33 that had to yield for oncoming vehicles.

But the semi truck drove fine, situated perfectly between a yellow and a white line. It wasn't speeding; the rig actually seemed to be traveling below the speed limit.

A car pulled up to the intersection and stopped. A red Ford Taurus. I could see the driver turn her head. There was something familiar about the car, or maybe it was the driver; I wasn't sure, and it wasn't something I dwelled on. I don't think I could have if I had tried.

The front wheels of the Taurus turned and the car accelerated, lurching forward and wheeling into the southbound lane of Old US 27. It passed the semi and continued along.

Five seconds. In five seconds, the rig would be at the intersection.

I heard another car came to a halt on M-33, but my eyes were glued to the semi. I was trying to get a look at the driver, trying to predict what might happen, if anything at all. Wondering if Death himself was behind the wheel.

Suddenly, tires began grinding gravel. Dust exploded and whirled like a hurricane. Air brakes screeched and squealed like a deranged elephant, and a monotone car horn blared. It was a pleading sound, I remember that much, a car horn that screamed *please no! No! No!* Then there was the awful, ear-splitting explosion of metal and glass as the semi truck plowed smack into the side of Joyce's green Dodge Caravan.

FOURTEEN

I t was nearing two in the morning when I arrived home.
There had been so much going on, so much to do.
So much that *couldn't* be done.

The coroner had assured me that Joyce, Justin, and
Molly hadn't felt a thing. The semi had struck the van and
had literally rolled over top of it within a split second.

And he called them 'occupants'. *The occupants didn't know
what hit them, Mr. Ryker.*

I wanted to scream that they weren't *occupants;* they were
my *family.* My *wife* and my *kids.* But I didn't say anything. I
was too numb, too enveloped in the protective cloak of
shock.

*All in all, a rather simple way to go. A bit messy, certainly. But
simple.*

B y the time I arrived home I was fatigued beyond
exhaustion, mentally and physically debilitated. I
stumbled out of the car and into the garage—one car
inside, not two, which was another unbearable
reminder—and entered the house. Turning on the light and
seeing Molly's Barbie on the floor induced another

spasmodic fit of sobs, and I sat down at the kitchen table, dropped my face into my hands, and wept.

When the crying subdued, I sat up in the chair. By now I was so tired that I was dizzy; yet, I knew that there was no way I'd be able to get to sleep. Not tonight.

Maybe not ever.

I stood up and walked to the sink to get a glass of water, and it was then that I saw the red flashing light from the telephone answering machine. It glared at me with an accusing red eye.

Blink, you did it.

Blink, you killed them.

Blink, it's you're fault.

Blink . . . .

I pressed the *play* button.

Beep.

"Hi Honey—"

Oh, God.

"—got your message that you might be late. But the kids need to be picked up from the park, remember? Don't worry . . . I'll go get them. See you tonight. Love you, baby."

The sobs came again, this time in such violent seizures that I thought my spine would crack. My legs grew weak and I succumbed to the overwhelming astasia, slumping to the floor, nearly unconscious.

Beep. Another message. This time—

"Mr. Ryker."

It was *him*. His voice was calm. Cold. So very, very cold.

"I'm certain the events of the day were a bit different than you had planned. Certainly different than what had been planned for you. I warned you, Mr. Ryker. I tried to warn you again. But I knew that you would somehow try to change the course of events. Congratulations, Mr. Ryker. You have done that."

There was a long, arid pause, as if he was taking a drag from a cigarette. I choked back a sob and listened intently.

"You see, when it appeared that things were possibly going to change, I was forced to make an—adjustment. I paid a visit here yesterday, Mr. Ryker, as you well know. I paid a visit to your wife and your children, to prepare them . . . just in case. I tried to warn you again. I tried to warn you, Mr. Ryker, and now you know: no one ever—ever—cheats death."

There was a click, a short buzz, and three beeps from the answering machine to alert that there were no more messages. The red light stopped blinking, and the unit reset itself.

Death was gone . . . at least for now.

SPINSTER

L ook at them.
Go on . . . *look* at them.
It's the work of the Devil going on, I tell you. Always has been. Nothing but the hand of Lucifer, being used to manipulate those poor, poor children. He's got hold right around their little throats.

Oh, but they know what they're doing, all right, the little beasts. Dressing up in those infernal costumes and parading out into the night, ringing doorbells and demanding candy. My mammy used to tell me every year. She'd say *'Eleanor, those children are doing the devil's work'*, and she'd go on to tell me that they were evil and wicked with hearts as black as night.

Not to worry, though. The Good Lord will take care of his own. How do I know, you ask? The Bible tells me so. Reminds me of that song that I still sing. *Jesus loves me, this I know, for the Bible tells me so.*

But they seem so *happy* about it! Look at them out there, right now. Wearing costumes and walking up and down the street. See how they giggle and laugh? It's not natural, what they're doing!

And their *homes!* Look across the street. Look at that pumpkin on the porch, with its infernal face glowing in the shadows. Oh, I know they'll tell you it's innocent, but it's not. Not one little bit. After all, it's right here in scripture. Let me see . . . ah. Here. Right here in Deuteronomy, chapter eighteen, verses ten thru twelve: *'Let no one be found among you who sacrifices his son or daughter in the fire, who practices divination or sorcery, interprets omens, engages in witchcraft, or casts spells, or who is a medium or spiritualist or who consults the dead. Anyone who does these things is detestable to the Lord'.*

You see? It's written right there. The Lord forbids this kind of behavior. Despises it, don't you know. In my seventy-seven years, I've never seen such blasphemy!

Don't tell me that it's just another day. It's All Hallow's Eve! It's a *pagan* festival! Why, these poor little children are worshiping the Devil and they don't even *know* it!

And you'll not start with that *'harmless fun for kids'* stuff. *I* know what's harmless and what's not. Why, at this very moment, there are wicked people performing their evil deeds. And those young children out there are a part of it! They don't know it, of course, but they are. Yep. If you're not part of the solution, you're part of the problem. *'He who is not against us is for us',* that's what Mark tells us in Chapter nine, verse forty.

And those little boys and girls out there . . . ooh. Heresy, I say. It's heresy. No . . . *worse.* They're little devil worshipers, that's what they are.

A clown, you say? You don't think that a child dressed as a clown is all that bad?

Let me tell you something. The mask of the deceiver knows no bounds. If the devil wants to be a clown, he'll be a clown. Or a cowboy or a hobo. He's deluded all of those little ones into thinking that this night is something fun, that everyone is doing it.

But the schools! They're the *worst!* Of course, what would you expect with *public* education these days. You know where I went to school? A small, one-room schoolhouse right here in Courville. Yep. We started school with a prayer, and we had scripture reading every day.

They don't do that, anymore, you know. Tossed it out. Said that it was 'unconstitutional'. Separation of church and state. Lord, if I hear that term one more time, I think I'll go mad.

But they still celebrate the most evil, wicked day of the year. They *force* it upon those poor little kids.

What do you mean, they *don't*? Of *course* they do. They make it fun for children by having apple-bobbing contests and pumpkin decorating. Why, the schools in *this very town* actually have a Halloween party after school! I've seen it. Teachers dressing up like specters and willow-the-wisps, playing scary music and decorating their windows with skeletons and goblins and witches. Well, they'll be sorry one day. One day, they'll be held accountable for all of their wickedness.

Oh! There's the doorbell.

Of course I'll answer it! Perhaps I can reach one—only one—of those miserable little urchins. They need to know that what they're doing is wrong, and that the day of judgement is at hand.

What do you mean *'not tonight'?* How do you know? The time is known to no man . . . not even the Lord himself knows the hour. Now, if you'll excuse me a moment . . . .

Oh, hello, hello, children, hello. My, my! Six . . . seven . . . *eight* of you! Goodness!

Trick or treat, you say. Tell me . . . does any one of you know what you're doing this night?

No, you're not simply trick or treating, and don't all of you answer at once. You'd think they'd teach you to raise your hands. But no . . . you all probably go to *public* schools.

You . . . in the white sheet. You're a . . . a *ghost*, if I may presume. Do you know what this *'trick or treat'* business is all

73

about?

Well? Are you going to answer me?

I didn't think so.

How about you? Why, you look simply repulsive in that silly mask of hair.

Oh? You're a werewolf? Is that *so?* Well, do you know that there really *are* werewolves, hmm? Oh yes. It's true. Years ago, men in Germany sold their souls to the devil so they could live out their carnal desires, and—

No, I will *not* tell you what 'carnal' means and—

No! It is not a carnal-covered apple! That's caramel!

Now, you listen to me. What all of you are doing is *wrong,* you hear me? Oh, I know that your mothers and fathers say that it's okay, that there's no harm in dressing up in costume and trick or treating. Tell me . . . how many of you go to church? No! Not all at once! Raise your *hands,* children. Now . . . how many of you go to church?

Only *six* of you?

You . . . little girl with all of the make-up. Why—

Don't interrupt me! I don't know who Britney Spears is. Probably some young prostitute that you children so pitifully idolize. And you—

No, I will not tell you what a 'prostitute' is. Go ask your father. I'm sure he'll be able to tell you. Make sure your mother is around when you ask him.

Now, where was I? Oh, yes. There are eight of you here. Six of you go to church. Does your church know what you're doing tonight?

What's that? Your church says it's okay?

Well, they're *wrong.* You know what? That's not the *real* church. You probably go to one of those smarmy, happy churches that ordains homosexuals and let—

No! I will *not* tell you what it means! Go look it up. And stop interrupting, you insolent werewolf-child.

Now, now, now, stop, all of you. Come back. After all, I *do* have a treat for you.

Yes, yes, there now. Gather round. I don't want you to leave here empty-handed. Now . . . is everyone listening?

Good.

Change your ways, children. Go home and repent, this moment. Confess your sins to the Lord, and He will forgive you. Cast aside your evilness, and the Father will take care of the rest.

Now, here's a pamphlet for each of you to take. Words from the Lord, they are. One for you, and you, and—

Go on, take it! Put it in your little bag with all of your ill-gotten treasures. At the very least, give it to your mother or father. Perhaps one of them will come to their senses. I doubt it, but it's my duty to the Lord to do what I can to save sinners and help the lost. And you, children, are about as lost as children could possibly be. It breaks my heart to see you like this, it really does.

Now. One for you, and you and you. And you, too, Miss—

—*Spears.* Yes. The little hooker. Make sure you take this and read it, then give it to your father. He's not fit to raise cabbage if he lets you out of the house looking like you do.

Now you children run along. I'll be praying for each and every one of you. Lord knows your parents aren't. Good-bye.

There. Heavens above, maybe there's hope for one of them. I doubt it, but I have to do my duty as a witness. It's all in His hands now and—

Goodness. It's the door again. Maybe one of them decided to pull one of their little tricks. We'll just see about that.

Why . . . it's a little girl! A beautiful little girl! Tell me,

75

young one, what are you dressed up as?

You *have* no costume? What kind of trick or—

Oh? You're not here to trick or treat? Then what are you—

Outside, dry, dead leaves tumbled through the late evening sky and danced across the lawn, scraping the driveway like fingernails on a blackboard. They swirled up and down and all around in swelling spiral patterns. Ghosts and goblins and hobos and witches ran along the sidewalk, swinging their bags and giggling. A group of children mobbed the front door of the home across the street. They jostled and jockeyed one another, and, one by one, they began to walk away, bags swinging, scurrying across the lawn to the next house.

But these were things that the old woman didn't notice. She saw only the small girl that stood in her doorway, wearing a ruffled pink dress that fluttered in the wind. A pink ribbon held her auburn hair back in a long ponytail. Her face was innocent and unblemished, her skin perfect and supple. She stood at the door, her buttery cheeks glowing, looking up at the graying, bitter woman.

"—here for?" the old woman finished. "Tell me . . . just what is such a beautiful little girl like you doing out on a night like this? And without a coat?"

The little girl tilted her head back and stared straight into the eyes of the old woman. "Why are you so *mean* to everyone?" she asked meekly.

The old woman drew back, her chin dropped, and the skin beneath her neck sagged.

"Mean?" the old woman replied in defiance. "Tell me, little one, what on *earth* are you talking about?"

"You are so *mean* to everyone. You don't say or do anything nice."

SEASON OF THE WITCH

The little girl's reply caught the old woman by surprise, and she drew back even more, staring at the little girl through her thick glasses.

"And what do you know about *mean,* hmm?" she sneered. "Tell me, young miss, just what is . . . *mean?*"

"You never say anything nice to anyone," the little girl in the pink dress squeaked. "All you tell them is that what they're doing is wrong and they are all terrible and evil and wicked and they'll pay for it someday."

The old woman suddenly realized what the little girl was doing, and why she was here.

"Oh, is that so?" she asked, scanning the porch and the yard through the open door in cynical supervision. She was certain that the other children had put her up to this, and she was going to get to—

—the bottom of this, I tell you. I'll get to the bottom of this. Those nasty children have put this sweet little girl up to this, I know they have.

Where are you?!?! Come out here, now, where I can see you, you wicked, wicked children!

What do you mean, 'there's no one else here'? Child, I know those menacing children put you up to this. Well, you're not to listen to them. Do you hear me? Unless you want to end up like they will. They'll—

Of course they're going to hell! And why shouldn't— *Child . . . did you just say . . . 'hell'?*

Oh, my. Lord, what have they put you up to? Listen here, young one. Don't use that word again. I know they told you to say that, but you shouldn't be—

What? They didn't tell you to say that word? Oh . . . you learned it from church. Yes, of course. Scripture *does* use that word. Nevertheless. It's just not . . . *proper* . . . for a beautiful young lady like yourself to be using that word.

Me? Mean and nasty? Here, here, child. And I thought that you had manners. I thought that perhaps you were different. Apparently not. You're just like the rest of them, all wrapped up in their silliness. Well, you'll see. You'll see, and—

"—you're a mean old lady," the child interrupted. "That's *all* you are."

The woman recoiled. Her eyes widened, then narrowed.

"Now, you listen here, you nasty little child." She leaned forward and waved a crooked finger in the girl's face. "You don't talk to me like that. I am doing the Lord's work! All of your hideous friends out there, running about and yelling and laughing and knocking on doors . . . if it wasn't for them, I wouldn't have to worry so much.

"But I *do* worry. I *worry,* because I *care.* Do you think I want to see them burn for eternity? Lord knows, I've tried everything I could to make them see the light. Why, child, do you know that I, personally, have visited every single house on this block? Oh yes. I begged and pleaded with everyone to stop this sinister 'Halloween' nonsense.

"They didn't listen. They *won't* listen. And do you know why?"

The tiny girl stood motionless in the doorway.

"I asked you a question, young lady," the old woman hissed invidiously. Her voice was taunting and intimidating.

"They won't listen to you," the little girl peeped, "because you're not nice to people. Everyone says that you used to be nice, but now you're not. Now you're just a mean, nasty, old woman."

"Child!"

"You're mean and you're nasty, and nobody likes you."

"Go home!" the old woman ordered. "Go home, and don't come back."

78

"No one comes to see you," the little girl in the pink dress said. "All you do is tell them what they're doing wrong. Even your own family won't come to see you."

The old woman glared.

"The older you got, the meaner you got," the girl continued. "And now, there's nothing left of the person you once were. You're just mean and old. You're mean and you're old and you hate people. You're . . . you're just a nasty, nasty . . . *spinster.*"

"Why did you come here in the first place, if all you have is hatred in your heart and the devil on your tongue?!" the old woman said, nearly shouting. She waved her hand, motioning the girl off. "Away with you, child, you disrespectful little juvenile! Away!"

But the little girl didn't leave. Instead, she took a step forward, and then another. Now she was standing in the breezeway. Her eyes bore into the old woman.

"I came here," the little girl replied icily, *"because I wanted to see what I've become."*

At once, the old woman shuddered and took a step back. Without a second's hesitation, the little girl in the pink dress took another step inside. A brown leaf swirled through the door, carried by a heavy gust of wind. The leaf scraped to a rest on the wood floor, flipped over, spun, and stopped.

"Get out!" the old woman shrieked. *"Child, get out of my house this instant!"*

The little girl said nothing. More leaves swirled up and around behind her, swarming like a flock of little brown sparrows. Several found their way through the door and floated to the floor.

"Who sent you here?!?!" the old woman demanded in a crackling gasp.

The little girl in the pink dress shook her head. "No

one sent me," she replied. "I just wanted to see." She took another step toward the old woman, and, again, the old woman took another step back.

"The devil sent you!" the old woman cried. She tilted her head back and closed her eyes tightly, raising her palms upward like a raving faith healer. "Lord Jesus, in your holy name, I command this evil spirit to depart!"

The little girl slowly shook her head from side to side. "I'm not an evil spirit," she said.

"Yes you are!" the old woman replied with a sudden, accusatory point of her finger. "Lord, Almighty! You've been sent by the Evil One! It's written all over your face!"

The girl began to walk slowly, very slowly, toward the old woman.

"Get out!" the woman screamed, backing into the kitchen. *"Get out now! Be gone! Devil be gone! In the name of—"*

The little girl stopped and calmly held her hand up, and the simplicity of the gesture alone silenced the old woman.

"Once, you were nice to people," the child in the pink dress began. She clasped her hands together behind her back. "You were kind and gentle and loving. People liked you. But that was long ago."

"Get out!"

"You became . . . *hard.*"

"Leave me alone!"

"You decided that *you* were right, and everyone else was wrong. You thought sex was dirty, so you never got married."

The old woman recoiled, pinning herself against the counter. Her mouth was open, her bulging white eyes swollen in disbelief, magnified even larger by the lens of her thick spectacles. Her hands grasped the edge of the counter with such a tight grip that her knuckles paled.

"You get out of this house this instant!" the old woman

shrieked. *"This instant! Do you hear me?!?!?"*

The little girl took a defiant step forward, mocking the old woman's demand.

"Do you know what I have decided?" the little girl asked in her sweet, innocent voice. "I've decided that, if you're the woman I'm going to turn into when I grow up, I don't *want* to grow up . . . *at all.*"

"You're mad, child! You're a possessed little girl, can't you see that!?!? There's a demon inside of you! In the name of Jesus, I command you, demon, to come out! Leave this poor child at once!"

Suddenly, the little girl began to shake. A confused look came to her face, and a short series of convulsions rocked her body. She trembled violently, and her eyes rolled up and down and around, her body paralyzed by the tumultuous shuddering.

Finally, after nearly thirty seconds, the quaking ceased. The little girl stood still, looking up at the old woman.

"I . . . I think . . . I think it worked," the little girl peeped shyly, gazing curiously at her own hands as if they were oddly foreign.

The old woman, still pressing herself back against the kitchen counter, stared in amazement.

"It did?" she asked.

The little girl looked up. A coy smile came to her face, and she shook her head slowly, mechanically. She winked, and her eyes twinkled devilishly. "Just kidding," she taunted. "Just kidding."

"You are wicked!" the old woman screeched. "Wicked, wicked *wicked!*" She began praying in a whisper, fervently trying to ignore the child before her.

"Our Father, who art in heaven, hallowed be thy name—"

"I have decided," the girl with the pink ribbon in her hair began, "that you would be better off not living at all."

The old woman wasn't listening. She repeated the prayer over and over, trying to drown out the words of the child, knowing that if she just prayed hard enough, long enough, the evil beast before her would leave.

Without warning, the little girl snatched a knife from the counter. She held it in her hand and brandished it like a sword, waving the shiny blade back and forth, carving the air with wide figure-eight movements.

The old woman stopped praying. Her mouth hung open in a silent gasp.

"Child! What are you doing!?!?! Put that down this instant!"

The little girl ignored her. "I have decided to end your misery once and for all," she said.

The old woman screamed and tried to flee. The little girl, however, was far too quick. She leapt to the side, easily cutting off the old woman's escape and cornering her in the kitchen. The blade flashed as the pretty little girl continued to weave it through the air, sweeping it back and forth and over and under.

"Once and for all," she repeated, her voice honey-like, the embodiment of youthful innocence. "If you are the person I'm going to become," the beautiful child said, "then I'm going to make sure that I never grow up."

The old woman watched in horror as the little girl raised the knife to her own chin. "Once and for all."

The old woman gaped, her face cemented in terror.

"No! Child, no! Don't—"

"I don't like what I've become. I don't like who you are. I don't want to be . . . me."

With a single, swift move, the little girl drew the knife across her tiny neck. A thin red line opened from artery to artery.

"Child!!!"

Blood gushed in torrents, splattering over the counter,

spraying the cupboards and cabinets, drenching the floor. It stained the little girl's pretty pink dress, her perfect, innocent skin. Her eyes rolled back into her head, and her smile faded. She coughed, causing even more blood to spew from the wound and from her mouth and nostrils. The knife clanged to the linoleum floor, and she reached up and placed a hand to her wound, then removed it, displaying a blood-covered palm. Oily red liquid continued to spew as the little girl reached behind her head with her stained hand and pulled the pink ribbon from her hair. Slowly, she held it out to the old woman, as if to hand it to her.

The old woman screamed.

D avid Fullmer sipped a cup of hot cocoa at the dining room table. A half-eaten piece of pumpkin pie sat on a plate before him. Across the table was his wife, Meredith. She, too, held a mug of cocoa in her hands.

"Man, I can't believe how tired I am," David said, glancing at his watch.

Meredith frowned over her cup of cocoa and smiled. "It's only nine, David."

"I've been up since four."

"Would you like a medal?"

"Some sympathy would suffice."

Meredith laughed. "The kids'll be home any time. Then you can go to bed. Finish your pie."

He leaned back and patted his slightly protruding belly. "Can't. It's great, but I don't think I can eat another bite."

"Well, next time don't—"

Meredith was interrupted by the terrified screams of children outside.

David sprang to his feet and was out the front door in seconds. "Stay here!" he shouted to his wife, and he bolted off the porch.

The sun had set, but the sky glowed faintly in the declining light. Street lamps lit up the streets, and porch lights burned up and down the block. Dead leaves scurried up the street, swept along by a chilly wind.

Two houses down and on the opposite side of the street where the old woman lived, a group of children were gathered at the door. One child, dressed in a superman costume, was in the yard. He was on his hands and knees, vomiting. Other children were fleeing the yard, gasping, their hands covering their mouths. A ghost started to run, then tripped over his white sheet and slammed to the ground. Instantly he was on his feet again, running across the lawn.

Bags of candy lay abandoned on the lawn and on the walk, their contents strewn everywhere.

David tore across the street, up the walk, and up to the group of children.

"Get back!" he ordered. "Everyone back, now!"

A sea of children split open, and David pulled away ghosts and goblins and witches and one girl who looked suspiciously like a tiny Britney Spears. When he reached the front door, he stopped.

Oh, God, he thought, upon seeing the gruesome scene.

"Everyone back!" he ordered again, waving his arms to shoo away the dozen or so trick or treaters that had gathered. "Go home! Go home, now!"

He turned back around, gazing in horror at the bizarre scene.

The door to the old woman's home was open. Several brown leaves lay on the floor, and while David looked on, another leaf sailed over his shoulder like a tiny paper airplane. Then it nosedived, lighting on the wood floor at his feet.

He raised a fist to his mouth and gagged as vomit rose

in his throat.

The old woman lay on the linoleum floor in the kitchen. Blood was everywhere—on the cupboards, on the cabinets, on the damned ceiling, for crying out loud. It dripped from the edge of the counter and splattered across the front of the refrigerator. Several leaves had found their way into the kitchen and were scattered about, marred with splotches of blood.

Oh my God, David thought. *Ho-lee shit. The crazy old bitch did it. She killed herself.*

Her body was on the floor, on her side. The woman's neck was sliced open, and her head was tilted at an oddly distorted angle. Blood still trickled from the wound, creating a thickening crimson beaver pond on the kitchen floor. Her gray hair had soaked up a large amount of the syrupy red liquid. A single kitchen knife was in one hand, and in the other—

A thin pink ribbon.

SEASON OF THE WITCH

In her place, one hundred candles burning
As salty sweat drips from her breast;
Her hips move, and I can hear what they're saying, swaying;
They say the beast inside of me's gonna get ya, get ya, get . . . .

—*Peter Steele/Type O Negative, 'Love you to Death'*

The face of evil is always the face of total need.

—*William S. Burroughs*

ONE

Guests began arriving at six.

The party had been hastily thrown together, and Curtis wasn't sure he was actually looking forward to it. While it was a happy occasion for him and his wife, he was a bit uneasy about facing a house full of people that had been privy to pretty much everything that he and Lauren had been through during a ten-year rollercoaster marriage.

That's the only problem with Courville, he thought, pouring himself another glass of Pepsi and watching the evening shadows grow long upon the grass. *It's like living in a goddamn fish bowl. Everybody is watching . . . especially if you've got problems. 'Cause if you've got problems, that gives the fish on the other side of the glass something to talk about.*

And brother . . . the people in Courville had things to talk about—especially when it came to Curtis and Lauren Stanton.

They were married in September, 1992. Lauren had her *first* affair the following summer, then another (with her boss at *The Wickerton Legend,* the newspaper office where she worked in a town several miles away) that winter. Through it all, Curtis had been blind to her infidelities, probably due to the fact that he spent a vast majority of his evenings hanging out at the local bar after work, exercising his bibulous endeavors.

It wasn't until Lauren was fired from her job (she left her boss for yet another conquest) that Curtis became suspicious. When he actually *did* find out the truth, he felt like the stupidest person on the planet. It seemed like everyone in Courville knew about the meretricious indiscretions of Lauren Stanton—except *Curtis,* of course.

There had been a messy confrontation that had escalated into a physical skirmish. It hadn't been all *that* serious, but Lauren wound up with a very blackened eye, and Curtis wound up in jail.

An attempt at reconciliation included a stay at an alcohol rehab clinic for Curtis, and counseling for Lauren. They received joint counseling for a year after that. Curtis had a few bruises from falling off the wagon, and there *had* been some pretty serious fights, but at least nothing of a physical nature. One particular shouting match at three in the morning brought numerous complaints from neighbors (and two police cars) but no one was hauled off to jail and things quieted down.

And for a few years, things had gone pretty smooth. Curtis had been able to stay away from the bottle, and Lauren had been able to keep herself at home. They'd even talked about finally starting a family, about *really* settling down for good.

Of course, things would have been far, far different if Lauren knew of her husband's shortcomings . . . that included much of his own improprieties. Behind her back, Curtis had courted more than simply a bottle at the local tavern. Amazingly, for a town as small as Courville, this was something Lauren hadn't found out about, and you can bet this wasn't something he was going to bring up during counseling. For Curtis, his infidelities were going to remain right where they were supposed to be—in the past. Besides . . . Lauren's trysts gave him something to hold over her head. If she knew of his own unfaithfulness, he'd lose his trump card. It was just like country music singer George Strait said: *You've got to have an ace in the hole.*

And then came last summer.

TWO

This time it had been Lauren who slipped. The affair had been brief, one of those supposed one-night-only-no-one-will-get-hurt deals.

Except Curtis *had* found out about it. And he left. He packed a suitcase and left in the middle of the night without leaving a note, without any indication as to where he was going. He was gone for over a month.

Lauren had filed a missing persons report, but it was obvious to most people that Curtis Stanton had had enough. He'd been cheated on one too many times, and the poor boy just couldn't take it anymore. Perhaps, some mused, Curtis had fallen off the wagon and had drunk himself to death, and it would only be a matter of time before they found his car on some remote two-track, his body slumped over the wheel, dead from alcohol poisoning.

When he showed up a month later, he announced to Lauren that he was at the end of his rope, that he couldn't trust her anymore, that it was over. And no, he hadn't fallen off the wagon. He'd driven far south, all the way to Louisiana, where he'd rented a motel room for the past four weeks. He'd done a lot of thinking—not drinking—and now he had some answers.

And an ace in the hole, of course.

But, lo and behold, miracle of miracles. They had been able to patch things up again . . . or at least make a last-ditch effort, anyway. One *more* for the Gipper before throwing in the towel. They knew that it wasn't going to be easy, that the road would be long and wouldn't ever end.

And one of the first things they decided was that they needed to make some life-changing decisions . . . one of which involved a brand-new start by moving somewhere fresh and unfamiliar. A place where their baggage could be left behind like trash on the curb. Somewhere where no one knew of Lauren's past infidelities and Curtis's battle with booze. A place where their secrets were safe . . . or at least, not on the front page.

And that's how they discovered the Old Mission Peninsula.

THREE

T he peninsula is a beautiful place, man," David Fullmer was saying. Fullmer and his wife lived directly across from the Stantons, and they'd been the first to arrive at their going-away party. David's hand was now wrapped around a sweating Budweiser, and he was in the kitchen with a few other arrivals.

"Yeah," someone else chimed in. "That place is cool. Lots of cherry and apple orchards and vineyards. And history. You're gonna love it there."

Curtis and Lauren had purchased an older home deep into Michigan's Old Mission Peninsula, a long finger of land that stretched north of Traverse City. The land mass was quite large—nearly thirty miles from beginning to end—and surrounded by the clean, clear waters of Lake Michigan to the east and west. The peninsula was narrow, too, sometimes as thin as a mile from shore to shore. It was speckled with old farms and rolling hills, a few lush vineyards, dense forests and several small lakes.

And no one knows us there, Curtis reminded himself as he glanced around at the smiling, chattering guests in his house. *We're anonymous. Mr. and Mrs. Anonymous, that's who we are.*

The Old Mission Peninsula was about a two-hour drive from Courville. Not a world away, but far enough. *Out of the yard,* as they say. Both he and Lauren agreed they'd like to stay in northern Michigan if at all possible, and when they'd found the old farmhouse for sale on the Internet, it seemed like the perfect place.

And it was.

They had met the realtor at his office in Traverse City. Chuck Hirsch was a tall man, thin, with a dark complexion and slick, black hair. In his suit, he looked more like a New York attorney than a northern Michigan realtor. He and Lauren chatted amiably, but Curtis was a bit standoffish and intellectually on his guard. When the realtor spoke to Curtis, his eyes darted around the room in perpetual surveillance. Not so, however, when he spoke with Lauren. When he spoke with her, she held his complete attention. He had stared at Lauren a bit longer than Curtis liked, but that was something he had gotten used to over the years.

"You two are going to love this place," he said, first looking at Lauren, then on to Curtis. He flashed a polished, confident smile. "This one is going to go quick. Not much property available on the peninsula these days, and *nothing* like this has been available for *years.*"

They drove up the peninsula in Hirsch's Ford Excursion, and he explained a few of the more pleasant amenities of the house they would be seeing shortly.

"I'm telling you: you're gonna love this place. Just listed. You guys are the first showing. The place is *gorgeous.*"

By the time they arrived, it was as if they had already been there.

The home had been built around the turn of the

century, and had been well-taken care of. It sat back from the road next to a field filled with apple trees, and the nearest house was nearly a quarter-mile to the north. The property itself was nearly five acres . . . not a palatial tract by any means, but certainly more than enough elbow room. And the price was fair. The owner, an older, graying woman who had recently lost her husband, wanted to sell quickly and move somewhere—*anywhere*—warm. She had complained that while the summer season on the peninsula was pleasantly mild, even quite hot at times, the winters were far too long and brutal for a woman who was getting on in years.

And, although she wasn't *giving* away the home by any means, she'd priced it to move.

"Go ahead, look around," Hirsch said. "Take your time. Walk the orchard if you want." The realtor returned to his car where he sat in the driver's seat and began chatting away on a cell phone.

"God, Curt," Lauren said as she walked through the yard and toward the field. She completed several turns, taking in the surroundings. "Look around." She shook her head as she continued. "It almost looks . . . familiar, doesn't it?"

"It should be. We saw a picture on the web site."

"Yeah, but it didn't do any justice. This place is incredible."

They stopped walking and stood at the edge of the lawn where the orchard and grass met, looking up at the large home that rose up beneath a cloudless, lazuline sky. Curtis didn't agree that the house and property looked all *that* familiar, but he *did* agree that the place had a unique charm to it.

"No, it's more than charm, Curt," Lauren said. "More than that. It's almost . . . magical. There is just something about this place. Can you sense it?"

"Yeah. Yeah, I guess so."

Curtis walked into the orchard, assessing the untrimmed apple trees and the dense forest several hundred yards to the west. Tall, wispy grass brushed against his jeans, depositing small, coarse seeds that stuck to the fabric of his pants like velcro. He brushed them away with a snap of his hands.

Lauren remained where she was, enthralled with the quiet, pastoral setting. She moved her head slowly, rotating her head from side to side in a panoramic survey.

Chuck Hirsch, for his part, continued chatting on the phone, but even from where Curtis was standing he could see that the realtor was staring at Lauren from behind the windshield.

Oh well.

Lauren spoke without turning.

"Curtis."

Curtis didn't answer, but, rather, turned and walked back through the tall grass and approached his wife. Her hands were on her hips, and her head was tilted back as if she was looking at the house.

But she wasn't.

When Curtis reached her, he could see that her eyes were closed, her face bathed in the midday sun.

"We have to have this place."

Curtis smiled. "You're that sure, huh?"

She turned, her eyes now open, her lips parted in a wide grin. "Yes. I am. This is it."

"It's the only place we've looked at."

"We can stop looking. Today. *Now.*"

On the ride back to the realtor's office, Hirsch had gone on about it being the smartest investment they'd make in their lives, that they could turn around and sell the place for twice as much in a year from now. Curtis and Lauren hadn't disagreed. They made an offer and secured a deposit; after several counter offers, they reached an agreement.

Moving day would be Monday, July 20th.

The party went well. Any discomfort Curtis had felt earlier was erased by the friendliness of well-wishers that stopped by. Curtis felt that they sincerely *would* be missed. He'd even joked to his friend Marc Ryker that of *course* they'd be missed: *after all, we've provided the neighborhood with quite a bit of entertainment over the past ten years.* Marc had laughed, but he had been distant.

"Everything all right with you?" Curtis asked. Marc didn't reply.

"Marc? Hey . . . hello? Earth to Marc."

Ryker re-entered the atmosphere and smiled. "Sorry about that," he said. And then, in response to Curtis: "Yeah, everything's fine. Really great."

Ryker had seemed uncomfortable about something, but whatever it was, he kept it to himself.

By midnight, everyone had cleared out. By twelve-thirty, the red plastic cups had been picked up, the scraps of chips and pretzels and nuts had been vacuumed from the carpet, and by one in the morning, Curtis and Lauren had showered and crept into bed. Curtis fell asleep, dreaming about a fresh start and a new beginning.

And Lauren did, too.

Friday, July seventeenth, had been Curtis's last day on the job. He worked for an architectural firm in Petoskey, and had been planning to go it alone for over a year. The move to the Old Mission Peninsula was the catalyst. With the booming construction industry and houses going up like tents at a Boy Scout Jamboree, he was sure that there would be plenty of work available.

The firm threw a small going-away party for him at the office, and he stayed a few minutes to chat with some of his friends, who were now officially *former* colleagues.

That's where he was when the phone rang at five thirty-three, Friday, July 17th.

Curtis was just about ready to leave the office when he'd received an hysterical phone call from Lauren. She was crying and choking as she explained that it all happened right behind her, she'd seen it in the mirror.

What? What happened? What did you see? What mirror?

More crying and sobbing. *Oh, Jesus, Curt. Oh God! Oh God! I saw it all! I watched it happen! Oh God!*

And something about Joyce. And the kids.

Joyce? Joyce Ryker? Kids?

FOUR

The funeral was held on Tuesday, July 21st, and Curtis and Lauren postponed their moving day so they could attend. The previous Friday, a semi truck carrying logs had lost control and plowed into the side of Joyce Ryker's minivan, killing her and her two children instantly. Curtis and Lauren had been good friends with the Rykers and they were well-liked by everyone in the neighborhood. The news was devastating.

And word was going around that Marc had been a witness to the whole thing. Getting gas or something at the convenience store. He had watched the whole thing as it happened, for crying out loud. Saw his family obliterated in a mass of twisted metal and wood. Life didn't get any shittier than that, for sure.

They picked up the moving truck Tuesday night, a big, silver and orange *U-Haul,* and most of the loading and packing was complete by nightfall. Wednesday morning, Curtis made a quick stop down the street to see Marc Ryker and again express his sympathy. They'd been good friends; they always would be.

Jesus, he thought, as he approached the Ryker home.

That is just some heavy, heavy shit.

He knocked several times on the door. No answer. He cupped his hands to his temples and his forehead and peered through the garage door window . . . empty. Marc wasn't home. He made a mental note that he would keep in touch, that he'd call from time to time.

He walked back to what was now officially his old home. Lauren was finishing up packing some clothes, and in a few hours they said their mental good-byes to their old house, and to Courville. A fresh, new start had begun.

Curtis sat behind the wheel of the moving truck, which was now parked in the driveway of their new home. Lauren's red Ford Taurus pulled up and stopped directly behind the truck; she'd followed behind him. Curtis would return to Courville to pick up his car next week.

He killed the truck engine and gazed out the bug-splattered window.

Man, Lauren is right. This place is perfect. It's just . . . perfect.

On their initial visit it was Lauren who had been enamored with the quaint old home. Now, knowing that the house and surrounding acres were now *theirs,* he was, like Lauren had been, mesmerized.

The house was two stories, white, and nearly immaculate, considering its age. New vinyl siding glared brightly in the afternoon sun, contrasted by a dark roof. The windows were trimmed in black, and, although there were no curtains, the house had a warm, inviting appeal. Cozy and clean. Maybe too clean. That could be remedied, and probably would be very soon.

The yard butted up to a field that stretched across several acres that bordered the dirt road. It was interspersed with several wide, bulbous maple trees, branches full and lush from ample sunlight, the dark bark on their stubby trunks wrinkled and gnarled with age. Several dozen apple trees—much smaller than the maples— grew in uniform rows stretching across the field. They'd been abandoned years ago and left to grow wild, as evident by the long, untamed grass that saturated the orchard.

And to the north, far on the other side of the field, was another house, very similar in size and shape to the one Curtis and Lauren now owned. A colossal maple tree obscured part of the structure, but there was—

Movement.

Something moved beneath the ancient maple near the distant house.

Curtis, still seated in the moving van, squinted as he gazed across the field through the leaden afternoon sun. He caught another flash of movement through the lemony haze and the drifting pollen and the buzzing insects. He and Lauren hadn't met their new neighbors yet, and neither the real estate agent nor the woman they had purchased the home from had offered much, if any, information. In truth, the old woman herself had been a bit evasive. Curtis spoke with her at Chuck Hirsch's office when the papers were signed, and he had asked her who owned the house to the north. She had just looked at him. Stared, actually, like the question had surprised her. Perhaps it had.

Then she proceeded to say that it was no one in particular, that she rarely sees any activity in the old farm house to the north. Then she had changed the subject entirely, talking about how wonderful the sunsets are, how beautiful the fall is, and how winter is long, yes, but the snow in the orchard is *magnificent.*

Chuck Hirsch had been equally ambiguous about the house to the north, and perhaps even a bit overly vague, stating that he wasn't sure *who* lived there, that he wasn't all that familiar with the property.

"Hey."

Curtis flinched, startled by the close proximity of his wife's voice. The driver's side window was down, and Lauren laughed, crossed her arms on the door, and rested her chin. Sandy locks of hair curved around her cheeks.

"Gotcha." She smiled. "Are you going to sit in there all day?"

Curtis smiled. "Just daydreaming." Then he shook his head. "Man. I can't *believe* this place." He made an expansive gesture with his hands. "I mean . . . it's really *incredible*. This is like something out of a movie."

"Glad you approve, now that we've spent over a hundred thousand dollars."

"I never said I *didn't* approve. It's just that it's growing on me more and more. I mean . . . even more than before."

"Like fungus?"

"Shut up."

"Ha."

"Ha yourself."

Lauren laughed. "Come on. It's just me and you, and we've got to at least get a mattress down so we have someplace to sleep tonight."

Lauren walked to the back of the truck, and Curtis watched her in the side mirror.

At thirty-four, Lauren had the body of a woman ten years beneath her age. Shapely hips, and a swaggering, sultry stride. Any man would be proud; he was no exception. It was easy to see how men like Chuck Hirsch would—

Knock it off, Curtis. You are the one who made the decision to drop it. One last chance for the Gipper, remember? Besides . . . there are a few old bones knocking around in your *closet.*

He glanced back at the house on the other side of the

field.

This time, he *did* see someone—and that someone was a *woman*.

He could see her shape, standing near the large maple. Her hands were in her back pockets, elbows pointed behind her. Blue jeans, plain white T-shirt. Jet-black hair whispered in the breeze. Sunglasses. He couldn't make out her facial features, but there was no doubt, even through the wobbling waves of heat, that she was a beautiful woman.

And she was looking at *him*.

He *knew* she was.

She wasn't looking *toward* him. She was looking *at* Curtis, seated in the truck, behind the wheel. She was watching *him* watching *her*. Just *how* he knew this he wasn't certain.

But something told him that she was.

"Hey . . . are you coming?" Lauren called out.

Curtis glanced at the side mirror to see his wife peering out from behind the truck.

"Hell, I'm not even breathing hard," he shot back with a smile.

Lauren smirked and shook her head. "In your dreams, pal," she said, and disappeared behind the truck.

Curtis turned and again looked at the house on the other side of the field.

The woman was gone.

FIVE

They began by screwing on the stairs, but that became a bit dangerous, as each received their share of oak barbs from the old steps. Groans of pleasure were sprinkled with giggles of *'ouch!'* and *'shit!'* Christening the entire house was going to take a while. Curtis and Lauren decided that they didn't need to perform the entire ceremony in one night, and instead retired to the frameless mattress that lay in what would become their bedroom on the second floor. Heated passions flared brightly until, exhausted and sweaty, they crumpled together atop wrinkled blankets.

Soon, Curtis heard his wife's rhythmic breathing, slow and steady. She was asleep. He, however, was not—and, after lying awake for an hour, he rolled gently off the mattress. He got up slowly, left the bedroom quietly.

The bright moonlight streaming through the curtainless windows provided ample illumination for him to find the upstairs bathroom, which adjoined their bedroom. He left the light off while he relieved himself. Naked, he strode back through the bedroom and stopped at the open door that led to the short hallway. Behind him, the makeshift bed glowed ghostly blue-white. Lauren lay on the mattress, the disheveled sheets crumpled at her feet, her unclothed body motionless in the light of the moon.

This is it, he thought. *It's now or nothing. The last chance, the last opportunity to make it work . . . if it will work at all.*

If they couldn't make a go of it here, they were going to call it quits. This wasn't something that he and Lauren had consciously discussed, but more of a clairvoyant agreement between them. Both knew that if they couldn't make it here, they couldn't make it *anywhere.* This was their last chance.

And, while Lauren *claimed* to love him, Curtis *still* wondered sometimes.

And he wondered if *he* loved *her* as well.

He thought that he did. But it had been too easy for her to find someone else, too early in the relationship for her to sleep around.

But, then again, so had he. It hadn't been too difficult for him, had it? He certainly hadn't had much difficulty finding a new mattress monkey from time to time. He told himself that everybody gets bored with the same old thing now and then. At the time, he couldn't have cared less if she'd found out or not. She *hadn't,* which was all the better.

For *him,* anyway.

But then again, those had been the blurry years. He'd been hitting the bottle like a major leaguer, and, if pressured, probably couldn't remember too many of the events from 1992 - 94. They weren't a blur . . . they weren't even fucking *there.* Old Grand Dad and Jimmy Beam had been at the home plate, Curtis had swung . . . and hit home runs over and over again. Hell, he might've won the pennant that year; he didn't remember.

Besides, he thought. *Everything is packed away at the Years Gone By Store—all inside that huge unit that you don't even look at anymore, much less inventory. It's way back there. Forget about it.*

Darkness, shadows, and blue moonglow.

Curtis walked down the stairs slowly, sliding his hand along the smooth wood handrail. Downstairs, timbers of moonlight plunged through the curtainless windows, illuminating the wood floor. Cardboard boxes sat piled along the far wall in the living room, along with numerous other items that had been unloaded from the truck. Unpacking and arranging would take a few days, that was for sure. No problem.

He went to the kitchen and leaned forward, pursing his lips beneath the faucet. They hadn't even unpacked glasses yet.

He turned the knob labeled 'cold' and puckered, sucking in the cool well water. The water in Courville was good, but it was nothing compared to the fresh water in . . . .

Shit. Where do we live, anyway?

Not Traverse City; that was too far south.

Old Mission?

No. That was the name of the peninsula. There was a village of Old Mission, but that was farther north, at the tip of the thin land mass that fingered into Lake Michigan.

What did the papers say? Shit, you bought the house, and you can't remember the address on the deed? What was the name of this community?

Oh, yeah.

Milcom. Our mailing address is Milcom. 13565 Wilshire, Milcom, Michigan.

He stood up, wiped a dribble of water from his chin, and stared out the kitchen window.

He froze.

Outside, in the orchard, was a shadow that shouldn't

have been there. Not a tree, not a murky trick of light.

Now, who the hell is that?

There was a dark figure—a *human* figure—standing in the field.

SIX

*N*o, it's not a tree. There are trees all through the field. That's somebody. That's a human.

The orchard seemed to float in bleach-blue moonlight, the trees nothing more than vague statues in an arid mist. The shadowy silhouette of the man was too far away for Curtis to see anything more than indeterminate features.

But there was *someone* standing there, you bet there was. There was no mistaking it for anything but what it was: a human form.

Does he see me? Curtis wondered.

No. Probably not. Too dark in the house.

He backed away from the window, just to make sure his own figure wouldn't be revealed in the light of the moon.

What in the hell is he doing, just standing there like that? In the middle of the goddamn night?

And then, as if he'd forgotten:

And it's my property. Our property. Shit. We own that field.

Considering it unwise to investigate further, at least in his standard-issue birthday suit, Curtis padded through the kitchen and peered cautiously out the living room window.

Still there. Shit. Who are you?

He clenched and unclenched his fists, his usual habit when he was tense or anxious. Some men chewed nails, some stroked their chin, some scratched their balls through their pants pocket; Curtis Stanton curled his hands into fists, opening and closing them like he was preparing for a prize fight.

And maybe he was. He was getting *pissed.* There was no doubt that someone, for whatever reason, was standing in the middle of the field,

—on our property, dammit—

and Curtis wanted to know *who.* He wanted to know *who,* and he wanted to know *why.* And the longer Mr. Longshadow loitered motionless in the field, the more determined Curtis was that *I am going to nip this in the old proverbial bud, right now, tonight, Mister. There's a new sheriff at this here ranch, pardner, and we don't take a likin' to strangers.*

He tiptoed across the living room, ducking beneath the window until he reached the mass of scattered boxes. Some of them contained his clothing; he'd have to find a pair of shorts or pants or sweats.

After popping open two boxes and not finding anything suitable to wear, he turned and looked through the window and into the field.

What the hell?

There were now *two* figures in the field.

Side by side, watching him. They *had* to be watching him. They weren't facing each other, and they sure as hell weren't chatting about the weather.

This only infuriated Curtis more, but it also alarmed him.

Thieves? Robbers? What would they want? Who are they? Kids? Kids just farting around with nothing better to do?

No. Kids would be running and hiding, ducking and

weaving. Spray painting *Jimmy loves Sally* on a wall in spray paint. Stealing vegetables to chuck off the freeway overpass.

The figures in the field were *not* kids. They were larger than kids, and they didn't *act* like kids. They were *adults*, whoever they were, and they were up to something. Nobody just stands in the middle of an orchard in the middle of the night for no reason at all.

Then he suddenly remembered where there *was* some clothing. Just some boxers and socks, but he was sure that they were right over—

Here. Next to a *Pampers* box labeled *plates* in felt marker. A milk crate-sized box labeled *Curtis-undrwr-sox.* He opened the box, found a pair of white boxer shorts, and slipped into them.

There's a new sheriff in town, boys.

He crept to the front door and opened it slowly, peering out into the orchard.

Still there. Damn. Who in the hell . . . .

He took a breath, an authoritative *gonna get to the bottom of this shit* breath, exhaled, and slipped out the door. His hands clenched open and closed.

The two figures didn't move.

Lotta guts they got, he thought.

Curtis walked across the cool, damp grass, unconcerned with his lack of stealth.

Across the driveway. He winced as gravel gnawed at the tender flesh of his feet. Then he reached clammy grass again, sopped with night dew, and his feet rejoiced.

And one of the figures vanished.

Curtis stopped walking. The second figure—the one on the left—had just pulled a Houdini.

Now yuh see'um, now yuh don't.

What the hell? Who was that? David fucking Copperfield?

The figure hadn't walked away, hadn't run off. Didn't

rise up into the air into the starry night sky. No noise, no footsteps, no swishing blades of grass. No tremor of feet crunching dried brush.

The shadowy form had simply *vanished.*

And, as Curtis watched, the remaining figure became fuzzy. At first, he thought that the form was moving, walking away from him. This prompted him to begin walking faster, toward the figure, until he realized that, no, it *wasn't* walking away. It wasn't walking away at all.

Then it was gone.

Curtis walked quickly across the lawn and into the field. Longer, stringy blades of grass swished at his calves. Dead twigs poked at his tender ankles.

The sparsely planted apple trees on either side formed a crude alley of sorts, and their awnings pooled shadows all around him. Still, there was no sign of the trespassers.

He stopped at the spot where he'd guessed the figures had stood.

Nothing.

Crickets droned like tiny motors. The moon was bright and he was again conscious of his near nakedness, but he refused to feel silly.

There was someone here. Two people. Stars and moon as my witness, I saw them.

He turned and looked back at the house. His house, now. *Their* house. Their home. This was their home, their field. Their orchard.

He turned again, looking north, and could make out the dark shape of a large house looming in the shadows beneath enormous trees.

And a light flashed.

In the house to the north, where he'd seen the woman the evening before, a light blinked on inside. A figure passed through the glow of the window.

The shape behind the glass was, of course, the woman; of that much Curtis was certain. Two other things he was certain about: *one,* there was no way the woman could have been one of the figures in the field. The house was too far away. She would never have made it from the orchard to the house in *that* short of time. Besides . . . the figures in the field hadn't run off. They had *vanished.*

And *two,* Curtis was no peeper. He didn't get his jollies in the middle of the night by prowling around to see just what the neighbors were up to, or who was doing what to whom.

And now he *did* feel silly, standing in the orchard in a pair of boxer shorts, draped in the light of a silvery disc high above.

Enough of this shit. Time to get the hell out of here.

Curtis shook his head, turned—and froze. His blood ran cold.

One of the shadowy figures had returned . . . only, this time, it was *moving.*

It was moving, and it was walking right toward him.

SEVEN

Adrenaline ravaged his bloodstream. He spun and clenched his fists. Unclenched them. Doubled them into fists again.

Then: *a voice.*

"What are you doing, Curtis?"

Lauren.

Anxiety released its vice grip on his heart. He exhaled a gushing sigh.

"Jesus!" he said. "You scared the shit out of me! You look like a ghost in that nightgown!"

"And when was the last time you believed in ghosts?"

"There was someone out here," he said, pointing at the ground. "Right here. Two people. I saw them."

Lauren looked around, then shook her head.

"I didn't see anyone."

"Lauren, *someone* was in the field. Right around here somewhere." He waved with his empty hand.

"Who?"

"I don't know. I couldn't see. Two people, though. They were just standing. When I got close, they—"

Oh shit. Better be careful here. Best not to tell her that the two bogeymen just vanished into thin air, no, no, no. Especially with the fact that it's the middle of the night and you're walking around in a pair of Fruit of the Looms.

"—took off," he finished. "Kids, probably. But I don't know."

He turned and looked around, looked back at the house to the north. It was dark; the light inside had been extinguished.

Lauren looked him up and down, and opened her mouth to speak. Curtis interrupted before she could begin.

"Don't ask," he said, shaking his head. "I couldn't find anything else to wear. Come on."

He began walking back to the house, and Lauren followed. She giggled, and Curtis playfully slapped her butt. He slipped his arm around her waist. "That'll be enough," he said.

And then: "How did you know that I was out here?"

"I woke up and you were gone," Lauren replied. "I got up to get a drink of water, and I saw you walking out here."

"How did you know it was me?"

"Shit, Curtis." She reached an arm up to the star-speckled sky. "It's as bright as day out, with the moon like it is. I could see you from the bedroom window."

"You didn't see anyone else?"

"No."

Lauren returned to the mattress and slipped beneath the covers.

Curtis looked out the bedroom window and across the orchard. The white curtains hung motionless, thin and limp on each side of the window. Pale moonglow iced the trees and the field. Crickets whirred, but they sounded far away, like the whine of a distant airplane. The cool night air pressed against his face. He squinted, his eyes searching the shadows for any movement.

People don't just vanish, he thought. *They run, they walk, they hide . . . but they don't just* disappear.

And then his eyes caught something on the other side of the orchard.

It was a light—very, very dim—coming from within the house to the north. Very tiny and faint, like a flickering candle in the window. In fact, that's exactly what it looked like.

A candle.

Curtis watched the small bead for a moment, then slipped into bed next to his wife.

EIGHT

I *got the job!"*
Curtis had watched his wife's car pull into the driveway
and stop, watched her emerge from the red Ford
Taurus. She'd been looking for a job most of the week,
hoping to find work at one of the papers in the Traverse City
area. Curtis was on the roof making some repairs around the
old brick chimney, and now Lauren was standing in the
driveway calling up to him, sharing the good news.

"That's great!" he shouted back. "Give me ten minutes
and I'll be down!" He wiped the sweat from his forehead
with the back of his arm, then gazed up into the September
sky. The day was hot, the sky devoid of clouds. *Nothing like
a little global warming to take off the autumn chill,* he thought. *This
is like living at the equator.*

He looked out over the orchard. Five weeks had passed
since they had first arrived, and the time had flown. There
had been lots to do.

While the house *was* in good shape, there were some
modifications and upgrades that Curtis wanted to take care
of before winter's assault. Much of the wiring in the home
was old. Curtis replaced the old knob and tube with more

modern, up-to-code wiring, a project that he had just finished. The leak around the chimney had been discovered several days ago during a heavy rainstorm. Nothing major. However, while on the roof, he'd made the painful discovery of a wasp's nest tucked under the eve near their bedroom window. He'd been stung, once on the forearm and again on his shoulder, but he hustled away without further attack. The nest's subsequent removal would be the next project . . . but today it was just too goddamned *hot,* and Curtis wanted off the waffle iron roof.

Below, in the orchard, the apple trees were barren, which Curtis thought odd. Regardless of their lack of care, they should at least have a *few* apples here or there.

None did. Not one.

Several of the trees in the orchard had been overcome by disease and died. Of the ones that remained, their leaves had colored prematurely, turning a waxy, pallid yellow. The lack of rain and the uncharacteristic feverish September temperatures probably weren't helping the matter.

And despite the grilling heat, fall *was* settling in. Several maples on the property were already changing colors, their deep green cloaks now splashed with hints of cinnamon and mango and plum. In a few weeks the entire countryside would be ablaze with more colors than a jumbo box of *Crayolas.* Nights were growing colder, dipping into the forties. On several occasions Curtis had awoken to a sugar-coating of satiny frost across the sickly orchard.

And curiously, there had not been much sign of their neighbor to the north. Only on occasion would he catch a glimpse of the woman outside, tending a garden or walking to the mailbox at the end of the long gravel driveway. But it was rare to see her. Not that he'd been *looking* for her; he'd had too much shit going on to think about social matters.

So when a movement near the home caught his eye, Curtis followed it.

She was wearing jeans and a plain white T-shirt, the same ensemble he'd seen her wearing five weeks ago. She was kneeling down, tending a small garden, her hair tied back in a thick ponytail. The fact that even at this distance she appeared to be strikingly attractive was not something he had overlooked, either.

"Hey, what the hell," he said quietly to himself as he stood on the roof next to the ladder, and reminded himself of that little saying about it still being okay to peek at the menu.

The woman looked up, saw Curtis watching her, waved. Curtis waved back.

"Curtis?" Lauren's voice echoed up.

"On my way," he replied absently, still watching the woman on the other side of the orchard. After a moment he looked away and climbed down the ladder.

NINE

It's a great job," Lauren explained while they ate. "Salary, plus bennies. Insurance, 401K, all that."

There had been an opening in Traverse City, some ten miles away, at one of the local papers. They were looking for a managing editor, which would suit Lauren's talents perfectly. She'd be working second shift, from two in the afternoon until ten or eleven, probably longer during the summer months.

"Make sure you rake in enough for both of us," Curtis smirked. He stabbed his fork into a heap of mashed potatoes. "The more you make, the longer I can kick back." He flashed her a grin.

"Right. How'd the roof go?"

"Fine. There's a wasp nest beneath our window, though. I'll take care of it when we get another cold night. Couple of the little shits hammered me good. When do you start your job?"

"Tomorrow. Can you believe it? Seems they've been without a managing editor for a couple of weeks, and the crew is getting fed up. I'll be doing pretty much the same work that I did at the *Legend* . . . editing, planning and coordinating stories. They use Quark, though."

"Didn't you use PageMaker at the *Legend?*"

"Yeah, but I've been wanting to make the jump, anyway. It'll take some getting used to. And they want me in right away. Like *pronto.* Asked me if I could stay today, actually, but I told them no."

"Sounds like they need you pretty bad," he said, and stuffed a fork full of pasty-white potatoes into his mouth.

"How are the potatoes?"

"Mmmm. Great."

"Here. Here's the last of them." She scooped the remaining blob of mashed potatoes from the bowl and onto his plate, then directed the conversation back to the job. "I'm just glad I found something so quick. Not much out there in my field. Not around here, anyway."

"Second shift. That kind of sucks."

Lauren winced. "I know. Nothing I can do, though, until an early shift opens, if one ever does. Does it bother you?"

"What?"

"Night shift?"

And here it was: rearing its head gently, quietly, so as not to disturb anything. *Shhh, the baby is sleeping.* She might as well have asked if he thought that she would use the 'late night at the office' bit to screw the sports writer. But no, there was more tact involved. It was unspoken and unseen, but if there *was* any tension on his part, Curtis didn't let it show. Truth is, he *was* a bit leery about Lauren working so late at night. When you get burned a few times, you learn to stay away from the fire. He'd had a few indiscriminate fires of his own, but hell . . . those were bones in the closet. He'd done a good job hiding the skeletons.

You've got to have an ace in the hole.

And as long as he was playing the old mental version of

Truth or Dare, he may as well admit that yes, there was also something inside of him that *didn't* care. That if she was screwing around on the side, he *wouldn't* care. *Couldn't* care. He wasn't going to waste his energy wondering and speculating. He could play the game just as well as she could; probably *better.*

"Nah," he said. "I just hope that you like it. We've got to pay for this place somehow. I've got about another week on the house, and then it's back to the drafting board for this boy."

"Yeah?"

"Yeah. I'll get my desk and the rest of my office stuff out of storage next weekend. I'm actually looking forward to putting the pencil back to work. In fact, I thought I might put my pencil to work a little later tonight." He winked, and Lauren smiled and rolled her eyes. She shook her head and said nothing.

Desires were satisfied early, and Curtis and Lauren remained in bed, awake, cuddled close. The window was open, and the new curtains billowed in the breeze. They swelled out gently; soft, cotton specters, rising, falling, rising again, falling back into place. The late evening air was humid and gummy; a storm threatened from the northwest. It would bring cooler temperatures, rain, and a definite change in the weather.

And Curtis and Lauren slept.

TEN

Curtis awoke in darkness to the sound of thunder. A distant burst of light illuminated the western horizon. The storm was nearing. The air remained thick and full, and the curtain twisted and swelled in the increasing breeze.

After an hour of tossing and turning, listening to the nearing storm, he stood up, found his boxers and his slippers, and went downstairs. He navigated the dark staircase and found his way to the kitchen, opening a cupboard and carefully retrieving a glass.

Thunder growled. It was one of those long, rolling rumbles, the sound of a slow-moving bowling ball down an alley. The storm would hit soon; it was only a matter of time before the ball would strike the pins and the clouds would erupt in a fury of rain and wind.

He finished the glass of water and made his way back up to bed. The curtains heaved in the wind, billowing in and out.

Curtis walked to the window and spread the curtains to look down at the field, then looked up into the dark, storm laden sky, but his attention was drawn to a twinkling orange glow to the west.

Fire.

Something was on fire. Something big. He could see flames above the trees, licking up into the night, flickering and licking like yellow and orange snakes.

And he knew one thing: a fire that big at this time of the night meant *trouble.* This wasn't any barbecue, that was for sure. The Boy Scouts weren't making S'Mores or grilling weenies on sticks. This was a major league three-alarmer.

"Lauren!" he hissed. *"Wake up!"*

No answer.

"Lauren!"

"Hmmmm?" Sleepy.

"There's something on fire!"

"Oh. Okay . . . ."

"Jesus Christ! Did you hear me? Something is on fire! There's something burning out there! Lauren! There's something out there on fire!"

No response.

Curtis drew the curtains farther apart.

"Lauren!"

Still no response. Lauren wasn't waking up.

Screw it. I'll go myself.

He hustled into his jeans that were crumpled on the floor, then fumbled in the dresser for a sweatshirt.

Glancing out the window, he tried to estimate where the fire was.

How far? A half mile? No, not quite.

Downstairs. He snatched his cell phone from the counter. Shoes at the door. His mind churned, his heart galloped. The fall had been dry, and the forest would ignite like gasoline. Or perhaps it was a house on fire; Curtis didn't know.

Lightning strike, he thought. *Lightning hit a tree and it's burning. That's all it is. Let's hope.*

A flashlight. Lauren had given him one of those heavy-duty metal ones for his birthday. Under the sink. He snatched it up and clicked it on, but the bulb didn't respond.

"Shit," he groaned.

He placed the flashlight on the counter where he would find it in morning and remember to replace the batteries, and went out the front door.

From where he stood in the yard, the orange glimmer in the sky didn't appear to be as big as it had from his bedroom window. Perhaps it had died down a bit, perhaps it wasn't as large as he'd thought.

But it was still burning, he knew that much. He could see the orange-yellow glow flickering, reflecting on the low-hanging storm clouds.

And then he saw something else.

Lights.

To the north, lights suddenly clicked on in the big farmhouse.

Maybe she's seen it. She's seen the fire, too.

And that's where Curtis headed. Toward the house on the other side of the orchard.

ELEVEN

He cut straight through the orchard, and his feet crunched on the brittle, dying grass. Earlier, the night had been comfortably warm, but now, with the nearing storm, the air had become chilly-damp. Thunder groaned louder, closer still.

Across the field, Curtis spotted a shadow moving across one of the windows of the home. When he was nearing the far edge of his field and the property boundary, the light in the house suddenly clicked off. A door banged closed.

He stopped walking, and his eyes scanned the yard until he spotted a movement, the shadow of a person walking.

It was *her*. Had to be. She was walking across the back yard, walking through the grass. Past a small barn. Curtis watched as she climbed over an old wood rail fence and continued across the field.

Toward the light in the sky.

Maybe she's seen the fire, he thought. *Maybe that's where she's going. To investigate the fire.*

"Hello!" he called out to her.

He expected her to stop . . . but she *didn't*. If anything, she moved faster, heading toward the dark forest.

What's up with that?

The prospect of getting lost in the woods at night wasn't an idea he was comfortable with. He hadn't explored much of the timberland that encroached the field and orchard, and had no idea if there were any trails or even homes nestled in the bosky forest.

Thunder boomed again, and a flash of heat lightning boiled within clouds that were not so distant anymore. The momentary blast of light gave off just enough glow for Curtis to see that there was a tiny, dark split in the forest. A trail, or perhaps a road. That's where the woman had gone, he was certain.

Why hadn't she responded when I called out to her?

He walked up to the cedar fence and easily leapt over it, following the rail until it stopped at the forest line. Then he crept carefully along the shadows of the woods, toward the place where he'd watched the woman disappear.

Another rumble of thunder, another flash of light. Which was a good thing, because he would have missed the small two-track that snaked into the forest.

He stopped and stared into the dark woods, searching for any movement, listening for any sounds. The dark canopy of tangled branches above him blacked out the sky, and he could no longer see the orange glow in the distance.

A droplet of rain fell on his face, and he stepped onto the trail, took a few steps, and stopped. Again, he saw and heard nothing, and he started walking along the two-track.

Rain began to sprinkle the trees, the tiny beads pattering on the leaves and branches. Curtis kept walking, taking soft but cautious steps, trying to make as little noise as possible. There was no sign of the woman on the trail ahead, however, it was so dark that she could have been twenty feet in front of him and he wouldn't have seen her.

An enormous explosion of thunder followed by an

expanding arc of lightning caught him by surprise, and Curtis jumped. His heart raced, then slowed. Rain fell harder, and it began dripping through the trees and onto him.

Screw this, he thought. *If somebody's house is on fire, then this rain will put it out. If it's somebody toasting marshmallows, the party's over for tonight.*

He turned around and began to retrace his steps.

"Hello, Curtis," a voice said.

He flinched at the sound, and stopped walking.

The woman—his neighbor, he was certain—was on the trail, only a few yards away.

TWELVE

He had passed her somehow, and now he could see her silhouette on the trail. Perhaps there was a side trail that turned off, and the woman had taken it, only to return to the main trail after he'd passed. Now she was before him in the darkness, motionless, her hands at her sides.

Curtis was confused. He'd never met the woman before, he was sure.

How does she know my name?

Seconds passed, and he hadn't responded to her greeting. The woman spoke again.

"You *are* Curtis, aren't you?" Her voice was quiet, and there was a knowing tone to it. She *knew* that she was speaking to Curtis; the question had only been one for him to acknowledge vocally.

"Yes, I am," he replied.

The woman stepped forward. It was still too dark to make out her features, although Curtis could tell that she was slim and probably a bit taller than his wife.

"Sarah Hendricks," she stated, extending a shadowy arm. Curtis shook her hand briefly. It was wet from rain.

"Curtis Stanton," he replied. "I was—"

"—following me?" Sarah interrupted. She didn't sound offended, and her voice had a hint of playfulness.

"No . . . I mean—"

Jesus, Curtis, get it together and quit fluttering like a junior in high school.

"—I saw the glow in the sky," he continued, turning a little and pointing behind him. The rain was really coming down now, and he was soaked. "I came out to find out what it was."

"Yeah, me too," she replied. "But I don't think there's anything to worry about with this rain."

"Are there any houses over there?" he asked.

"No. Probably just kids having a bonfire. There are a lot of trails that wind through here. Lots of fields and swamps." Then, right out of left field: "I have coffee brewing at the house. Would you like a cup?"

"No. Thanks, though," he said.

Did she pick up on that? he wondered. He had hesitated slightly—very slightly—before he'd answered.

"Okay. Another time, then."

"Sure."

Coffee brewing? At this hour?

Curtis began walking, and Sarah walked with him. He felt awkward and clumsy, and for good reason: here it was, the middle of the night, and he was walking in the rain with a woman who, he was certain, was very attractive. Her clothing, as his, was sopping wet, which only heightened his awareness of her. Sure it was innocent, sure it meant nothing . . . but it would be hard to explain should anyone see them come out of the forest together, in the middle of the night.

And feelings stirred once again, jarring old bones in the back of the closet.

No. Those aren't wise thoughts. Isn't a wise idea. Just because I got away with it before—

They reached the edge of the forest. Here, without the thick cover of the tree branches, the rain came down in torrents.

"It was nice meeting you, Sarah," his voice raised over the pounding rain.

"Likewise, Curtis. I'll see you."

Lighting flickered, and Curtis caught a flash of a smile in the darkness. Then Sarah turned and began walking across the field toward her home.

He turned and walked toward the orchard. When he reached the old cedar fence, he stopped and looked behind him, toward Sarah's house to the north.

She was there.

Far on the other side of the field, where the cedar fence formed a dividing line between the long blades of grass and the manicured lawn, she stood. And although it was very, very dark, Curtis knew that she was looking at him. He could *feel* it.

Then she turned, and she was gone.

He draped a leg over the fence, then another, then made his way through the orchard. Every now and then he shot a glance over his shoulder. He saw a light turn on in Sarah's home, saw it extinguish, only to be replaced by the faint glow of what could only be a candle.

Does she drink coffee in the dark? Curtis wondered. *At three in the morning?*

As he approached his own home, he took one more look across the orchard, and again saw the faint flicker of a candle in an upstairs window.

He did *not* see his wife staring down at him through the curtains, watching him, didn't see her peering through a crack in the curtain as he returned from the orchard.

141

When Curtis went inside, he discarded his wet clothing in the bathroom and draped them over the shower curtain rod. Then he strode back into the kitchen and drew a glass of water. He stood there, looking out the kitchen window, listening to the rain pummel the roof. He could see the silhouettes of several apple trees in the orchard; nothing more.

He looked at the glowing numbers on the microwave.

It's the middle of the night. Who's having a bonfire at this hour? And why would Sarah go to investigate if that's what she believed it was?

A bolt of lightning lit up the clouds and the orchard was alive for a brief, bright instant. Then the light was gone. Thunder cracked a moment later, and a low growl rolled over the fields and forests, finally dispersing in the night. Curtis filled the glass again, sipped slowly, then placed the empty glass on the counter.

When he went upstairs, Lauren was as he left her, huddled on her side in bed. He crept next to her and fell asleep.

THIRTEEN

I watched him get up and leave last night. He saw the fire." Lauren pressed the telephone receiver to her ear and spoke quietly.

"He didn't know that I watched him. Came home soaked." Pause. "Yes, it *did* rain hard last night."

She paused, listening to the voice on the other end of the line.

"No, he doesn't know a thing, I'm sure. He hasn't been doing much work. Drawing, anyway. He's been doing a lot of things around the house."

She paused, glancing up the stairs to make sure that Curtis hadn't awoken.

"Yes," she replied. "I want to see you, too. Tonight." She smiled, listening. "Yes," she said. "That would be great."

She quietly returned the phone to its cradle, then craned her neck to look upstairs. Satisfied, she opened the front door and went outside.

Curtis awoke around nine. The scent of fresh coffee drifted through the house. Girders of sunlight streamed through the motionless curtains, and birds chattered in the old orchard. The storm had passed on, leaving the morning air cool and damp.

Curtis slipped into a pair of sweats and a flannel shirt and went downstairs.

"Lauren?"

No answer. He poured a cup of coffee and strode to the living room window. Lauren was outside, toiling in what would be a vegetable garden next spring. He whistled and she turned, saw him through the window, smiled, and waved. Curtis walked outside and met her in the yard.

"Heavy rain last night," she said, standing up. She was wearing blue jeans, and dark, wet patches stained her knees. White gloves, dirtied from work, covered her hands. She'd been holding a rusty trowel; now she dropped it into the churned earth.

"Yeah, don't I know it," he said.

Lauren looked at him, puzzled. "What do you mean?"

"You don't remember me getting up?" he asked. "Talking to you?"

Lauren shook her head. "No. What was wrong?"

"I saw a fire." He pointed into the distance. *"Somebody* was having a fire. I woke you up. You don't remember?"

She shook her head. "No. I was out."

"Anyway, I got up and went to check it out, just in case someone's house was on fire."

"What was it?"

He shook his head. "Don't know. Maybe just someone having a bonfire. If it was, I'm sure the rain put out their little party. It sure came down last night. I got soaked. Didn't the thunder wake you up?"

"No, not at all. I slept right through it."

I'm probably going to be late tonight," Lauren said, snapping up her purse from the counter. "I'll call you when I'm on my way home. You need anything from town?"

Curtis shook his head. "Just you," he said, and he gave her a kiss.

"See you tonight." Lauren walked out the door, got into the Taurus, and left.

Curtis stood over the kitchen sink and watched his wife drive off, and mentally inventoried his list of things to do.

I'll see you.

The voice interrupted his thoughts. It was Sarah's voice, as she had spoke to him the night before. That's what she had said.

I'll see you.

She had suddenly come back into his mind, unprompted. He certainly hadn't forgotten their curious encounter in the early morning hours, but the voice came to him clear and resolute, as if the words had been *spoken,* as if he would turn around to see Sarah standing in the living room. Just for kicks, he *did* turn around.

The living room was empty.

The storm windows would be first. They were stored in the cellar during the summer months, and the first task would be to pull them out and wash them. Then he'd affix them in their proper sills around the home.

The entrance to the cellar was outside, on the east side

of the house. Old hinges groaned as Curtis opened the heavy, wooden door, exposing a stone stairway that led down to a dark, musty room. He propped the door open with a rock and descended the steps.

The floor of the cellar was soft sand, chalk-like, and the walls were old brick, faded dark gray. The air was musty and thick and smelled of old paper.

A single forty-watt bulb hung from the low ceiling like a fat spider clinging to a black thread. Curtis tugged at the dangling chain and the light came on.

There were odds and ends of all sorts, mostly old equipment that had been used around the farm. Several rusty shovels, rakes, and hoes, and the remains of what could have been an air compressor. Next to the compressor sat an old, grease-splattered mower which probably didn't work anymore, and Curtis wasn't going to put the effort into finding out. There were several ancient doors that leaned against a wall, and next to them, a dozen storm windows.

But it was the sand floor that caught his attention.

What the hell is that?

There was a design on the floor in the sand. It was faint and had probably been drawn long ago. Curtis could make out the straight lines and curves. A five-pointed star with a circle around it. It was nearly five feet in diameter. Someone had devised it, probably with a stick or a finger, then traced over it a second time.

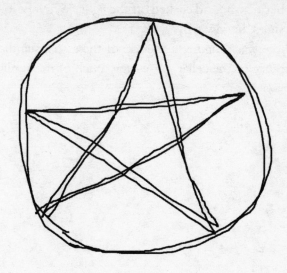

The design puzzled him for a moment, and seemed to jar a memory. He'd seen the design before, he was sure. It could be any number of things. A sheriff's badge came to mind. The insignia looked similar to what was emblazoned on many law enforcement vehicles. He was sure he'd also seen this symbol on jewelry, but he couldn't be certain. Whatever it was, it meant nothing to him other than a vague familiarity.

He thought nothing more of it, other than speculating that children had doodled on the sand floor. The old woman they'd purchased the house from had said that her grandchildren visited frequently. The cellar would undoubtably be a place of high interest among youngsters.

One by one, Curtis carried the windows up the steps and leaned them against the side of the house. When he pulled the final window away from the wall, he extinguished the light. He was about to begin the careful ascent up the steps, but he stopped. The cellar seemed murky, colder than it had been. It was a bit darker than it should be, and not simply because he had clicked off the light. When he looked up the stairs, he saw why.

There was a figure at the top of the steps, standing at the entrance of the cellar, obscuring much of the sunlight.

Sarah.

FOURTEEN

I *'ll see you.*
  He heard her voice again, but the woman at the top of the cellar steps had not yet uttered a sound.

Curtis squinted as he looked up.

Sarah's dark silhouette was haloed, framed by tangled, blinding sunlight. Thin beams splayed out around her head, her shoulders, her entire body, in a kind of misty corona. The appearance was striking, almost angelic. She was carrying a basket or a bucket; in the fragmented curves of dark and light, Curtis couldn't tell which.

"Howdy, neighbor," she said cheerfully.

"Hi," Curtis replied.

Then, realizing he was still standing at the base of the steps, he placed a foot on the first stone stair and ascended.

Sarah's shadow backed away as he approached the top.

"You won't regret those," she said, gesturing toward the large window in his arms. "Anything you can do to stop the wind in the winter." She waved her hand, gesturing across the orchard. "Not much stops the wind here, I'm afraid."

And now, for the first time, Curtis could see that he had been *right*.

Of *course* he was.

Sarah was more than simply beautiful; she was gorgeous.

He guessed her to be about thirty, maybe thirty one or two. Sinuous, curving features that were all woman, and more. And yet, her two most stunning features were what held Curtis spellbound.

Her hair was the color of the pit of night. It was beyond black; it was *eternal.* Not dyed black, not black with red hints . . . but deep, rich, black fibers that glistened in the sun. Silky tendrils fell past her shoulders, and one side of it fell in front of her shoulders and completely covered her right breast.

And her *eyes.*

They were green—

No, not green, Curtis thought. *Neon green. But—*

They were blue. And gray. The sun seemed to pick up variations of hues, and flecks, and Curtis found himself baffled.

Which is it? Green? Gray? Blue?

And while he was about to settle on one of the three colors, another tint bloomed.

Orange. A dazzling, pumpkin orange. Only for a moment, but it was there. Her eyes mirrored the season, as if they had stolen the coppery-orange of the rapidly changing maples that dotted the perimeter of the orchard.

And it was a *basket* she was carrying. A tattered straw basket that looked like it was about to fall apart. One arm looped around it, guarding its contents—shiny, red-green apples. Big ones, too, with an array of colors from pomegranate reds to viridescent greens. Some of them were a bit larger than a baseball.

"I thought you might want some," Sarah said, and she plucked an apple from the basket, held it up to her mouth, and took a bite. Her eyes never left his.

"Delicious. Here. Try one." She held out the apple that she'd bitten into.

Curtis must have hesitated, although he didn't think he had. Regardless, Sarah picked up on the momentary delay.

"Come on," she urged with a scintillating smile. "Try it. They're very, *very* good."

Curtis returned the smile and reached his hand out. He took the apple and raised it to his lips. The juicy fruit crunched in his mouth, full-bodied and sweet.

"Mmm. Great. Thanks."

"I brought you a few of them. I'll never eat them all."

"Where did you—"

"I have a tree that produces every year," Sarah interrupted, reaching into the basket and withdrawing another apple. She took a bite. "It's a shame. There are hundreds of apple trees in the area, but the only one that bears any fruit is the one in my back yard near the edge of the field. I've got more apples than I know what to do with."

She took another bite. "So . . . how do you like the neighborhood?"

Curtis laughed, and Sarah did, too.

"Well, if you can *call* it a neighborhood," he replied. "There seems to be no crime and no traffic. And as far as a *neighborhood* . . . well, you're our only *neighbor,* and so far your parties don't seem to be too wild."

"Wait 'till you get to know me." She winked playfully. *I'll see you.*

There it was again. Her voice played in his mind again. Why now?

I'll see you.

"Oh?" he replied. "Did we move next to a party girl?" Now it was Curtis's turn to smile.

"Oh, I've been known to be a bit lively. Walks in the middle of the night, you know. And I *love* storms. Especially the one last night. That was the most beautiful storm we've had in a while. Don't you think?"

"Haven't been here long enough to be an impartial judge," Curtis replied. "I don't really know much about the storms that move through the peninsula."

"Oh, you will. Especially the *fall* storms. You know, right before winter sets in? Next month—October—and November, too—will bring some bangers."

"Pretty bad, eh?"

"Depends on whether you like storms or not."

Sarah took another bite of her apple. "Anyway, I know your busy. Just wanted to drop these off." She handed the basket to Curtis. "And if you want more, the tree is loaded. At least for another few days. They're starting to fall. If you want any, help yourself."

"Thanks, I will."

And boy, he thought, admiring her as she walked away, *I'd love to help myself. Like you wouldn't believe, Sarah.*

All of a sudden, Sarah stopped.

For no reason.

Then she turned and looked directly at Curtis. No wave, nothing. Just a smile. Then she turned back and continued walking.

Shit. It was almost like she heard me thinking.

He went to work cleaning the storm windows, finding cause to gaze across the orchard every few minutes to see if he could catch a glimpse of his neighbor to the north.

FIFTEEN

Darkness. A car door closing. The front door opening. Footsteps on the wood floor at the bottom of the stairs.

Curtis awoke and turned in bed. Looked at the clock. Two. Two a.m.

His immediate thought was anger, but he pushed it aside. He'd stayed up, waiting for her to call like she said she would, but the phone never rang.

What do I care, anyway?

Lauren slipped quietly, silently, in bed next to him. He feigned sleep.

"Curtis?"

He didn't answer. She snuggled closer, draped an arm around his chest, and didn't say anything more.

Curtis was indeed awake, and he wasn't at all happy that she'd gotten home so late. But that went with the job, didn't it? She knew—and he did, too—that she'd have some late nights.

He began to fall asleep, teetering on the slim edge between consciousness and sleep. His mind took leave of command, leaving him in a murky terrain, the doorway to sleep.

And he could *see* her.

I'll see you.

Yes.

I'll see you.

Yes . . . .

They're starting to fall. If you want any, help yourself.

Yes . . . .

You want to fuck me, don't you?

Who? Me? No. I'm—

Come on, Curtis. I saw the way you looked at me. You want to screw my brains out. I can stand a fornicator . . . but a liar? Never.

No.

What? You'd never *fuck me? You'd better clarify yourself, Curtis. You've fucked three different women in your ten years of marriage . . . four, if you feel so inclined to include your wife. Tell me, Curtis . . . is she* really *that good that you want to stay with her? If she is, then why have you been eating apples from someone else's orchard? And why is* she?

No. Haven't . . . no. I've . . . .

I'll see you.

Huh?

I'll see you, Curtis.

He fell asleep.

SIXTEEN

It was an odd way to grow apart.

Lauren had become distant in just the short time that they had lived in their new home, and the late nights became more and more consistent. She became quieter, not sharing details of her late evenings at work . . . if, indeed, that was what she was doing. Curtis had his doubts. She'd been there, done that, and he recognized the pattern. Maybe it was a boss, or someone she met in Traverse. Maybe it *was* the sports editor. More than once he had heard her on the phone, talking in quiet, muffled tones, only to hang up abruptly when he came into the room.

And he *didn't* care, he told himself. His behavior toward her became a reflection of how *she* treated *him:* cordial, friendly. Smiles. They had sex, but it wasn't what could be called *lovemaking.* That was for people who *cared.* For people who *loved* one another.

Has it really come to this? he wondered one Friday morning. It was late September, and they'd been in the house for nearly two months. The woodland surrounding the farmhouse was aflame with the delights of autumn, blooming with bright yellows and vinaceous reds and rust orange. The air was crisp, and winter's breath was upon every breeze. It was morning, and Curtis stood at the dining room window and gazed, admiring the idyllic fall day.

Thinking. Gazing. Thinking . . . .

Lauren had left early for work, telling him that she hoped she wouldn't have to be out so late. Curtis knew that she would, indeed, come home late, and she'd have a dandy of an excuse.

The damned features editor didn't get her story in until late, she would say. *And it's the weekend edition, you know. Everyone is behind.*

Yeah. Right.

And he was beyond following her, beyond checking in and checking up. He'd done that in years previous, played the part of the covert sleuth, the shadowy private eye, and he hadn't liked what he had found out. It resulted in too much spent energy, too much anger and anxiety, too much rage and jealousy. Curtis tried to tell himself that *she* was the reason for his own past infidelities, that *she* had been first to wallow in the pool of infidelity. Which, of course, she *hadn't* been the first to be unfaithful in the marriage . . . but Lauren Stanton didn't need to know that detail. Or *any* of the details of his flings, for that matter—and that was the way it was going to stay.

Besides . . . Curtis had another interest. And right now, that interest was in her yard, on a stepladder, gathering up the remaining apples on the orchard tree. Curtis watched her through the living room window. A thick mane of black hair, tied back in a long ponytail, swayed between her shoulder blades as she pulled apple after apple from the bountiful tree.

And he wished her house was closer. He wished he could see her better, wished he could smile at her from time to time, and have her smile back. Maybe talk with her now and then, maybe share a coffee. He hadn't spoken to her in nearly two weeks, when she had brought over the basket of apples.

The basket of apples, he thought. *The basket of apples. I never returned the basket.*

He turned. The basket sat by the door, next to his Nike's.

I can talk to her. I can see her.

Without another thought he got up from the table, slipped his shoes on, picked up the basket, and walked out the door.

S he was still on the stepladder as he strode through the orchard and made his way through the long, dry grass. He stepped over the cedar rail fence and began walking across Sarah's tightly trimmed lawn. She had her back to him; she hadn't seen him approaching.

Not wanting to surprise her, especially while she was on the ladder, he opened his mouth to speak. However, before he could get any words out, she turned and looked directly at him as if she had known he was there all along.

"Good morning, Curtis," she said. Dark sunglasses concealed her eyes.

Jesus. A smile that would sink a ship.

"Hi," he replied, and he waved the basket. "Forgot to return this."

"Perfect," she said, reaching her arm down in a gesture that told him she needed the basket. Curtis walked up to the ladder and held it out to her. Sarah took it and returned to picking apples, placing them in the basket Curtis had given her.

"Not many good ones left," she said, plucking a large,

red-green fruit from a branch. "Most have fallen off. Winter is going to come early this year."

"How can you tell?" Curtis asked, watching her as she picked apple after apple and placed them in the basket.

"Lots of things," she replied. A breeze swept a lock of hair in front of her face, and she reached up and pulled it away. "Squirrels, for one. They've been gathering food for the past month. Other animals, as well. The animals can predict the weather a lot better than we can."

After a few moments the basket was full. She handed it to Curtis, who then backed away from the ladder as Sarah descended. She picked up another basket that lay in the grass, overflowing with apples.

"Could you bring that in?" she asked, nodding to the basket in his arms.

"Sure."

They walked across the lawn.

"You must be pretty busy," Sarah said. "I don't see you out much. Or your wife."

"Yeah, you know. That time of the year. Lauren is really busy with her new job at the paper. I'm just getting back to work."

"You're an architect."

It wasn't a question, but rather an acknowledgment.

"Yeah. How'd you know?"

"I have special powers," she replied, raising her eyebrows whimsically. Then she laughed. "I saw you moving in a drafting table the other day. Just a lucky guess."

"Good guess. I work—*worked*—for a firm in Petoskey. Now I'm on my own."

"How's it going?"

"Really great," he fibbed.

Actually, it probably *would have been* going fine, but he hadn't really applied himself. There were several jobs waiting to be finished, and several clients that were becoming impatient. He blamed his lackadaisical attitude toward work on his preoccupation with things that needed to get done around the house.

Curtis followed her inside her home, which was laid out very similar to his own. The kitchen, dining, and living rooms were nearly identical in size and shape. The two homes seemed almost interchangeable.

"Right over here," Sarah said, walking into the kitchen, and Curtis followed. She placed her basket of apples on the counter and took the basket from Curtis. Then she took off her sunglasses and turned to him.

"How about that coffee that I promised you a while back?" she asked pleasantly.

Curtis couldn't have said no if he tried.

Twenty minutes later they were still seated at the kitchen table. They chatted surface elements: the weather, the change of seasons, how much snow they'd get this year. Topics were light, and the conversation floated easily.

"This place looks almost identical to ours," Curtis said, nodding as his eyes gazed from the living room to the dining room, then to the ceiling.

"They were both built by the same guy," Sarah answered. "A long time ago. I guess he built one for his family, and one for his brother's family. Both families worked the orchard together, but that was years ago."

He looked at an unlit yellow candle that sat in the window sill. The blackened wick was short and curled like a burnt finger.

"I've seen that burning a few times," he said. "You

must be a real night owl."

"If I can't sleep, I'll get up and make a cup of hot tea or coffee, light a candle . . . you know. Just relax. I'm not much of a television person."

"You know—"

He suddenly felt silly, and he stopped.

"Yes?"

"Oh, forget it."

"What?" She smiled. "I can't forget it if you don't tell me what I'm supposed to forget." She smiled, and it drove him wild.

Goddamnit, stop it. Stop looking at me like that. You don't know what you're doing to me.

"Curtis?"

"Oh, it's no big deal. Really. It was . . . well, last month. I saw someone in the orchard. Two people, actually. It was three or four in the morning. I went to see who they were, but they—"

He caught himself.

"—were gone." He did not tell her that they seemed to vanish before him.

"Have you seen them again?" Sarah asked.

"No."

She sipped her coffee and looked at him over the mug.

"You'll probably see more."

Her reply stunned him. Her tone was very matter of fact, as if nothing at all was out of the ordinary. She gazed at him, and Curtis wondered if she was searching his face for a response.

"What do you mean?" Curtis asked.

"It's fall. Nearly October. The area draws quite a few during the season."

"Not in the middle of the night," Curtis asserted.

She smiled, and took a sip of her coffee . . . and it was

then that Curtis saw her necklace. He had been aware of it, a thin silver chain that hugged closely to her neck. But he hadn't seen the pendant . . . until now.

Affixed to the silver chain was a small, round object. The same design he'd seen in the sand in the cellar. A circle—with a five pointed star.

SEVENTEEN

Curtis didn't inquire about the necklace, but he certainly caught the similarity between the charm around her neck and the design in the sand in the cellar.

But he wanted to know more about what she had meant when she said that he'd 'probably see more people' around.

"Why do you think that more people will come around?"

She looked out the window thoughtfully. "Some people," she explained, "believe that this part of the peninsula is a very . . . *special* . . . place."

"In what way?"

"Many people think that this particular area is sacred. That it is a pivotal point of unique powers, especially during the month of October and the arrival of Samhain."

"Who is that?"

Sarah laughed. "It's not 'who', it's *what*. Samhain is a Gaelic word meaning the end of summer. Samhain is the night of the Feast of Souls. It's kind of a holiday for some."

Curtis took a sip of coffee. "And when is that?"

"October 31st, usually, or thereabouts."

"Halloween?"

"Yes. Although the festival of Samhain has been around much longer. I thought perhaps you might have come to the region for the same reason that others do."

"Me? Sorry. I came here because we fell in love with the area, and the price was right."

"Everything does have its price, doesn't it?" Sarah mused.

Curtis smiled and searched her eyes for something hidden, something clandestine, as if he might spy a hidden door that contained a treasury of secrets.

And he wondered if he *really* wanted that door opened.

She returned his smile. "I'm baking apple pies this afternoon. Would you like one?"

"Mmmm, that would be great."

"I'll bring it over."

She sipped her coffee, and Curtis caught another glimpse of the silver pendant around her neck. He was curious about that, too, but he didn't ask her about it. He looked at his watch.

"Wow," he said. "Time flies when you're having fun." He stood up to leave. "Thanks for the coffee."

"Anytime."

Sarah stood and walked him to the door. "See you later today," she said, and she closed the front door behind him.

Curtis walked home, but he didn't go inside. Instead, he went around back and opened the cellar door. The wind took it out of his hands and it banged against the stone foundations.

He walked down the steps, reached the sand floor, and pulled the small chain that dangled from the bulb. Light burst forth.

Curtis turned and looked at the ground. He had disturbed the sand when he'd retrieved the storm windows, but the insignia was still visible, if a bit scrambled.

He knelt down in the sand and retraced the lines, connecting the broken arches and turns. In a few moments, the design was complete again.

That's what it is, he thought. *That's the same thing she was wearing around her neck. A circle with a star in the middle.*

He stood, turned off the light, walked back up the steps, and closed the cellar door behind him.

EIGHTEEN

A fine mist began to fall by midday. The air grew cold and clammy, prompting Curtis to shut the windows tight.

He had just closed the bedroom window upstairs when there was a knock at the front door, and a twinge of anticipation surged. He'd been waiting; he was beyond trying to tell himself that he wasn't. He'd been waiting for her to come over since the moment she'd told him that she'd bring over a pie. He'd replayed their earlier conversation over and over in his mind. Not so much that he needed clarification on anything. She'd been vague about all that *Samhain* mumbo-jumbo, the *Feast of Souls.*

Hey, to each their own, he thought.

No, what he went over in his mind was *her.* The way she spoke, the way she smiled. The way her eyes seemed to glow, and the way they contrasted with her black hair. He undressed her in his mind and saw the curve of her hips, the soft skin of her breasts and shoulders. In his mind his fingers gently kneaded her hair, her delicate lips met his.

He walked down the steps and reached the door, opened it wide.

And suddenly, there she was. Same blue jeans and flannel shirt that she'd worn this morning. Same dazzling eyes and hair.

"Special delivery," she said with a wide grin. In one hand she carried the pie, in the other, a small paper grocery bag.

"Remind me to sell my stock in *Domino's,*" he said. "You've got them beat by a mile. Come on in." He stepped back to allow her inside.

Sarah kicked off her sneakers as she stepped in. "Getting muddy out there," she said.

The mist had ceased, but the ground hadn't soaked up the light drizzle. Small puddles had formed in the gravel driveway. A gray canopy of stippled clouds hung dismally over the field, the orchard, and the nearby forest.

Curtis took the pie from her and placed it on the counter. It was deliciously warm, and the sweet aroma filled the kitchen. "Smells incredible," he said after he sniffed the air.

"I make a mean pumpkin pie, too," she said, placing the bag on the counter. It made a dull *thud,* and she reached in and pulled out a wine bottle. There was no label on it, nothing to indicate what it was. The liquid it contained was a deep red-black.

"And my specialty," she announced proudly. "Homemade blackberry wine. Much, *much* better than anything you can buy, mind you," she boasted.

Curtis smiled, but he never even *thought* about uttering the phrase that he'd learned so well several years ago.

No thanks, I don't drink.

It had been a hard phrase to use at first, especially with most of his friends popping over to watch a game, or when he went to someone else's for an evening get together. And bars didn't even come into play. He stayed away from the local watering holes, and for good reason. Gradually, *no thanks, I don't drink* became easier and easier, until most of his friends had realized that, son of a gun, Curtis Stanton *was* serious, that he *wasn't* going to have a drink. Coffee was fine, as was Coke, Pepsi, tea, whatever.

Today, however, the *no thanks, I don't drink* phrase was tossed out the window like well-chewed gum, along with other realizations that he had begun to acknowledge. Such as the fact that Lauren was probably banging someone in Traverse City, and the fact that he now believed their marriage was in a tailspin. A regular *Mayday,* an irrecoverable nosedive—only no one was radioing the tower. Their union was no longer on the rocks; it had been swept out to sea in a fury of tumultuous waves and spume.

But a ship had been on the horizon. A beautiful, mysterious ship, with a cargo of surprise and newness and adventure.

No, thanks, I don't drink, became—

"You're amazing," as he picked up and admired the bottle. "Homemade wine. Pies. Anything you don't do?"

"Windows," she replied with a laugh, then a roll of her eyes. "Sorry . . . that one came out of retirement. But I *do* love to cook and bake."

"You don't show it," he said, resisting the urge to give her body a once over.

"Oh, I can't eat *everything* I make," she said with a grin. She pointed at Curtis. "That's what neighbors are for."

"Glad to be on the receiving end," Curtis replied.

His mind was spinning. The innocence of a simple neighborly relationship was wearing thin, at least for him.

And her? Does she feel the same? Does she want the same, or is this just how she is? Am I reading this whole thing totally wrong?

Some women—and men, for that matter—were simply perpetual flirts. Some of them didn't even know that they were doing it. Regardless how they acted or how someone might take their actions, their intentions *were* innocent. Curtis didn't want to make a mistake of misidentification.

But God . . . how clear does she have to be? It's in her eyes and her smile. It's in her body language. She brought over a pie, for Chrissakes. And wine. She wants the same thing I do. Doesn't she? And is she wondering the same thing?

Yes, he'd played this game before. It was the same game, but the players were different. Each person brought their own challenges, their own set of variables. The rules of the game were the same, but the board was laid out differently.

He opened up a kitchen drawer, found a corkscrew, and cranked the instrument into the cork. The bottle opened with a *pop*.

"It should breathe for about ten minutes," Sarah said.

Curtis placed the bottle on the table and pulled out two wine glasses from the cupboard. Then he opened the drawer again and pulled out a knife.

"I've got to try a piece of this pie. The smell alone is driving me crazy."

He cut a small piece and served it to Sarah on a plate. Then he cut one for himself. "You know," he began, sitting on a barstool, "you didn't say too much about that Samhain thing. That 'Feast of Souls,' or whatever it's called. I'm kind of curious about that." Which he wasn't, of course, but Sarah seemed to know quite a bit about it, and it would get the conversation moving. The first roll of the dice in the game.

"It's quite ancient, actually," Sarah replied without hesitation. "It began in Ireland in the 5th century, B.C. October 31st was the day summer officially ended, and the beginning of the Celtic new year." She paused only to chew a piece of pie, then continued.

"On that day, it was said that all of the disembodied spirits of the people who have died that year come back in search of living bodies to possess. The Celts in Ireland believed that the laws of space and time were suspended for that night, which allowed the dead to coexist with the living."

"Sounds spooky," Curtis said with a smile. He winked. "Gotta watch out for those damned disembodied spirits."

"Which is exactly how the practice of dressing up for Halloween came from," Sarah continued. "No one, of course, wanted to be possessed, so they wouldn't light any candles or have any fires. They did everything they could to make their homes uninviting. Then, they would dress up that night in creepy costumes and make all kinds of noise in hopes of frightening away the spirits. 'Halloween' was actually a concoction of the early catholic church, in an effort to undermine the pagan celebration of Samhain."

"And why is it that people are drawn here at this time of the year?" Curtis asked, biting into another piece of pie. He nodded at his plate. "Very good, by the way."

"Thanks." She smiled, and it drove Curtis bananas. "People are drawn to this area for its power. You really don't know about this?" she asked with a look of genuine surprise.

"No. Should I?"

"It's fairly common knowledge, but you won't find it in any of the local history books. Kind of one of those things that people want to sweep under the rug. In the mid 1800's, a coven of witches settled here."

"Get out of here."

"No, really. It's true." Sarah raised her hand for a moment, as if she were pledging an oath. "As you can imagine," she continued, "this didn't set well with locals. Long story short: all of the so-called 'witches'—which included entire families—were burned at the stake. Just like what went on in Salem, and over in Europe."

Curtis stopped chewing and listened intently.

Jesus, she's serious.

"Witches," he remarked skeptically. "Seriously."

"Yes. Well, that's what the townsfolk thought. In truth, the group was more of a pagan clan than anything. Not much was known about them except for the fact that they kept to themselves and practiced their own kind of religion—a religion that was in a dark contrast to the conservative orthodoxy of the day."

"All of them were killed?"

Sarah nodded. "Men, women, children. Everyone. Their land was seized and divided among a few people from the peninsula. In fact, this field and orchard is the exact place of their settlement."

The whole thing seemed a bit outlandish to Curtis, but the fact that an entire group of people—men, women, and children—had been burned to death . . . that was unconscionable, regardless whether they were 'witches' or not. There were other places in the world where this had happened, of course, through various periods of history. It seemed crazy to Curtis that a group of people would condemn an entire population to death—especially by such extreme measures—simply for what they believed in.

"That's insane," he said.

But he had been right. He had struck upon a topic that Sarah seemed to know a lot about, something that seemed to be more than just a general interest.

"There are many people today," Sarah said, "who believe that the souls of those people—the witches—return here every year to find souls to possess. It makes this area a very powerful place in the realm of the supernatural. Many people believe that they can harness the powers of these dead souls and use that power for their own benefit in the natural world."

"But if these supposed 'souls' are coming back to possess people," Curtis asked suspiciously, "why would anyone want to risk becoming possessed?"

"There are ways to keep manifestations from harming humans," Sarah replied. Her answer was matter-of-fact, maybe even a bit flippant, and Curtis began to wonder.

"You know entirely too much about this stuff," he said with a smirk. "Next thing you'll tell me is that *you're* a witch."

Sarah smiled and shrugged casually. "My reasons for being here are very similar to the reasons others are drawn here," she confessed.

Curtis felt his smile fading, then caught himself.

She's a nutcase. She actually believes in this shit.

"And those reasons are . . . ?"

She shrugged again. "You know. Power. Contentment. Satisfaction, and a sense of being a part of something that is greater than your physical self. Look."

She reached behind her neck with both hands, unclasped her necklace, and held it up for Curtis to see. He nodded.

"This is an ancient occultic symbol. It's an inverted pentacle. Among other things, it is believed that the inverted pentacle keeps the souls of the dead from taking over your physical being."

Curtis held out his hand and Sarah dropped the necklace into his palm. He studied it closely, pressing the shiny medallion between his thumb and forefinger.

"Hold it up and I'll show you something," she said.

Curtis did as she asked.

"Now . . . turn it over," she continued, "so that the star is pointing up."

173

He turned the pendant around. As he did, Sarah stood up and placed her chair next to him. She sat down and leaned forward, placing an elbow on the table. He could feel the warmth of her body and smell her perfume, a sweet, gentle aroma that was at once deliciously intoxicating.

She reached up and pointed to the pendant that Curtis was holding up, and her hand touched his.

"It's called a pentacle when it's worn alone. As an insignia on a wall or paper, for example, it's usually called a pentagram. Look."

She raised a finger to the object in Curtis's hand. "Each point represents an element. The lower left point represents Earth. It's symbolic of Stability and Physical Endurance. This one—"

She moved her finger to the lower right point of the tiny star within the circle. "—this represents Fire. It is the symbol of Courage and Daring."

Instinctively, Curtis moved his finger up to the upper right-hand point.

"And this one?" he asked.

"Water. Emotions and Intuition."

Again, he moved his finger to another point, to the upper left.

"Air," Sarah said. "Intelligence and the Arts. And the top point—"

Now she took his finger in her hand and placed it at the top of the small pentacle.

"Spirit," she explained. "Symbolic of Deity and the Divine, and the All that Is. And around the star," she continued, releasing his finger and tracing the circle in the air, "represents sacred space, in which the spirit controls the four earthly elements."

"But you wear it," Curtis said, flipping over the pendant so the star pointed down, "like this. What's that mean?"

"The inverted pentacle represents winter," Sarah replied nonchalantly. "It is believed to ward off offending spirits." She said nothing else, and Curtis knew that there was more that she wasn't telling him. He turned to her and held out the necklace. She took it from him and returned it to her neck.

She looked at him, and she knew.

She knew that *he* knew that there was a lot more that she wasn't telling him.

And he was right, of course.

"So, this is kind of like . . . a religion?"

A warm smile flowered on Sarah's lips.

"One of the oldest—if not *the* oldest—of all of today's religions. Much older, in fact, than any of our modern day misguided faiths. In fact, the five-pointed star was actually a secondary symbol of the Christian faith, representing the five wounds of Jesus on the cross. One in each wrist, one in each ankle, and those made by the crown of thorns. The spear wound in his side wasn't counted, as Christ was dead at the time. To the early Jews it represented the five books of Moses. The insignia also has been called the 'star of life' being that five-fold symmetries are found in so many living organisms. Fingers, many flowers, starfish, apples—"

"Wait a minute," Curtis interrupted. Cynical, yet noncombatant scorn, flared in his eyes. "How is five represented in an *apple?*" He smiled. Truth is, he thought that what he was hearing was Grade-A, prime *bullshit*.

"Do you have one?" Sarah asked.

Curtis got up and walked into the kitchen. Several apples were in a small basket next to the toaster, along with a few oranges and two bananas. He picked up an apple.

"And a knife," Sarah said.

Curtis opened a drawer and snapped up a knife. He walked back to the table and sat down, placing the fruit and the utensil on the table.

Sarah turned the apple so that it sat upright, with the stem pointing upward.

"Now, cut it in half. Horizontally."

Curtis picked up the apple and cut it in half. He placed one of the halves on the table, along with the knife.

"Look at the slice."

Curtis smiled a *golly gee, how about that* grin. Cutting the apple in half, crossways, revealed a perfect, five pointed star—the core, cut crossways—with several dark seeds in the middle.

A pentagram.

"You see?" Sarah said, tracing the star within the fruit, and then running her finger around the edge. "They are everywhere. Some people believe that the five-pointed star is the most powerful symbol in the universe."

Curtis placed the apple on the table and looked at her, again searching her eyes.

"And this is your . . . your *religion?*" Curtis asked, trying to sound noncommital or inoffensive, but he wondered if his cynicism was transparent enough for her to detect his derisive disbelief. "Witchcraft?"

Sarah smiled, but her lips did not part.

"No," she said, gently shaking her head. "Not witchcraft. That's . . . that's not really what it is at all. It's . . . much different."

Curtis thought she was going to continue, but she didn't. Still, he was curious, regardless of whether he understood her spiritual doctrine or not.

"Do you believe in God?" he asked.

Her smile faded, leaving a faint, almost undetectable smirk. Curtis wondered if she was merely patronizing him.

"Yes, Curtis, I believe in God." The smile returned. "The God I believe in just doesn't happen to be the God that I worshiped in Sunday school."

The look of surprise on Curtis's face betrayed him, and Sarah laughed.

"What?" she replied to his silent response. "Hard to believe that I was raised a good Catholic girl?"

Curtis laughed, and the curtain of curiosity remained. It hung before him like an invisible wall.

"And so . . . what *do* you believe?" he pressed.

"I believe," Sarah replied with a Machiavellian smile that was at once so striking, so enticing, that Curtis froze. Her face gleamed with beauty and the oh-so-tantalizing unknown. She placed her elbows on the table, kneaded her fingers together, and rested her chin on her folded knuckles. *"I believe that it's time for that glass of wine."*

NINETEEN

Curtis rose to his feet. "Glass of wine, coming up."
He walked to the counter and poured two glasses, hoping to divert the discussion of ancient, dead souls to something—*anything*—a bit more rational. Truthfully, he had been interested in hearing about her beliefs; now the game was taking another turn, progressing around the board, and the only spirit he wanted to raise resided in the bottle Sarah had brought.

He handed a glass to Sarah, placed the bottle on the table, then sat down.

"Cheers," he said, raising his glass in celebration, to which Sarah nodded and raised hers. Glasses clinked, and Curtis placed the glass to his lips without a single thought of his old *AA* meetings and the twelve-step program.

Hi . . . my name is Curtis, and I couldn't give a rat's ass.

The wine was delicious, savory. Curtis never *had* been much of a wine drinker, but he did have memories of blackberry wine, back in his high school days when he and his friends would pool their money together, find a willing buyer (none of them at the time were of legal age to purchase booze) and buy all the Manischewitz blackberry wine that they could afford. At under three dollars a bottle and eleven percent alcohol, a dandy buzz could be had by all . . . or at least enough of one to start feeling wobbly. Plus, the bottle said that it was a *kosher* wine. Curtis and his friends thought that fact alone made it better somehow, although at the time, he nor his friends really knew what it meant. *It's the Jewish word for 'cool'*, one of his friends had insisted.

But *this* blackberry wine was *nothing* like the wine of his youth. This wine was deliciously sweet—but not overbearing. The tang of blackberry wasn't overpowering, and there was a tiny hint of tartness that made it nearly semi-dry and light. The wine seemed to be a blend of the seasons; of spring, summer, and fall.

"This *is* really good," he exclaimed, gently swirling the dark liquid in the glass.

"You were expecting less?" Sarah replied, flashing another grin.

Curtis looked over his glass and into her eyes, shook his head, and smiled. "You really are pretty amazing, Sarah Hendricks," he said.

Sarah said nothing. She simply returned Curtis's gaze, and sipped her glass, displaying a contented, satisfied grin.

They talked well into the afternoon, about many things, most of which centered on more 'earthly' matters. Sometimes the topic turned back to the history of the area, but Sarah always steered the issue onto another subject. It was clear to Curtis that, at least for the time, she was unwilling to share much more about her knowledge of metaphysical canons that others in the area—perhaps even Sarah herself—had faith in. Or maybe she thought that she had told him more than she should have.

Another topic they had averted: he didn't ask her about her family, and she didn't ask about his wife. Something told

Curtis that there just wasn't much to know about her family, and he knew that it would be pointless to ask. As such, she didn't press for many personal details about himself.

It was sometime around five that Curtis realized three things: one, he was buzzed. Two—

He liked it, goddammit.

Hi . . . my name is Curtis. I'm just here for the beer.

But the third realization was a bit more disturbing. Sobering, in fact, and he *didn't* like it. He didn't like it because he couldn't *explain* it. His third realization was this: he and Sarah had been drinking wine all afternoon. They had laughed and chatted and poured and sipped for several hours. Each had probably had four or five *full* glasses.

Yet—

The bottle on the table was only half empty. The bottle looked as if only two or three glasses had been poured from it.

He had become aware of it after pouring the third glass of wine for each of them. He had thought that there should be less wine in the bottle, but he didn't think too much of it at the time. After another glass, however, he was perplexed.

"Be right back," Curtis said, and stood up to go to the bathroom. He glanced at the bottle before he turned away.

Half full. Shit. We drank way more than that. Way more.

He walked into the bathroom, clicked the light, closed the door, and looked in the mirror.

"Great," he whispered, seeing the embarrassingly long stain of wine that began at the corner of his mouth and ran down his chin. *"I'll bet that really impressed the lady."*

He reached up to wipe it off, but the stain didn't immediately rub away.

Instead, it *flaked* off.

It had dried, and had dried like a scab. A scab that was the color of—

No. You are drunk.

Somewhere within, his consciousness tried to take hold. It told him that hell yes, she was beautiful, but she was *strange*. There was something going on here, something that wasn't adding up. Something rotten in Denmark, as his father used to say.

Nope. You're drunk, Curtis Stanton.

There was blood on his chin.

No, it's not. It's blackberry wine. Homemade blackberry wine.

He ran water in the sink, wet his finger, and rubbed the rest of the stain until there was no trace of it.

Blackberry wine. That's all it was.

He relieved himself, and gave himself another once-over in the mirror.

Weird shit, he thought. *All that talk about the 'Feast of Souls' and people using pentacles and pentagrams to—*

He suddenly remembered the strange circle with the star that he'd seen in the basement, how it was identical to the one that Sarah wore around her neck, but his recollection was hazy, dream-like.

He shook his head while staring at his reflection in the mirror.

Hell. Hang around her long enough and she's liable to make me believe anything.

He shut off the light, opened the door, and strode into the hall.

Sarah was standing by the fireplace, admiring some old photos on the mantle. Her back was to him, and again he admired the perfect curves of her body, her trim waist and firm hips. Desire flared brighter.

He walked up to her to explain some of the older photos, pictures of his grandparent's home in Harbor Springs. He reached out over her shoulder and pointed. "This one is—"

Sarah suddenly turned, and her eyes met his. They were

close. Curtis felt a jolt of awkwardness, like he had within his grasp something that he so strongly desired—only now that he had it, he wasn't sure if it was what he wanted, after all. The moment, however, passed quickly, as the internal computers and mathematicians and bean counters weighed their options and calculated the answer.

He lowered his hand and touched her hair, then gently touched her neck. Sarah closed her eyes.

Superficials tumbled and fell. A wall crashed down.

They were afire instantly, an inferno of passion and lust. He kissed her lips, her chin, her neck. She moaned softly as he gently nibbled on the soft skin beneath her ear. Then he took her by the shoulders and pushed her against the stone fireplace, pressing his lips on hers. She responded equally, fervently, her hands on his back, pulling him to her.

After a moment, Curtis withdrew. They stared at one another, silently, each reading into the depths of one another's eyes. Nothing was said as Curtis took her by the hand and led her upstairs.

It was dark when he awoke. His mind was fuzzy from the wine, and he shook his head in the dark. He was snuggled next to Lauren in their bed.

And outside, a car door slammed.

A car door?

Reality flew about in his mind like a buzzing gnat, and he fought off sleep and grogginess.

A car door?!?!

Suddenly, he was wide awake

Thoughts exploded as he realized that the woman in bed next to him *wasn't* Lauren Stanton, his wife of ten years.

It was *Sarah*.

They'd made love, here in the bedroom, and they'd fallen asleep.

They'd fallen asleep . . . and Lauren had come home.

TWENTY

His heart hammered in his chest, bludgeoning his rib cage. His skin constricted and his face flushed. Blood raced through his arteries, pounding rhythmically in his temples with feverish intensity, seeping into every vein and tiny venule.

Downstairs, the door of the house opened, and his delirium spun out of control. He'd had only enough time to make it to the bedroom door before the kitchen light blinked on.

This is it. Caught. No way outta this one. Not now, there isn't.

His heart was pounding so hard he could literally feel his arteries swelling. His lungs heaved as he gasped for breath. It was like all of the air in the house had been drawn away. Curtis was at the top of the stairs and was about to turn and race back into the bedroom—

Too late.

Lauren suddenly appeared at the bottom of the stairs. She looked up, and their eyes met.

"Curtis?"

Red-handed. She isn't going to like this one bit.

"Curtis? What's wrong?"

Lauren was still at the bottom of the stairs, but now she raised a foot, and, with some hesitation, placed it on the bottom step.

Curtis shot a panicked glance behind him, into the bedroom where Sarah was—

Gone.

Jesus, she's trying to hide! She's trying to hide in our bedroom!

He turned and bolted into the bedroom. From the bottom of the stairs, his wife called out again, and her voice echoed through the house.

"Curtis! What's wrong?!?! You're scaring me."

Curtis raced around the room. Sarah wasn't in the closet, not under the bed, nor the adjacent bathroom. Nor were her clothes anywhere to be found.

Where in the hell is she?!?!?

Footsteps climbed the steps, painfully echoing the drumming of his heart. Closer.

Behind the door!?!? Jesus! Is she crazy?!?!

Louder footsteps. Lauren was nearing the top of the stairs. Curtis felt like his heart was about to explode, and his mental turbulence whipped his senses into a frantic hurricane of disorientation.

In a frenzy, he swept the door away from the wall. There was nothing there. But—

"Curtis! What is going on?!?!" Lauren was at the top of the stairs. In five steps, she would be in the room.

—but he felt *cold.* His skin tightened with fleshy goosebumps. Cool night air frosted his sweaty skin. Curtis spun.

The window was open.

He sprang to it and looked outside, his eyes searching the darkness some twenty feet below.

"Would you mind telling me what's going on?!?!" Lauren's

voice was close, and the room dimmed when her figure reached the doorway, blocking the light above the stairs.

Then the bedroom light clicked on.

Curtis turned. His mouth was open, and he was swallowing quick, shallow breaths.

Make this one good, Curtie. Make this one good.

"Man, Lauren," he began, shaking his head. He ran his fingers through his disheveled hair. "I just had the most bizarre dream." He sat down on the bed and wiped his cheeks with the palms of his hands.

And maybe it was. Maybe that's all this was . . . a dream.

"God, Curtis. You scared me. I thought something was wrong."

"A dream," Curtis repeated, shaking his head. A bead of perspiration dribbled down his temple, and he wiped it away.

No. When I woke up, she was here. She was in bed with me. I felt her, I could smell her. She was here. Sarah was here.

Lauren walked over to him. "You're sweating," she said, sitting next to him on the bed. "What were you dreaming about?"

His fabrication was hardly original, but it sufficed. He made something up about people chasing him through the forest, and him not being able to get away.

Lauren looked at the tattered sheets on the bed. "Yeah, it even *looks* like you've been running."

His mind was whirling, and he hoped that Lauren didn't see the panic in his eyes.

Did I put everything away? Is there anything she might see to make her suspicious?

He'd had the mental clarity earlier in the evening to cork the bottle of wine (it was still nearly half-full) and stash it behind some books in the room that had become his study. He'd washed the wine glasses and returned them to the cupboard. Wiped off the table and the counter. No, any evidence downstairs had been eliminated.

"Well, it was just a dream," Lauren said. She brushed a light kiss on his cheek. "I'm going to jump in the shower." She got up and closed the bedroom window, then walked into the bathroom. Curtis waited impatiently until he heard the water running. Then he leapt up and fumbled through the sheets.

Stains wouldn't be a good thing, he thought. *That wouldn't be something I can explain away so easily.*

He found nothing.

Satisfied, he went downstairs just to double-check everything. The glasses were, indeed, sitting on the shelf in the cupboard, just like he'd placed them, and the bottle in his study was tucked neatly behind some large text and reference books.

Curtis, you are one lucky son of a bitch. Careless . . . but lucky.

Relieved, he turned off all the lights and walked back up the steps and into the bedroom. He heard the water shut off as he climbed into bed.

Something clinked on the floor beside the bed. Something metallic, something small. He rolled sideways and peered over the edge.

Sarah's necklace.

The thin silver chain was bunched and twisted, covering up the small pentacle that rested on the floor.

Whoops, Curtis thought, and he quickly reached down and snapped it up. He cupped it in his fist just as the door to the bathroom swung open. The bathroom light clicked off, and Lauren slipped into bed next to him. She touched his shoulders, and ran a finger down his side to his hips.

"Curtis?" she whispered in the darkness.

"Hmmmm?" he feigned in his best sleepy-groggy groan.

Her hand was resting on his hip and she drew it around

to his belly and caressed his soft skin with a single finger.

"Mmmm. Sleepy . . . ."

"You're no fun," she said, snuggling up to him.

"Should . . . Shoulda been here earlier," he continued in simulated drowsiness. Then, realizing what he'd said, he smiled in the darkness.

And fell asleep.

TWENTY ONE

Curtis awoke early, well before the sun rose. He'd awakened several times during the night, each time squeezing his fist to make sure that Sarah's necklace was still there.

Lauren was still sleeping, and Curtis arose and threw himself into his work. There were several projects he was behind on, and there was one commission in particular—the Martin home—that he was in danger of losing altogether. His deadline to have that one complete had passed weeks ago. If he pushed it, he might be able to finish it up today.

While he worked at the drafting table, his mind wandered, reconstructing the previous day's events. Several things puzzled him. One, of course, was the wine. Half of the bottle remained, yet he was *certain* that both he and Sarah had consumed five or more glasses *each*. That would have meant that *each* of them could have polished off a bottle, without help from the other.

But what puzzled him the most was—

How in the hell did she get out of there? How did she leave the bedroom? Through the window?

It seemed impossible. *Was* impossible. The bedroom

was on the second floor. If she jumped, she would've broken a leg or two—or *worse*.

There was, obviously, the most plausible explanation, and that was the fact that she left before he had woken up. Before Lauren had come home from work.

Of course.

Now, with the clarity of morning and several cups of coffee, he wasn't so sure if Sarah had been next to him in bed when Lauren had returned, after all. Maybe he'd only *imagined* that she was lying next to him, and had simply *fantasized* that she was in bed when Lauren came home.

Yes, that *had* to be it. If she had been in the room, there simply would have been *no way* for her to leave—not without going down the stairs, anyway.

And the wine. That had something to do with it, for sure.

He smiled beneath the bright light in his study, huffed through his nostrils as he shook his head in disbelief. He worked furiously.

Lauren awoke around ten. Curtis had polished off a pot of coffee, and another had just finished brewing when she came down the stairs. He heard her on the steps and called out to her.

"Fresh coffee, on the counter."

"I could smell it from upstairs. Thanks."

He heard her slippers skid on the wood floor, heard a coffee mug clunk, heard liquid pouring. She came to his study. Curtis was hunched over the drafting board, a ruler in one hand, a drafting pencil in the other.

"How's it going?" she asked, placing a hand on his shoulder. He turned, and she knelt. They kissed briefly.

"Good, really good," Curtis replied. "I think I can

finally finish up the Martin project today."

Then, from nowhere:

"Curtis, I'm sorry about the late nights. I *really* am."

The abrupt apology took him by surprise. Her voice was apologetic, genuine.

Curtis set down the pencil and ruler and reached for his coffee. "It's not a problem, Lauren," he said, facing her and smiling. "It's really not."

And he meant it.

He worked tirelessly the rest of the morning, and by noon he was *certain* that he'd have the project complete by days' end. It felt good to be so involved, so lost in a project again. Lauren had brought some work home with her and she had papers spread out across the kitchen table and counter. The morning was peaceful; neither spoke much to one another, unwilling to disturb the steady flow of work that needed to get done.

A movement out the window of his study drew Curtis's attention, and when he realized what he was seeing, his entire body tensed.

Sarah. Sarah Hendricks was walking up the driveway.

Their driveway.

She was coming to *their* house.

TWENTY TWO

What in the hell does she think she's doing?!?! his mind screamed. *She's coming* here! *She's actually coming* here!

He remained huddled at his desk, his body rigid, his hand clenching and unclenching against his thighs. He was facing the drafting table, but his eyes never left the woman walking up the driveway.

The morning was chilly, Curtis presumed, noting the thick wool sweater she was wearing. Her hair hung long and straight and full. Twice, she sidestepped one of the many small puddles that had pooled on the hard-packed drive.

Jesus. What in the hell....

Then she slipped from view as she strode across the lawn and to the front porch. Curtis cringed when he heard the doorbell ring.

"Sounds like we've got company," Lauren called out, getting up from the table.

"Wonder who it could be?" Curtis replied, trying to conceal his nervousness.

He heard the door open, heard voices. He froze at the desk, listening. His hands balled into fists, and he held them.

Sarah: "Hi! I'm your neighbor. Sarah Hendricks."

Lauren, sweetly: "Lauren Stanton. Nice to meet you."

Sarah: "Likewise . . . and I'm sorry to bother you. Something's wrong with the power at my house. I see you have electricity, so, whatever is wrong, I think it's just with my place."

Lauren: "Uh-oh. That's not good. Curtis!"

Shit. Get your best poker face on.

He stood up, took a breath, and walked out of his study and into the living room. Both women looked at him.

"This is Sarah Hendricks," Lauren said.

Curtis approached the two women and extended his hand to Sarah. He smiled a very unpolished *I can't believe you're doing this* smile.

"Curtis Stanton," he said, his eyes boring into hers. "Nice to meet you."

He felt awkward, but he had articulated the greeting without betraying his discomfort. At least not to his wife, anyway.

"Sarah says something's up with the electricity at her house," Lauren said.

Curtis acknowledged with his best concerned frown. "Oh?"

"I think it's something with the fuse box," the dark-haired woman said. "It's one of those old ones. Usually, I can fix the problem by replacing a fuse, but I think it's more than that, this time."

"Can you take a look at it for her, honey?" Lauren asked.

Curtis raised his eyebrows. "Yeah, sure, I suppose."

"Curtis just finished re-wiring our entire home," Lauren explained.

"Oh?" Sarah said.

Curtis nodded.

I can't believe you're doing this.

"Yeah," he said, "we replaced the fuse system with a two-hundred amp circuit box. Those old fuse boxes aren't up to current building codes anymore."

"I think this one is about on its last leg," Sarah said with a bemused smile.

"Well, I can see if we can at least get some power back on," said Curtis, amazed at how cooly he was handling the situation. Just twelve hours ago, the woman at the door had been beneath him, naked, his sweaty skin against hers, in a passionate tryst.

Without another word, Curtis opened the closet door and found a parka. "Let me grab some tools from the garage." He walked past Sarah and out the door.

"If you still have a problem, come back over," Lauren said. "You can use the phone, whatever."

"Thanks," Sarah said. "It was nice meeting you. See you soon."

"Take care."

Sarah walked out the front door and traced Curtis's steps to the garage.

TWENTY THREE

"Y ou are un-*fucking* believable."

He spoke the words without looking at her. He and Sarah were walking along the dirt road, the 'long way around', as Curtis suggested, instead of traipsing through the orchard.

Sarah replied simply with a laugh.

"Jesus, Sarah. You've got the balls of a rhinoceros to do something like that."

"Like what?" she replied, flashing a satisfied grin.

"Like showing up at my front door with my wife home. Jesus! Are you out of your mind?!?!"

Sarah laughed, and Curtis chuckled and shook his head. It *had* been a ballsy move, but now that the discomfort had passed, he felt smug, like he had gotten away with something. The old *ring the doorbell of the old man's house and run off* gag.

"I've got your necklace," Curtis said.

"I know," she said without looking at him.

T he panel is down here."

He followed her into the cellar, which, like Sarah's home, was laid out nearly identical to his own. Sarah had grabbed a flashlight from the porch, and the two descended into the murky, tomb-like room.

When they reached the sand floor, there was no need for Sarah to show him the fuse box, no need for Curtis to ask where it was, no need for any explanation of the sort. He set his toolbox on the floor. Sarah extinguished the flashlight, and the cellar glowed from the light that streamed in from the open cellar door above.

And suddenly, they were in each others arms, forcefully, powerfully, grasping at one another, lips upon lips. Clothing was discarded carelessly, and hot flesh met hot flesh. They made love furiously, aggressively, bodies entwined and writhing, gritty sand sticking to their skin.

Suddenly Sarah pushed him off of her, twisting around and pulling him beneath her in a single, controlling movement. Her hips gouged rhythmically, pounding and gyrating, her needs now divulged in the frenzy of her motions. She worked herself faster and faster until she came in a scalding fury, until her cries of pleasure echoed through the dark cellar. Curtis urged her on, each hand grasping her buttocks and drawing her to him as his own thrusts matched hers. His own orgasm was explosive, and he cried out as a mountain of passion erupted. He continued pumping wildly, his movements frenzied, like that of an unbridled animal.

Finally they slowed, quivering hips decelerating slowly, precisely, until all movement ceased. Lungs that had been gasping out for air were now satisfied, and breathing eased. A drip of sweat fell from Sarah's breast and onto Curtis's chin.

He placed one hand on her shoulder and pulled her to

him, gently placing a nipple to his lips. Sarah groaned softly as he flicked his tongue back and forth, over her areola and around her breast. Then he brought her to him and they lay together silently, unmoving, listening to the sound of each other's pounding hearts.

A s circumstances dictated, their time together was brief.

"Tell me," he said softly. One hand was on the small of her back, the other on the back of her head. Her cheek was resting against his chest, rising and falling with every breath he took.

"Hmm?"

"How did you get out?"

"Hmm?"

"Last night, Sarah." His voice grew tense. "How did you get out of the bedroom?"

"Hey, you never know," she replied softly. Her voice was teasing, playful, but calming and languid. She remained motionless, her eyes closed, satisfied. "I just *might* be a witch, and I escaped on my broom. Or maybe I cast a magical spell that made me invisible."

"I'm serious," he replied. "It would be funny if I could figure out how you did it," "But I can't. There is *no way* to get out of that room, other than the door. And the window is twenty feet off the ground."

She drew up and rested her chin in the middle of his chest, just above his sternum. Her eyes were wide, serious. Beautiful.

"Curtis, do you like to fuck me?"

Her head bobbed as she spoke, and her chin dug into his chest. Curtis said nothing, and he felt a pang of surprise at her bluntness. Sarah let the question hang, and it drifted like still smoke.

"Then leave it at that," she finished, responding to his silence. She turned her head away and again rested her cheek on his chest.

Curtis, do you like to fuck me?

She had said that. Those very words. It surprised him to hear her say the 'f' word, as she had never used it before. It didn't seem to fit her, and he began to wonder if there was a part of Sarah that he didn't know. A part he didn't *want* to know.

After a few minutes, he took a deep breath. "Well, I think your electrical problem is taken care of," he said, kissing her neck.

Sarah leaned back, placed her palms to his chest, and slowly got to her feet. Curtis rolled to his side and stood up. Both were covered in powdery, grainy dust that was difficult to wipe off completely. Their clothing was filthy as well, and already Curtis began percolating excuses that he would reveal to his wife.

Panel is in the cellar, he would tell Lauren. *Dirt all over the place. You can't work on the box without getting filthy.*

They dressed in the gloom, and walked up the stone steps in silence.

"Oh, shit. My toolbox is downstairs. Hang on."

Curtis went down the steps quickly and found his toolbox. He picked it up and was about to start back up the stairs when his eyes saw something in the sand.

Below him, the soft earth still held the evidence of his encounter with Sarah. He could make out the outline of his back and shoulders, the concave depression made by his head, and the cup-like indentations from Sarah's knees.

But around the perimeter where their bodies had been was a crudely drawn circle. And within the circle, faint lines were visible—most of which had been disturbed by their frantic desires—that had most certainly been the same criss-crossing lines that he'd seen in his *own* cellar. The same design that was on Sarah's necklace.

A five-pointed star.

TWENTY FOUR

W hat is up with that shit?"
He had just emerged from the cellar and was standing at the top of the stairs.

Sarah looked confused. "What 'shit' are you talking about, Curtis?"

"That design. That drawing, whatever it is. The circle with the star. There's one in the sand in the cellar. Right where we were."

"I told you what those are, Curtis," she replied. Curtis picked up on the subtle annoyance in her response. It was faint, just beneath the surface, but it was there, all right.

"Well, you didn't tell me enough," he said, not masking his own irritation. "Like . . . do you really *believe* all that crap? Spooks and spirits and shit?"

"The question isn't whether I believe," she replied, her voice controlled and restrained. "The question is, Curtis: what do *you* believe?"

"That's not answering my question."

"Curtis, you can't handle the answer."

"I can't handle your vague responses."

"You can't handle what I'm all about."

"Try me."

"I just did. You were incredible."

She stepped toward him and looked into his eyes. She placed a hand to his cheek, then traced the outline of his jaw with her index finger. Her eyes glittered, staring into his. Then her finger found his chin, his lips.

Curtis, do you like to fuck me? He heard her voice, but she hadn't spoken a word. Her eyes glanced from his lips, his chin, back up to his eyes . . . .

She gently followed the soft flesh of his mouth until his lips parted. Now her finger was on his tongue, and he closed his mouth around it and sucked lightly. She withdrew her finger and drew her face closer still, her eyes never leaving his.

"And what was your question?" she asked, her eyes glowing, the sides of her mouth stretching into a mischievous grin.

He shook his head, mentally discarding his confrontational stance, then kissed her. "Forget it," he said. "Oh . . . speaking of which, before I forget—"

He shoved his hand into his pocket and withdrew the necklace. He held it out, but Sarah shook her head.

"Keep it for now," she said.

"Can't," replied Curtis, shaking his head. "I can't take a chance of Lauren finding it."

He reached out and took her hand and held it out, then dropped the necklace into her palm. Then he gently bent her fingers over into a fist.

"I have to go," he said.

"I know."

Lauren was gathering up her work from the table when Curtis returned. Her brow furrowed and she grimaced as she saw him.

"You're filthy," she said as he closed the front door.

"Her fuse box is in the same place ours was before I replaced it. The cellar is nothing but sand and dust." He glanced down at his soiled clothing.

"Did you get her taken care of?"

You bet I did.

"Yes, there's power there. She's going to need to get that old box replaced, though."

"She seems nice."

"Yeah. Yeah, she is." He kicked off his shoes and walked to the staircase. "I've got to wash up," he announced.

"And I'm off to work," Lauren said, gathering up the remaining papers. She walked to the stairs and gave Curtis a cautious kiss on the lips, then drew away, frowning with overdramatized repulsion. "God, you're dirty, and you *smell,*" she said, giving him a head-to-toe. "Don't put those clothes in the hamper."

He grinned. Lauren turned and left, and Curtis walked up the stairs, happy with the fact that he hadn't had to lie to his wife, after all.

He showered and dressed. Went downstairs into his study. There was still some more work to be done on the Martin home, although he no longer believed he would complete the project today. He was already weeks behind; one more day wasn't going to matter.

She's just plain weird, that's all, he thought while he worked at his drafting table. But in this case, he admitted, weird was just *fine.* Weird was *okay,* and probably a perk: if you can screw like that, it's *okay* to be weird. With a body like hers, being weird didn't matter. Just because she believed in freaky shit and returning souls and God knows what else didn't mean *he* had to. He could care less. Hell, he might be a believer *himself* after he slept with her a few more times.

And there *would* be more times, that he was certain of. Until then, he could celebrate.

Yes, yes . . . a toast in honor of the beautiful Sarah Hendricks.

He removed several books from the shelf and found the bottle of blackberry wine. He left it on the shelf, retrieved a glass from the kitchen cupboard, and poured the red-black liquid until the glass was nearly full. Then he held it up, looked out the window across the orchard at the old house under the huge maple, and spoke.

"And here's to you, beautiful Sarah," he said. He sipped the glass, then licked his lips. *"And all of your weird shit."* The wine was sweet and wonderful.

At five o'clock, he put down his pencil and turned off the light in his study. His eyes were bothering him from staring at lines and curves, and his mind was blurry from the wine. He'd sipped all afternoon, losing track of just how many glasses he'd had. No matter. He felt *good,* and the wine buzz kept his feet off the ground most of the day. He kind of floated along as he worked, the sweet liquor purring through his bloodstream. The project was coming along great, he was doing an awesome job, he was sure.

But enough was enough. His vision was clouding, and he was having a hard time concentrating. The wine was still on the clock, working overtime.

He left his study and wobbled into the kitchen.

Okay Curtis, he thought. *You're shit-faced. No bout-a-dout it.*

Yesterday's newspaper was on the counter, and he turned it to glance at the headlines.

RAZOR KILLER ARRESTED, was in bold at the top of the paper. Beneath the headline was a photograph of a blonde-haired man in orange prison garb being escorted by police.

"They finally caught the son of a bitch," Curtis said aloud.

For several years, Michigan residents lived in fear of a sadistic serial killer that struck at random, torturing his victims before decapitating them and placing their head in the nearest toilet. The act was beyond brutal, and the killer was so unsystematic in choosing his victims that virtually everyone in the state live in fear, thinking they could be next.

And the killings seemed so *senseless.* There had been no sign of the victims being robbed or sexually assaulted, and it was widely assumed that the perpetrator didn't know the victim. The only clues the killer left was a crude, handwritten note for the authorities, taunting them, taunting everyone, stating that the murders would continue until the killer saw fit. He was trying to teach a lesson; however, it was unclear just what that lesson was.

Curtis glanced through the article and shook his head.

Sure is a crazy planet to live on, he thought. *One weirdo down, one million to go.*

He folded the paper and pushed it aside. Then he shuffled through the cupboards, wondering what to nuke for dinner. Nothing looked good.

And it had grown colder in the house. Or maybe it was just the effect of the booze. The hair on his arm stood up, his skin tightened.

He stumbled upstairs to put on a sweater, and had just pulled it on when he looked out the bedroom window.

He stopped with his hands around his waist, still grasping the wool fabric. The collar of the sweater clung above his chin, then snapped down and clung around his neck. He stared out the window.

There were two figures standing in the orchard below.

TWENTY FIVE

Anger boiled, ignited and fueled by the liquor that raced through his bloodstream. He tugged his sweater to his waist and stormed to the window. He grabbed the bottom of the sill and yanked upwards. The window banged open.

"Hey!" he shouted out across the orchard. *"What are you doing over there?!?!"*

The two figures turned and looked, but they were too far away for Curtis to make out features.

"What are you doing?!?!" he shouted again.

The two figures began to walk away, heading for the thick forest. They moved slowly, not hurried, like they had heard him and were leaving, but they were going to take their own sweet time about it—which simply infuriated Curtis even more.

The two forms suddenly became blurry, as did the surrounding orchard and the trees . . . more effects of the intoxicating blackberry wine. Curtis rubbed his eyes, blinked several times, and the haziness went away.

Fine, he thought, slamming the window closed. *Then I'll come to you.*

He raced down the steps and nearly fell, catching himself on the railing. He put his shoes on clumsily and darted out the front door, flew around the house, and sprinted into the orchard.

The figures were still in view, but they were near the forest. If that was where they were headed, and Curtis thought that they were, they would have a good head start.

But if they were in a hurry, they didn't show it. Curtis was running as fast as he could—as fast as he *dared,* anyway— in the tall, thick grass. He might have a chance if they kept poking along like they were.

Weirdos, he thought. *Like Sarah said. People that come here because they think the area has special powers. Well, you can be attracted to the area all you want. You can dance and sing and talk to spooks or your Aunt Bernice and your Uncle Freddy. . . but you're not going to do it on* my *property.*

The two figures slipped into the forest and disappeared, and Curtis thought that they had probably followed the thin two-track. If that was the case, his odds of catching up with them would be better. He couldn't really *do* anything, since he didn't own the property in the woods. But he could *warn* them, hell yes. He could tell them to stay away from his orchard.

He came to the rail fence and bounded over it. It was hard to focus, hard to remain coordinated being as intoxicated as he was. His pace was quick but his steps were unsteady, and he came close to falling several times.

Finally, he reached the edge of the forest and raced along the tree line until he found the two-track. He turned and flew up the path. Pine and cedar branches smacked at his face in some of the more narrow, overgrown parts of the trail, forcing him to sweep them out of his way as he ran.

But there was no sign of the two trespassers. He tried to keep an eye out from right to left, but the forest was thick.

It would be easy to hide from him, especially if they knew the woods.

He charged along the path, cursing the alcohol for making him woozy, cursing the two intruders.

And suddenly, he *did* fall. He tripped on an exposed root that was growing across the two-track, and the result of his carelessness slammed him to the ground. There was no time for head over heels or falling and rolling, not even time for an *oh shit, I fucked up* thought. The root snared his foot and he smashed straight into the ground face-first.

He was dazed. The force of the fall not only jarred his head, but knocked the wind from his lungs. He lay sideways, doubled over in pain, gasping and wheezing for breath. He tasted hot liquid in his mouth and spat a stream of splattering blood into the sand.

Still heaving for air, he forced himself up on his hands and knees. Blood drooled from his mouth and nose and formed ruddy pools in the sand. He struggled to stand, felt nauseous, and decided to remain where he was.

Damned . . . damned roots, he thought. *Shit. Coulda . . . coulda killed myself.*

There were several roots that crossed the trail, and he placed his hands on one that ran beneath him, steadying his balance. He closed his eyes and forced a long, deep breath.

There. Better. That's . . . better.

He opened his eyes and leaned back, balancing himself on his knees. He brought one arm to his face and wiped away the blood from his chin and mouth. His tongue was on fire, and he decided that if the extent of his injuries was nothing more than a severely-bitten tongue, well, he was pretty damned lucky.

He stared at the pattern of blood in the sand, knowing that something wasn't right. The fuzziness in his mind worked against his reason, and he struggled with

213

comprehension.

What? What's the matter with the blood?

And then, after a difficult effort to drive off the effects of the alcohol, he realized what it was.

No, not the blood. The roots. It's the roots.

Below him, exposed roots squirmed across the two-track like thin, spiny fingers.

No. It's not the roots. It's not the roots at all. It's what the roots are doing. How they're growing.

The roots at his feet twisted and turned, curled and coiled, forming a large circle that encompassed a perfect five-pointed star.

TWENTY SIX

Enough. He'd had enough.

He turned on the path and wiped the blood from his face again. The salty taste in his mouth was going away; his tongue wasn't bleeding as badly anymore.

Sarah. He was going to see Sarah. *Now*. There was shit that she wasn't telling him, he knew it. She knew what was going on, and she probably knew the people that were trespassing in the orchard. Goddamn freaks.

He turned and started back over the snaking two-track, slowly this time. The alcohol wasn't as much of a factor anymore, but the fall and the blow to his head and face were. He spat a wad of blood and it hit a leaf. The force of the red goo caused the branch to bend but the leaf captured the careening gob, and it slowly dribbled to the edge and ran over, dangling like a string of gooey, red snot.

This is all just a huge, steaming pile of bullshit, and I'm going to put a stop to it right now. Just *how* he intended to do this he wasn't quite sure, but he was going to start with Sarah.

W hat the *fuck* is going on?"

"*Curtis?* God . . . what happened? What's—"

"What is going on around here, with those goddamned symbols all over the place? Is everybody out of their fucking minds around here?"

He had walked straight across the field to Sarah's home, banging his fist on the front door. Sarah had answered, and her first expression was one of shock. Seeing Curtis standing at the door like that, blood smeared over his chin and across his cheeks, dirt caked in his hair and speckled on his shirt and pants.

"Come inside," she said, taking him by the arm. "You're a mess." She led him to the dining room and sat him down in a chair. Then she hurried off, returning with a wet towel and a tube of antiseptic gel.

"Who *are* they, Sarah?" he asked, as she dabbed the wet rag to his chin.

"Who are *who?*" she asked.

He drew back, grabbed her arm tightly, and pushed it away from his face.

"Ouch! Curtis! That *hurts!*"

"*Who are they?!?!*"

"*Let go!*"

He released his grip and was immediately sorry for the unnecessary display of force.

"Sarah, I'm sorry. I didn't mean—"

Sarah dabbed the cloth to his chin. "Who are *who?*" she asked again.

"I saw them again. Today. Two people in the orchard. I chased after them, into the woods. I tripped and fell."

He turned toward her, and saw that she was wearing the necklace that he had returned. He reached out and placed his finger on the silver charm. "*This,*" he said. "What is *this* all about?"

216

"I told you."

"Not everything. You know what?" He tapped the charm that dangled from her neck. "There's one of these in the forest. That's what I tripped on, Sarah. *Roots.* They form one of these . . . these *pentagrams* . . . perfectly. I *saw* them. Shit, I *tripped* on them. Nobody made them. They *grow* that way, Sarah. How do you think I did this?" He pointed to his face.

She continued to dab at his face, wiping away the smeared blood. There was only a small scratch on his chin; most of the blood had been from biting his tongue.

"So . . . no answer?" Curtis said.

Sarah placed the wet towel in the kitchen sink, then walked back to Curtis. She held out both hands. Curtis took them in his. She stared into his eyes. Gone was the playful sparkle, the child-like mischief. Her expression was that of seriousness and serenity. Her eyes were luring, deep and enticing, glittering with wondrous temptation.

"Come with me, Curtis. If you really want to know, I'll show you."

TWENTY SEVEN

Curtis had a feeling . . . a twinge of premonition, of *ignis fatuus* . . . that told him that he didn't *want* to know. He shouldn't know. Wouldn't understand. One moment he wanted to turn and run, to tell Sarah *no, it's okay, really, I don't want to know. Let's go screw and make up.*

And yet, he *was* curious. He wanted to know more about what was going on, what Sarah was all about.

She led him upstairs and to a closed door. The hall was dark, and Curtis detected a hint of fragrance in the air, the luscious scent of sweet autumn apples.

"Come with me, Curtis," Sarah said softly. She grasped his hand, squeezed it, and opened the door.

"*oly shit.*" He hadn't meant to speak the words, but they came anyway, softly, beneath his breath.

"Come, Curtis." She stepped into the room first, and her body was instantly immersed in the light of dozens of candles. Curtis did as he was told, and followed her into the room.

Everything was black. The floor, the walls, the ceiling had been painted a shiny, achromatic black. Even with the dozens of candles that glimmered from shelves in the walls, the room was hopelessly dark and cheerless. The only furniture was a massive, wood-framed bed with a satin red and black bedspread. The walls, floor and ceiling were inscribed with strange symbols and designs. On one wall was the now-familiar upside-down pentagram. Inside the star was the image of a goat's head, its elongated chin situated in the single point heading south, its two horns filling the two points directed upward. On the floor, encompassing nearly the entire room, was a full pentagram, perfect, drawn in white. Several symbols were drawn near each point. There were no lights and no light fixtures in the room; candles provided nothing more than a gloomy, disconsolate illumination.

Curtis was stunned. This was like the shit he'd seen in those idiotic slasher films years ago. All those silly witchcraft and devil worshiping movies that were good for a cheap thrill or to scare your date. Stuff Hollywood came up with to make teenagers cough up a few bucks at the theater on a Saturday night.

But the shit's not real, he thought. *It's just for movies. No one really* believes *in this stuff.*

"You're wrong, Curtis."

He looked at her. Blinked. Then blinked again. He hadn't said anything. Not out loud, he hadn't.

"What? Wrong about what?" he asked.

"You're *wrong.* I *know* what you're thinking. People *do* believe in this '*stuff*' as you call it."

He stared.

"Don't look so confused, Curtis. You *know* that I know what you're thinking. It's something that I'm very good at."

"How . . . how do you—"

"Look around. What do you see?"

Curtis looked at the walls, looked at the floor. He shrugged.

"You see *devotion*, Curtis. Look around you. You will see devotion and commitment and power."

"But . . . what's this . . . what's this all about?" he stammered.

Sarah smiled, and if her grin was a knife it would have cut out his heart. She was incredibly, *stunningly* beautiful—that was without question. But there was now a deviousness, a dark side to her that wasn't to be trusted. He saw something behind those crystal eyes that he hadn't seen before. Something that was so misleading, so maliciously seductive that he wanted to recoil. Again, as he had felt in the hall, he wanted to run, to get out of this room, this house. Wanted to get away from Sarah, to never see her again.

As if sensing this, Sarah's smile changed. The sinister, deceptive countenance faded. Suddenly, she was the lovely, lovely Sarah that he had first seen up close at the top of the cellar stairs.

"*About*, Curtis?" she finally replied. "What's it *about*? It's about making dreams come true. It's about having the power to make things happen. To make *your* dreams come true. For instance . . . ."

She stopped speaking, and her hand rose to the top button of her blouse. One by one she unbuttoned her shirt, revealing a black brassiere. With a simple snap she unfastened the clasp in front. Her shirt and bra fell to the floor. She stood before him, naked from the waist up.

"Curtis, *this* is what it's all about. It's what it's *always* been about." She took a step toward him. "It's about pleasures, plain and simple. Carnal desires, needs, passions of the flesh. It's about all of the things we all want and crave, but spend our lives trying to suppress, as if it's not natural. As if fulfilling these needs would somehow be *bad* for us."

She took another step forward and placed her hands at the front of his pants. There was an audible *snap* sound as she unbuttoned his fly.

"Tell me, Curtis," she whispered, her hand exploring further and further. "Tell me . . . *am I bad for you?*"

TWENTY EIGHT

The ensuing bedroom events were a mixture of extremes that Curtis had never before experienced. Sarah had insisted that their lovemaking take place on the floor, in the middle of the pentagram. Seconds seemed to turn into hours, which seemed to turn into days.

But the sensations were mixed, split into arenas of elation and torment. Explosions of exquisite intensity suddenly blossomed into strange fits of terror, and Curtis found himself powerless, puppet to some alien, unseen force. Indeed, there had been a time when she was on top of him that he couldn't move. He tried, but his arms—his entire body—was pinned to the floor. No amount of strength he could muster would allow him to move. Above him, Sarah thrashed wildly, exercising complete control.

Other times, it was *he* who seemed the wielder of power, the master of the game. Once, he had taken her from behind, when she was on her hands and knees. Sarah had cried out, screaming in pain, but she was helpless in his grasp, and he pounded and wailed while she struggled and screamed. Curtis was appalled at his own behavior, but again, he was powerless to the unseen force, and was merely a witness to an event he could not contain. Soon, her cries of pain turned into pleas of desire, until his primitive thrusts were synchronized with her own feral movements. Both screamed in excruciating ecstasy as simultaneous orgasms exploded.

But strangest of all were the pictures that flashed in his mind. He tried to push them away, tried to expel them by concentrating on the surge of the moment, by admiring Sarah's body and watching her movements responding to his own, but his efforts were in vain. Strange pictures, designs, and symbols flew through his mind's eye, and he had a recollection of *The Wizard of Oz,* when the tornado struck and Dorothy was caught up in the windstorm. People and events swirled past her in a violent turbulence, and all poor Dorothy could do was watch.

And *voices.* Chanting. Haunting voices stirred from somewhere. He couldn't understand the words, but he was certain the language wasn't English. He became entranced, and Curtis was no longer himself, but a vessel of transmission, a mere artery for a strange, dark heart that beat somewhere, unseen and unheard, from some unearthly dimension. At times, in the very heat of pleasure, it was like he *could* feel the foreign blood coursing through his body like an evil, writhing snake, and his only release from its grasp would be his *own* release, through a massive, cataclysmic orgasm. Both he and Sarah came over and over again, until their bodies collapsed from sheer exhaustion.

Finally, they lay spent, he on top of her, in the candlelight of her bedroom. His fatigue was absolute; he couldn't move if he tried. Every muscle in his body was drained, depleted of energy. Curtis had never before experienced such extreme physical intensity.

But the *voices* . . . .

He could still hear them in his head as he lay on top of

her, lips against his neck, her warm breath breezing his
sweaty skin.

Ave, Ave, Satanas . . . .

He heaved a breath. Sarah moaned softly. The voices
in his head continued.

*Ave, Ave, Satanas . . . Regie, Satanas . . . In nomine Dei nostre
Satanas Luciferi excelsi!*

The words and phrases didn't make sense. It was a
language that he didn't understand, couldn't comprehend.
Latin, perhaps, but he wasn't certain. He was sure he'd
heard something in there that sounded like 'Satan', but he
couldn't be positive, and he didn't give it any more thought.
Besides . . . it didn't matter, anyway. The only thing that
mattered now was—

Sarah. She was everything, now. And if all of
this—whatever it was—came with her, well, all the better.
He could no longer see himself continuing his present way
of life, living the same boring ritual day after day, caught in
some fairytale dream of make-believe and pretend. After all,
isn't that what he and Lauren had been doing for years?
Pretending?

He could almost hear Lauren's voice.

*I'll pretend that you love me and that I love you. You pretend
that you don't know that I'm fucking the guy down the street, and I'll
pretend that I don't know how much you drink. 'Kay?*

He wanted to stay here forever, lost in the moment, her
body against his, his sweat fusing with her own. Candles
flickering, ghostly shadows darting. Strange emblems and
symbols—whatever they meant—he wanted them, would do
anything to prolong the moment, to repeal the laws of time.
Let time and space whirl about them, around them, above
and below them.

Right here and right now.

He slept.

TWENTY NINE

C urtis awoke alone.

He was confused at first, unsure of his surroundings and where he was. Then it came back to him like a pleasant dream, and he closed his eyes for a moment, savoring the brief *deja vu*. Panic seized him for an instant when he realized he did not know how long he'd slept or what time it was, but a quick glance at his wristwatch eased his fears.

Eight. A few minutes after Eight. Plenty of time to get home before Lauren.

He stood up and assembled his clothing, fumbled with his pants, his shirt and socks and shoes. Looked around the room.

Candles illuminated the strange symbols on the walls. He remembered how they had seemed to flash into his mind while he and Sarah lay on the floor, entwined within one another. He had still been buzzed, that was it. It was the liquor that had caused the bizarre cinematic images to flash through his mind and manipulate his thoughts.

He looked at the pentagram on the wall, the one with the upside down star and the goat's head. He *had* seen this one before, he was certain.

Where?

He couldn't remember. But he *had* seen it, that was for sure. Most likely, it was probably something he remembered from some 70's horror flick, where scantily-clad teenage girls were chased through the wilderness by an axe-wielding devil worshiper.

Satisfied, he opened the door and walked out of the dark bedroom, then closed the door behind him. The hall was dim, and there was only a faint light coming from the kitchen. Curtis strode into the living room. There was no sign of Sarah.

In the bathroom?

He glanced around the corner to see the bathroom door open; there was no light on.

"Sarah?" he called out quietly.

No reply.

He walked over to the dark living room.

The moon was high and full, and its effect was ghostly upon the orchard. A few leaves remained on the apple trees, and they glowed shiny, luminescent in the lunar haze. Long shadows hugged the ground like crouching black cats, wary and watchful and waiting. The large oak that shrouded the house was like an immense squid, its arthritic tentacles kinked and twisted. The branches seemed alive, as if at any moment they would reach down, spiraling and coiling, to snatch an unwary prey.

And in the orchard, figures moved. Curtis couldn't be sure how many, but he saw several. They were only shadows among the apple trees, but they were definitely *people*. He could see nothing more.

In the next moment the figures began to disperse, all except for one. It grew larger, coming closer, walking toward the house, and he knew that it was Sarah.

He met her at the front door, opening it for her. She seemed surprised to see him.

"Oh?" she said as she walked inside. "Finished with your beauty sleep so soon?"

"Yeah." He smiled, then motioned toward the field. "Who were they?"

Sarah looked at him, then drew close and put her arms behind his neck, pulling him closer still. Curtis draped his arms around her waist.

"You curious boy," she said. "Do you have to know *everything*? Isn't it enough just *having* everything, hmm?"

He looked into her eyes. Smiled. Shook his head.

"You really are incredible," he said, and this pleased Sarah immensely. Her eyes lit up and her grin widened.

"Good," she said. "Wanna do that again sometime?"

"Do you have to ask?"

"No. I never have to ask, Curtis. *Never.*"

He walked home through the field, beneath a single, silvery sphere. The moon bathed the orchard with a frosty, blue glow. The night was cold, and there were no other sounds save for the crunching of dry, fragile grass beneath his feet. The crickets and katydids and locusts and cicadas were all snuggled in their little insect condos for the winter.

The house was dark. When he'd left earlier in the day in pursuit of the two people in the orchard, he had no cause to leave any lights on. The moon, however, flared in the sky like a beacon, allowing him to see his way to the front door without stumbling into or over something, like he'd done earlier that evening in the forest.

Remembering the incident, he flicked his tongue in his

mouth. The throbbing had vanished long ago, and he hadn't recalled any pain or discomfort for a while. Indeed, when he probed his tongue by running it against his cheek and over his teeth, he couldn't find the wound at all.

He went inside, and the first place he went to was the downstairs bathroom where he flipped a switch and squinted in the bright light. He leaned toward the mirror and stuck out his tongue, swishing it back and forth, searching for a cut, a scar . . . *anything.*

There was nothing there.

No incision, no gash where his teeth had ripped into the pink muscle. No scar. The wound seemed to have healed perfectly.

If it ever happened at all, he thought. Then:

Oh, it happened, all right. I remember that just as well as I remember everything else. I guess that's just one of the fringe benefits of screwing a witch, or whatever she is. Sticks and stones may break my bones, but my witch can fix them all. Ha.

He went upstairs, showered, and put on a pair of cotton sweat pants and a ragged gray sweatshirt. Then he retrieved his dirty clothing and carried the bundle into the laundry room, where yet another pile of dirty clothes—the ones he'd soiled earlier that morning in Sarah's cellar—waited. He placed the whole heap into the washer, tossed in enough soap to launder the men's department at *K Mart,* closed the lid, and went into the kitchen.

And he was *hungry.* God, was he ever. Starving. He hadn't had a bite to eat since—

Shit. Did I even eat today? Oh yeah. A bowl of corn flakes for breakfast. And blackberry wine, of course.

There would always be plenty of that.

He inventoried the cupboards. Lauren hadn't had a chance to go grocery shopping, judging by the sparse contents on the shelves. He supposed that *he* could have gone to the store and picked up some things, but Lauren had always done that.

He looked at the clock on the stove. Eight thirty-five. Lauren said she'd be getting out of work at nine.

She could run to the convenience store on the way home, he thought. Maybe pick up a pizza or something.

He picked up the phone, and suddenly realized he'd never called her at work before. Didn't even know the number.

He placed the phone back down and dug a phone book from the top kitchen drawer. He flopped it down on the counter.

"G . . . G . . . ." he said quietly, flipping pages and skimming with his finger. "G . . . Grand . . . . Grand Traverse Gazette & Times," he said, holding his finger beneath the number on the page. He picked up the phone, dialed the number, then withdrew his hand from the page.

The number rang several times. When it was finally picked up, Curtis could hear noise in the background, the sound of presses running, computer keyboards being tapped, and a few voices.

"GTGT," a young female voice said.

Curtis paused, confused. "What?"

"Gazette and Times," the woman clarified.

"Oh. Gotcha. Sorry. Lauren Stanton, please."

"One moment, sir."

There was a click as the line was placed on hold, and a polished, radio-trained voice was in mid-sentence, telling Curtis that the *Grand Traverse Gazette and Times was one of the fastest-growing daily newspapers in Michigan's northwestern lower peninsula, and that it was the recipient of—*

"I'm sorry to keep you waiting," the young woman broke in. "Can you spell that last name?"

"Stanton. S-t-a-n-t-o-n. Lauren."

Pause. Then:

"I'm sorry, sir, there's no one here by that name."

"What?" Curtis asked. "Can you check again, please?"

While he waited, he flipped open the phone book and double-checked the name of the newspaper.

"I'm sorry," the girl finally said. "I'm new here . . . but I still don't see anyone by that name listed in our directory. Can anyone else help you?"

"No," Curtis said slowly, robot-like. "No, that's all right." Pause. "Thank you."

He hung up.

THIRTY

The drive to town took him twenty minutes, and he located the newspaper offices easily enough. He searched the parking lot, looking for her car, already certain that he wouldn't find the Taurus. Then he took a short cruise downtown, searching for her car in front of bars, coffee houses, whatever. Once he saw a Ford Taurus tear out of the parking lot near a small restaurant. His heart pounded and he whirled his car around only to discover that the Taurus was green and not red, and it was being driven by a kid that didn't look old enough to pilot a *Radio-Flyer* wagon.

The goddamn bitch, he thought. He spun the car around and headed back up the peninsula. *The goddamn bitch doesn't even work there! How fucking stupid does she think I am?!?!*

Before he'd set out, he'd called all of the other papers, just to be sure. It was possible that he'd gotten the name of the paper confused, as there were several papers published in Grand Traverse region. Every phone call resulted with the same response.

I'm sorry, sir . . . but there's no one here by that name. Yes, I'm sure. There is no 'Lauren Stanton' that works here.

He was enraged. *How could I be so dumb? How could* she

be so dumb? What in the hell is going on?

But he knew. Oh, he'd had his *suspicions,* up till now. He'd *wondered* if she was screwing around again, with all of those 'late nights' at the 'office'.

Now he *knew.* He knew beyond any shadow of a doubt.

But why the lie about the job? Jesus Christ . . . did she actually think she'd get away with that?

He barreled up the peninsula, his car hitting nearly eighty miles an hour at times. Yellow dividing lines came at him like furious needles.

Calm down. Calm down. He eased up on the accelerator, and the shadows on the side of the highway slowed. *Calm down.*

And by the time he arrived home, he was calm. He was cool, he was composed. Lauren hadn't arrived home, which was good. Curtis went upstairs and strode into the dark bedroom.

Across the orchard, in Sarah's house, a single candle glowed in the window. Curtis walked back to the bedroom door, clicked the light on. He walked back to the window. The glare from the overhead light in the room prevented him from seeing outside, but that's not what he wanted. He wanted Sarah to see him, and he knew that she would be able to see his silhouette in the window.

He raised his hand and placed the palm to the glass. After a moment he withdrew his hand, then turned the light off. When he looked across the orchard, the single candle in the window was extinguished.

He undressed and climbed into bed, curled on his side. From where he was, he could look out the window across the dark orchard.

And he waited.

Soon, headlights swept the field. White, hazy cones swished, dipped and jerked around as the car drew nearer.

Then the lights froze, illuminating a few apple trees and the tall, overgrown grass.

The lights blinked off.

Lauren was home.

THIRTY ONE

He heard the door open, heard her footsteps on the wood floor. Heard her walk quietly upstairs.

She entered the bedroom without turning the light on. Curtis turned groggily, fabricating sleep.

"Hi honey," Lauren said softly.

"Mmm. Hi," Curtis replied, using his best *just-woke-up* voice. *"How was work?"*

"Long," she said. "Sorry I'm late. I stopped at the grocery store, though, and picked up a few things. Did you have a good day?"

"Mm-hmm," he mumbled.

"Good. I'm going to take a shower."

Yeah, Curtis thought. *You do that.*

The bathroom light blinked on, then faded as Lauren closed the door, leaving only a glowing band of light at the bottom.

And Curtis fell asleep.

He awoke to an early, hazy-gray morning, and the only thing he could think of was food. His appetite was enormous, with not having eaten since the previous morning.

Lauren was still sleeping beside him. He had no recollection of her coming to bed, and figured that he must have fallen asleep while she was showering.

He got up quietly, slipped into the same clothing he had worn the previous night, and crept downstairs. Corn flakes were going to have to suffice, and he wolfed down a bowl, and then another. Lauren had, however, picked up some bread and juice and muffins, and he helped himself.

Then he started a pot of coffee and went into his study, but he had a hard time concentrating. He held his pencil in one hand, ruler in the other. He wasn't focused, and his mind traveled.

How could she think that she could get away with lying about her job and where she worked? he thought. *And if she wasn't at work, then where was she?*

The answer, he decided, would be easy enough to find out.

He would follow her. Today. He would follow her and find out where she was going, where she'd been all these days that he *thought* she was at work.

He tried to focus on the project spread out on the drafting table, but his mind whirled blindly. *Where could she be going? What is she doing? Who is she doing?* Just wondering about it was driving him mad.

The coffee pot growled in the kitchen, indicating that the decanter was full. He got up, poured himself a cup, and walked back into his study. Tried to work again, but only succeeded in making pencil doodles at the bottom of the page. He tried to remember some of the drawings that he'd seen in Sarah's bedroom. Soon, the entire bottom of the blueprint was sprinkled with tiny insignias and symbols.

Lauren awoke an hour later, and she was so business-as-usual that he thought he was going to puke. Here he was, thinking that he was the King of Deception, when she'd been the Queen all along. She'd dethroned him, right behind his back.

"How's you're coffee, honey?" she chirped from the other room.

Puke. Jesus. I've got to hand it to her. She can act. Of course, she's had a lot of practice over the past ten years.

"It's fine, thanks," Curtis called out. "How'd you sleep?"

He heard her slippers pad the floor, and then she was at his side. She kissed his cheek.

"Wonderful," she said. "I was *so* tired."

"Problems at work?" Curtis asked, looking straight into her eyes.

Does she know? Does she know that I know?

"Yeah. One press went down, and we had to run with one short. Supposed to be back up today, though. And one of the main computers is on the fritz. It's the one that does the payroll register, so you can imagine the nightmare that's causing."

No. She doesn't know.

"I'll bet that was a pain in the ass."

Lauren nodded and sipped her coffee. "You're not kidding. Everyone's running around thinking that they're not going to get paid until it's fixed, which, of course, isn't the case. Sure has caused a lot of panic for no reason."

She left him in his study, went upstairs, dressed, then busied herself around the house. At two o'clock she left for

239

work.

And Curtis followed her.

THIRTY TWO

He'd waited until her car was nearly out of sight before rushing to his own vehicle and speeding after her. He caught up with her after only a few minutes, and he remained a quarter of a mile behind her. As they drew closer to town, however, he had to creep up closer so as not to lose her in traffic.

Her car wound downtown, through several traffic lights. Then she made a quick left and turned into the parking lot of the *Grand Traverse Gazette & Times.*

What in the hell? thought Curtis. *What's she doing here? She doesn't work here. She's—*

He pulled his vehicle into a parking place on the other side of the street. Watched her emerge from the Taurus, carrying her purse and a folder of papers. She strode through the parking lot, stopped to chat for a moment with a woman who was getting into a car. Then she continued walking and finally disappeared through the front doors of the newspaper building.

Curtis was dumbfounded.

She doesn't work here, he thought. *They have no one that works here by that name.*

He exited the car and walked down the street, ducking into a phone booth. A fat, weather-beaten phone book dangled from a coiled steel snake that was tethered to the booth itself, and he flipped through it until he found the number he was looking for. Then he picked up the phone and dialed the newspaper. It rang once, then was picked up.

"GTGT," a male voice answered.

"Yes, Lau—um . . . Managing Editor, please."

"One moment."

Curtis was placed on hold, and smooth-talking voiceover guy told him that *advertisers with the Grand Traverse Gazette & Times could expect results, like hundreds of other businesses in the Grand Traverse region. All for just—*

"Lauren Stanton," his wife said, very business-like and professional. Curtis froze, holding the receiver to his ear.

It's her. She's there.

"Hello? Hello?"

He hung up.

When he returned home, he saw Sarah outside, walking down her driveway carrying the day's mail. He honked and she turned and waved. Tires crunched gravel as he pulled the car back out of his own driveway and drove to Sarah's. She had stopped, waiting for the car to arrive.

The car came to a halt, and Curtis got out. Sarah smiled, but her grin was strained, or perhaps a bit forced.

"Hi Sarah," he said.

"Hello Curtis," she replied. There was an awkward moment of silence, followed by another, then another. Finally, Curtis spoke again.

"Can I see you today?"

"No."

No explanation, no excuse. Just . . . *no.* Curtis was a bit surprised . . . and disappointed.

"Okay. When can—"

"Soon," she interrupted, and her strained smile grew cheery and bright. "I'm . . . I've got some things to take care of."

"Anything I can help with?"

"No. No, Curtis, you can't. If you can—*when you can*—I'll let you know." She held her hand out and he took it. Then he pulled her close and kissed her on the lips, on her cheek, then he nuzzled her ear. She closed her eyes.

"I want to be with you," Curtis whispered.

"I know."

THIRTY THREE

There was more to it; he was certain. Somehow, there had been some confusion about Lauren working at the paper. After all, she said that one of their main computers had been down. There had been a lot of confusion at the newspaper offices. And the woman who'd answered the phone was new, too. But it still did nothing to ease his suspicions of her with someone else. He occupied his mind with these thoughts all day, going over the things she'd said to him, trying to put the pieces of the puzzle together.

And of course, when he wasn't trying to figure out Lauren, he was thinking about Sarah, recalling the incredible—if bizarre—episode in her bedroom just yesterday. Yeah, she might be freaky, and all of that supernatural bullshit was just that—*bullshit*—but damned if he was going to let that bother him. He didn't care if she worshiped the fucking tooth fairy if it made her the sexual dynamo that she was.

And the more he thought about her, the more he *needed* her. Wanted her, right now. He kept glancing out the window of his study, hoping to see her outside, hoping to catch a glimpse of her.

Finally, when he could stand it no longer, he got up, put on a parka, and went outside.

Sarah opened the front door before he even knocked, as if she was expecting him.

"Hello, Curtis," she said. There was no smile on her face, no indication of a hidden desire or secret passion.

"I have to see you," he said.

"I know."

"I have to be with you. *Now.*"

"I know."

"Do you know *everything?*"

"No."

"It sure seems like it sometimes."

She smiled a tantalizing grin. *"I know."*

They lay together on the floor of her bedroom. Candles burned. The episode had been a repeat of the previous day, with all of its extraordinary dark passion and fury.

"I'm beginning to think that there is a lot more to you than I could ever know, Sarah," he said quietly.

She chuckled lightly. *"That's not the half of it, Curtis."*

They were silent for a minute, until Curtis shifted a little, drawing his face to hers.

"I want you for my own, Sarah. I do. I want you forever."

"I know you do."

"I don't think you *do.*"

"Curtis . . . you don't know what you're asking."

"I know what I *want.*"

"And what if you get it?"

"Then I'd be happy."

"You're not happy now?"

"I . . . yes. Yes, I guess I am. But I could be *happier.* With *you.*"

"You're married, Curtis. You have a wife."

He laughed out loud. "Yeah, you're right, Sarah. I'm married, all right. It's a marriage that's been messed up from day one. She cheated on me so many times I lost count." He didn't mention his *own* diversions, and Sarah didn't ask. He wondered, however, if she knew that his encounters with her hadn't been his first breach of his marriage vows.

"I want to be with *you,* Sarah. *You're* the one I want to be with."

"Take a good look around this room, Curtis. This is *me.* This is who I *am.* It's not just a part of me . . . it *is* me. I am *it.* You haven't begun to understand who I am or what I am about."

"I want it all," he whispered. "I want you, and everything about you. All of you."

She stared into his eyes, and Curtis watched the tiny candle flickers reflecting in her pupils.

"You don't know what you're asking," she repeated. "You have no *idea* what you're asking."

"I know that some of the 'people' that I've seen in the orchard aren't people, Sarah. I know that much."

She drew back, a bit surprised. Her eyes flickered. "No," she agreed. "No, some are not."

"They're those . . . those *spirits,* or whatever. Aren't they?"

"There's a lot more to it than that."

"Then tell me. *Show me,* Sarah. Show me what I need

to do. I want to be with you. I'll do anything you say."

"And your wife?"

"What about her?"

"I think she'd find your sudden—*disassociation*—a bit unnerving. In fact, she'd probably *hate* you, Curtis."

"I don't love her. I'm not *in* love with her. I'm in love with *you,* Sarah. I love *you,* Sarah. *You.*"

At this, Sarah drew back further. Then she kneeled beside him as if in reverence, her naked body bathed in soft candlelight. She placed one hand on his arm, gently moving it along to his wrist until she found his hand, which she grasped gently.

"Do you want to be with me, Curtis?"

"Yes?"

"No matter what I ask of you?"

"Yes."

"Who are you more loyal to: me, or your wife?"

"You." No hesitation. He sat up. "You are the one I want, Sarah. *You.*"

She smiled, and Curtis could see the upside down pentagram from the wall reflecting in her dark eyes.

"I know, Curtis," was all she said.

THIRTY FOUR

That was too much to ask.

As he stormed through the orchard toward his home, he told himself that he drew the line with cold-blooded murder . . . regardless who it was. Remnants of the their conversation whirled in his head.

She's crazy. She's out of her mind.

Sarah had told him all about the coming Feast of Souls—Samhain—on October 31st. How the souls of the murdered witches would return to this place, looking for a human to possess. How every year, a group of believers came to offer a sacrifice—a *human* sacrifice—to the souls. Strange rituals help participants utilize powers that were only available to those who knew how to harvest them, those who knew how to dance with the dead.

Can't you feel it? she had asked. *Can't you see it? Think, Curtis. Even Nature—the most powerful force of all—knows. Look at how special this area is. You yourself saw the pentagram in the roots. No one put it there, Curtis. It was created . . . by Nature. And there are more. Many, many more.*

Pentagrams? Symbols?

Oh, more than simple symbols. Nature has harnessed its own powers, its own forces, all in defense of unearthly manifestations. But we can harness the energy from those souls, Curtis. We can become like gods. We can become God.

That's just a bunch of bullshit.

Come, Curtis, she had said. *How do you think it is that I can do the things I have done? How do you think I was able to leave your room on the second floor? How is it that I know what pleases you? Surely, you've seen enough.*

No, he hadn't.

I will not kill someone, he had told her, no matter who it is.

I'm not asking you to do anything, was her response. *You will have to do nothing. Just answer with a yes or no.*

His answer was no.

You said you'd do anything.

Murder wasn't a considered option, Sarah. No.

Perhaps, Sarah had said, *perhaps you will change your mind if you travel to see your wife tonight. If you follow her after work to see where she goes.*

What? What are you talking about?

Follow her, Curtis. Tonight.

You . . . you think she's seeing someone else?

I don't think. I know, Curtis. I know.

He went home, his mind raging as he got into his car and sped into Traverse City. It was still early in the evening, and Lauren probably wouldn't be getting out of work for a while.

Unless she got out early to be with . . . with whoever.

He arrived at the newspaper office and immediately spotted her car in the parking lot. He circled the block several times until he found a place in an adjacent lot that allowed him a clear view of the front of the building, as well as Lauren's Taurus.

He waited.

At nine o'clock he saw Lauren exit the building, and he watched her walk through the parking lot and get into her car. As soon as she had closed her car door he turned the key in the ignition. His eyes never left her car as it pulled out onto the street and headed south.

Well, if you're going home, you're taking the long way around, he thought with bitter satisfaction. He screeched out of the parking lot and followed her.

The Taurus wound through downtown, past West Bay, and finally turned onto a side street. He followed at a distance as the car traveled several blocks before pulling into a dark driveway.

"Son of a bitch," he breathed. *"I was right. I've been right all along."*

And yet, through his anger, he felt relief, as if Lauren's unfaithfulness now legitimized his *own* improprieties, validating his *own* behavior.

He waited until she got out of the car and walked to the porch. She let herself into the home without knocking.

When the door closed behind her, Curtis exited the vehicle and darted up the sidewalk. Heavy brush grew in front of the windows of the home she had entered, cover that would work to his advantage. However, the shades were drawn, and he couldn't see inside.

He stole to the back of the house, slowly, listening.

There.

A window near the back glowed yellow. The curtain had been drawn, but there was a crack in the middle about a quarter of an inch wide. To make it even better, the bottom of the window was open several inches.

He slunk beneath the sill, immersed in the shadows, and listened.

"I don't have a lot of time," he heard Lauren say. "My husband is expecting me home."

"Your husband is always expecting you home," a male voice replied. "That's what husbands do."

And his voice was . . . *familiar*. Shit. Where had he heard that voice before?

He strained his neck up to peer through the crack.

No fucking way! Curtis thought. *Him?!?!?*

It was the realtor. Chuck Hirsch. The same guy who had brokered the purchase of their home on the peninsula.

Rage boiled, and Curtis clenched his fists, trying to suppress the urge to lunge through the window and strangle the son of a bitch. Lauren, too, for that matter.

"Do you think he knows?" Chuck asked.

"Oh, I think he knows *something*," Lauren replied. "But I don't think he's quite figured it out yet."

"Too bad for him," Chuck said with a laugh.

"I know," Lauren replied. *"I know."*

THIRTY FIVE

His car tore up the driveway and skidded to a halt in front of his home. How he had managed to pull himself away from the window, to *drag* himself from it, was beyond his own explanation. He *had,* however, and he'd managed to keep his cool . . . at least until he made it home.

He left the car parked in the gravel and got out, storming into the house. The phone was ringing.

He hurried over to it and picked it up.

"Hello."

"What did you see," Sarah said smugly. It was not a question, nor did it sound like one. Curtis knew that she knew what he saw.

"I saw enough," he replied, his voice blistering with anger. "I saw and heard plenty."

"Enough to change your mind?"

Fuck her. Let Lauren burn in hell.

"Yes. Enough."

"Good. Now listen to me, Curtis. You can't let on that you know. She *mustn't* know that *you* know. Understand?"

He didn't reply.

"Curtis . . . *do you understand?*"

"Yes."

"Just act as if you know nothing, as if you suspect *nothing.*"

"Yes."

"There are still a few more days before the Feast. Don't screw it up *now.*"

"When can I see you again?"

"When do you want me?"

"Now."

She laughed. "Go to bed, Curtis. I'll see you soon." The line went dead. He hung up the phone.

I'll show her, he thought with greedy satisfaction. *This will be the last time Lauren fucks around on me.*

He went upstairs and into the bedroom, turned on the light. And—

Sarah was there.

She lay in his bed, the covers pulled up to her breasts.

"Hello Curtis," she said softly. Her lips pursed in a smile that was both sensual and haughty.

Curtis's mind spun. What he was seeing wasn't possible. He'd just talked to Sarah on the phone, and now here she was, in *his* bed on the second floor of *his* home.

"How did you—"

"You said you wanted me *now,* didn't you?" Her smile widened, and Curtis flashed a roguish grin. He was beyond asking her how she had pulled off *this* one.

And besides—it didn't matter, anyway. Not anymore.

"Yes," he answered, and he began to undress. "Now." And he went to her, drawing the covers back and slipping into bed beside her.

"Are you happy now, Curtis?" she whispered as he took her into his arms. "Is this what you want? Am *I* want you want?"

He nodded, and kissed her on the lips. "Always. You're perfect, Sarah. *We're* perfect."

"I—"

"Don't say it," he interrupted with a pretentious grin. "I already *know* that you *know.*"

Sarah smiled, and gave herself to him.

THIRTY SIX

October 31st.
The day was unseasonably warm and arid, the air uncharacteristically gauzy and dry for this time of year. Most of the trees were now mere skeletons, their bare limbs lacing up into the sky in a maze of interwoven tresses. Leaves, browned and curled like brittle soup ladles with fingers, had fallen to the ground. They tumbled across the lawn and swirled in the orchard like dizzy insects.

And there had been a sudden change in Lauren.

Not long after the night Curtis had followed her to Chuck Hirsch's home, she had become withdrawn. Distant. She had been such a good actor up until this time, but now she seemed to be intentionally avoiding him. Which, of course, was fine with Curtis. After what he had agreed to, it was becoming increasingly harder to face her.

But he *had* been able to keep his cool, to maintain his normal behavior, if not in spirit, certainly in deed. He hadn't seen as much of Sarah as he wanted, but she had told him that the time was drawing near, that preparations were being made, that soon, very soon, they would be together.

And today was the day. Samhain. The Feast of Souls. All Hallow's Eve.

He could feel it. By God, he could actually feel it in the air. This place *was* special. There was something going on that he didn't understand, something happening in the supernatural realm. It was an undercurrent of electricity, a certain charge to the air.

And he *knew*. On October 31st, the sensations were so strong, so powerful, that he was certain that it was going to happen tonight. Exactly *what*, he wasn't sure. All he knew, all that he cared, was that he and Sarah would finally be together. No more pussy-footing around, no more pretending in front of a cheating, lying wife.

Of course, he thought, *I haven't necessarily been a Ward Cleaver poster child. Not by a long shot.*

But none of that mattered now.

Not long after Lauren left for work, Curtis saw a strange thing. A car that had been traveling along the highway suddenly slowed. It pulled off to the shoulder of the road and a man emerged. He locked the car, walked across the street, and into the orchard. Curtis watched the man as he stepped over the cedar fence and continued off toward the woods.

Curtis immediately went after him. He did not hurry, did not run. He simply strode through the orchard, stepped over the fence, found the winding two-track, and began to follow it. He came across the place where he'd fallen not long ago, and he once again saw the mysterious roots that made a perfect pentagram. He continued walking.

The forest grew dark. Thick cedar trees blotted out the sun, and the trail wound through a dense swamp. In places, the two-track ran through a patch of gooey mud, where Curtis saw something else:

Footprints. Others had been through this way, and not long ago. He hadn't seen anyone else, though, other than the man that had left his car at the side of the road.

And then he saw another inverted pentagram.

At first, he wasn't sure what he was looking at. He just noticed that the branches of a tree near the two-track seemed oddly deformed. He stopped walking and stared. It took him a moment to recognize the symbol, but now that he had, he wondered how he could have missed it. The pentagram hadn't been *fashioned* by anyone. The branches hadn't been bent or broken to form the emblem, but rather, had *grown* into the exact form over the years.

And suddenly, they were *everywhere.* In almost every tree around him, an upside-down five-pointed star with a circle around it was somehow formed. Some of them were harder to see than others, but they were there, all right.

He kept walking. He walked deeper and deeper into the forest, and the trees around the trail grew thicker and thicker.

And then he heard a noise. A loud crunch. A snapping sound. Not far off, either.

He moved quickly but quietly toward the sound, stopping every few feet to listen.

There it was again. More noises, like several people moving through the forest. More branches snapping.

He kept walking, slowly, making his way along the trail, until he could see a place up ahead where the trees diminished and gave way to a clearing.

Then he *did* see someone. Someone moved ahead of him. It was a man, and he was carrying a large branch. Then the figure moved out of Curtis' field of vision.

Curtis left the trail and slowly slipped into the woods,

making an arc around where he thought the meadow to be. He took slow steps, cat steps and carefully made his way to the edge of the field, finally huddling behind a clump of cedars.

There were over a dozen people in the field. All seemed to be working together, walking into the woods and returning with large sticks and branches. An enormous pile of these were stacked in the middle of the field. In the center of the debris, a single, jutting telephone pole rose up like a lance. Curtis watched, horrified, yet fascinated at the same time. None of the people appeared to speak to one another. They worked tirelessly, bringing more and more wood to place on the pile.

He had seen enough. He knew what they were doing, knew why they were there. The thought chilled his blood, but he pushed it away, warming himself with thoughts of Sarah and all her mystery and wonder and power. Silently, he turned and made his way back to the two-track and hurried back to the orchard.

He had only knocked once when he heard Sarah's voice from inside.

"Come in, Curtis."

He opened the door. Sarah was in the dining room, seated at a chair. A single candle glowed on the table.

"They're preparing for tonight," she said, before he could pose the question.

Curtis walked over and sat down at the table. Sarah detected a hint of remorse and reservation in his face, and she reached out and took his hand.

"Curtis," she began, "you won't even *miss* her. She is of no use to you anymore."

He nodded. "I know. But—"

"There's nothing to be afraid of, Curtis. No one will be caught. Do you think that legal authority could take precedent over the powers that we have harnessed? Over the powers that you will have?"

"I just . . . ."

He didn't finish his sentence, and Sarah said nothing more. He stared at the burning candle for a long time. Finally, Sarah stood up. She drew near to him and sank to her knees.

"Curtis."

He looked at her, kneeling at his feet like a slave.

"Yes."

"I can't explain everything that will happen tonight. But I can tell you this: she won't feel a thing. I *promise* you."

She stood up and walked into the kitchen, returning a moment later with two glasses of blackberry wine. She handed one to Curtis as she again knelt at his feet. She raised the glass in a toast, and Curtis followed. Glasses tinked lightly.

"*Ave, Satanas,*" she said.

"*Ave Satanas,*" Curtis repeated numbly.

They drank.

THIRTY SEVEN

"Go, Curtis. Sleep. I'll wake you when the time has come."

Sarah kissed him on the neck as she ushered him out the front door, and Curtis began walking across the orchard. The night had grown overcast and the air was cold—much colder than it had been the previous few nights.

Or maybe it was just *him*. Maybe it was *he* that was cold. Maybe the air had nothing to do with it at all.

He stumbled, but caught himself before he fell. Then, not two steps later, he stumbled again. This time he did fall, but he leapt back up to his feet and saw—

A light?

There was a light on at his house. Several windows glowed.

Shit. She's home already. She's home early.

His heart began to race faster, wondering how this turn of events would change things. Would Sarah have prepared for this? How? And what would he say to Lauren? He hadn't expected her home so soon. Where would he say that he had been?

He reached the edge of the orchard, stumbled again.

Jesus, Curtis, he scolded. *It was only one glass of wine. You can't be drunk.*

But as he approached the house, he realized that, indeed, he was inebriated. His hand fumbled with the doorknob, and when he did finally get the door open, he damned near fell into the foyer.

Lauren was in the kitchen, and she saw his distressed state.

"Curtis?" she said, hurrying toward him. "What's wrong. What's—"

She stopped speaking when the scent reached her. She frowned, and a look of anger replaced her expression of concern. She nodded confidently, with contempt, already knowing the truth.

"You've been drinking."

"No . . . Lauren . . . no. Just one. One drink." It was an effort just to speak, and he slurred the words.

"You're drunk."

He fell to his knees, but his dizziness grew. The room spun. "I'm . . . I'm sorry."

"Sorry? Sorry for what? God, Curtis, you fell off the wagon. Where have you been?"

"I was . . . I am . . . *sorry.*" His thoughts clouded.

Lauren smiled.

Curtis looked up at her through a strange, misty haze. His vision was distorted, and objects around the room appeared to be slanted at odd angles.

"Lau . . . Lauren," he stammered, but he stopped speaking when he saw the shiny object, the tiny silver charm around her neck . . . .

He gasped and slumped forward, then fell to the floor, unconscious.

His head hurt. His body ached. He couldn't move his feet, and his arms were numb, pulled behind him. He was aware of sounds, of chanting, but his head was too foggy to understand. He tried to shake it off, and succeeded somewhat—at least enough to slowly raise his head.

He was in a standing position, held fast by a tight binding around his wrists. Below him, a quagmire of sticks and branches. This made no sense to him, other than to add to his already murky confusion.

He raised his head further. Blurry lights glowed around him, and he tried to shake away his double vision. Gradually, the yellow flares grew apart, and he could make out a row of shadowy figures circled around him, each illuminated in the glare of their own yellow flare.

Torches. They're . . . torches.

A voice boomed from somewhere, but he couldn't see its source. Nevertheless, he was certain it was a voice he'd heard before.

"The Eleventh Key!" the deep voice proclaimed.

"The Eleventh Key!" the solemn group echoed. Torches raised, then lowered, and the deep voice began to speak.

"The mighty throne growled and there were five thunders that flew into the East. And the eagle spake and cried aloud: Come away from the house of death! And they gathered themselves together and became those of whom it measured, and they are the deathless ones who ride the whirlwinds."

Curtis shook his head again, unaware of what was happening around him. People and places were slowly coming back to him. He felt like he was waking from a long, long sleep.

"Come away! For I have prepared a place for you. Move therefore, and show yourselves! Unveil the mysteries of your creation.

265

Be friendly unto me for I am your God, the true worshiper of the flesh that liveth forever!"

"*Regie, Satanas!"* the group replied in unison.

Silence. Curtis could only hear the gentle hiss and pops of torches. They were all around him, these strange shadowy figures. They were shrouded in tunics, their faces covered and hidden beneath large hoods.

"*What . . . what . . . ."* he managed to stammer. "*No. No. Not . . . ."*

Two of the figures slowly walked toward him, their faces concealed within the dark shadow of their hoods. They reached the base of the pile of wood and stopped.

"*Why . . . why am I . . . ."* He was having trouble speaking. "*Why . . . ."*

One of the figures reached up slowly, very slowly, and pulled the hood back.

Curtis gasped.

"*But . . . but . . . ."* he gasped. "*Why . . . how . . . ."*

Sarah smiled, her face radiating in the glow of the torch she held. Dozens of tiny torches reflected in her dark eyes.

"Curtis, my love," she began. "This is what you wanted. What *we* wanted. To be together forever. To be *one."*

"*No . . . not . . . No."* He was still having a difficult time thinking and speaking, but the realization was approaching like a rumbling freight train.

"Curtis?"

"*Not . . . not me,"* he gasped, managing to shake his head. "*Not . . . me. Lauren. I thought that—"*

Sarah's face took on an expression of surprise. Then, she smiled. Not the passionate, beautiful smile that he'd remembered, but a devious, sinister smile, the smile of a coiled viper.

"Curtis," she said, her voice both mocking and playfully scolding. "When I was talking about a human sacrifice, surely, you couldn't have possibly thought that I meant . . . *your wife.*"

Suddenly, the figure next to Sarah reached up and pulled away the hood. A shadow fell and the face of Lauren appeared, her expression burning with haughty triumph. Her eyes glistened with scorn, her smile dripped venom. She said nothing.

And in the glow of the flickering flames, Curtis could do nothing but watch as his wife dropped her torch into the accumulation of wood beneath him. Sarah, too, dropped her torch, and, as if a silent word had been given, the other figures that surrounded him came forward, each dropping their torch onto the ignited pyre.

Through the growing flames and the crackling embers, through the wisping orange sparks and the rising streams of smoke, Sarah spoke to him.

"*I promised you, Curtis,*" she cooed, the glow of the escalating fire igniting in her eyes. "*I promised you . . . your wife wouldn't feel a thing.*"

Curtis screamed, screeching in terrible agony as the intense heat licked his feet, his legs . . . .

The flames spiraled, blooming upward in a flowering pillar, higher and higher, scorching the October night.

THE
HOUSE
AT
2629
WOODLAND
STREET

AUTHOR'S NOTE

The House at 2629 Woodland Street was originally written in October of 2000, exclusively for audio presentation. Hence, it was never printed (nor intended to be printed) in its 'original' state.

Writing audio drama is quite different from writing for the 'printed word' so to speak. What you will read is, of course, the story in its entirety, and then some. It has been slightly revised from its original form, but only to allow the reader to experience scenes and intent that would have been exclusive only to the audio version.

—CK

ONE

It is Wednesday evening, October 26th. A few minutes past eight. I am sitting in room twenty-three of the Lakeshore Inn, in the small town of Wickerton, Michigan. For the past fifteen minutes I've done nothing but stare blankly at the ivory colored wall before me, wondering what to do next. In my years on the job (actually, it's only been four years—it just seems longer) I've never heard or seen anything like what I've just experienced.

It started a week ago, at the offices in Chicago. The offices of PPI—that's the abbreviation for Paranormal Phenomenon, Inc., the firm I work for—are in a large warehouse building on the west side of the city. I received two phone calls last week from a man named Arnold Dalton. Dalton claimed that the home in which he lived was haunted, complete with the usual shimmering objects and things that go bump in the night. All the stuff that I hear about everyday. PPI gets hundreds of these calls every week. Rarely do any of these reports ever pan out to be anything that could be considered *paranormal* activity.

Still, we personally investigate a handful. I'm what's called a 'scout' at PPI. The low man on the totem pole, so to speak. Not that I mind . . . a 'scout' works alone . . . I happen to work better by myself. No inter-office politics, no red tape to cut through. I get sent out first to do initial surveys, a bit of 'fishing', to search for paranormal activity. A 'Ghosthunter', is what my neighbor Jerry Carter calls me. Shana, my ten-year-old daughter, calls me a 'spook dude'. I am *neither* . . . but I guess that's just what you're called if you're a paranormal investigator. The layman's terms, I suppose.

Ghosthunter.

Last week Arnold Dalton called twice; the first time, my receptionist, Holly, took the call. I hadn't gotten around to returning his call by the following day, so he called me again, this time . . . *at my home*. My number is unlisted; how he got it I don't know and he wouldn't tell me, and it's strict policy of PPI to keep all information regarding their personnel confidential.

Mr. Dalton went into great detail about how his home had suddenly become 'haunted'. I asked him a lot of questions; most homes or areas that suddenly begin to show paranormal activity usually are a result of some recent tragic death or violent occurrence. Hardly ever are these hauntings of a harmful nature, and will usually disappear in several weeks. I told him to wait it out, and in a month or two if there was still evidence of paranormal activity, to call again.

But Dalton was insistent. He wanted to meet immediately. I finally agreed—at his strong urging—to meet him at his home . . . the 'haunted' house in question . . . this very evening at five o'clock. I made some arrangements at the office, called Mr. Dalton back to confirm, and packed my bags. I caught an American Eagle plane out of O'Hare this morning, was delayed two hours because of high winds, but finally made the hour-long flight to Traverse City, Michigan.

I rented a car and drove an hour and a half to

Wickerton, a small village about ten miles southeast of Cheboygan. I found a small motel, the Lakeshore Inn, where I am now. Checked in, and headed for the home of Arnold Dalton.

2629 Woodland Street.

Over the phone Dalton had relayed to me a very detailed map; and for all practical purposes, the directions Dalton gave me were perfect. I found the house easily enough . . . but it certainly wasn't anything like I'd *expected* to find.

Quite the *opposite,* actually.

As I pulled into the gravel drive that was overgrown with weeds and brush, it was pretty obvious that Arnold Dalton wasn't around. No one was, for that matter, and there probably hadn't been anyone around in years. The windows of the house were boarded up, and the whole building looked to be falling apart. The lawn was disheveled; long and stringy blades rose up and bent over by their own weight. The grass probably hadn't been mowed since the Nixon years.

I left the car running a moment as I surveyed the weathered building. I inspected the map again on the seat, checking and re-checking the address. I had it right: 2629 Woodland Street. The numbers on the house were faded, but I could still make them out. After a moment I shut off the car engine and stepped out to have a look around.

The home was average-sized. The closest other building was a small house back up the road about a half-mile. The house at 2629 Woodland Street had no neighbors; whoever had built the home wanted their privacy.

I walked around the yard and to the back. There was no doubt that the house was abandoned. It was just too weathered . . . too battered and bruised by the elements to be livable. And another thing: there was no power to the house. The lines ran along the street, but never stretched out over the yard to connect to the house itself. I also searched for a phone line. I found none.

All of the windows were boarded up, except the ones on the second floor. Most of those windows had been broken long ago, no doubt by young boys with nothing better to do on an afternoon except throw rocks at the abandoned structure. I did things like that when I was a boy . . . I imagine kids still probably do those things now. Shingles were falling off the roof. *Shambles,* is what it was. The house was in *shambles.* Bob Vila would take one look at this place, shake his head and say 'no'.

I stepped up and onto the porch. It creaked and moaned under my feet like a feeble old woman. I paused a moment, uncertain as to whether the porch could support me or not. I bounced up and down a little bit on one leg. The graying boards beneath my feet sagged a little bit, but they felt solid.

Satisfied that I wasn't going to break my neck, I took a step toward the door, and, just for kicks, knocked. I could hear the hollow taps as they echoed through empty rooms in the house.

After knocking several times, I called out for Mr. Dalton. I felt silly, standing there at a vacant, dilapidated building, thinking that someone would actually come and answer the boarded-up door. Of course no one answered, and no one came to the door.

I stepped back again, checking the house numbers for the umpteenth time.

2629 Woodland. I was at the correct address.

The house was not anything like what I had expected. Arnold Dalton hadn't gone into great detail about the home in which he lived, but I was certain beyond any measurable doubt that the house before me could not be the house he had explained to me over the phone.

I must have heard Dalton wrong. The address was sure to be 2629 Wood*mere,* or Wood*crest,* or wood something or another. I decided I would go back to the motel, call Arnold Dalton and apologize, and ask for directions again.

At the Lakeshore Inn, I held the phone to my ear, rehearsing my apology as I dialed the number. *Mr. Dalton,* I would say. *I'm so sorry. I took down your directions wrong. Could you give them to me again?*

Suddenly, three shrill tones squealed from the receiver, and I was coldly told by a recorded voice that *the number I had dialed was no longer in service.* I hung up and dialed again. Same thing. This I couldn't figure out. I had called Dalton twice at this very number less that twenty four hours ago. Both times I connected; both times he had answered.

I scanned the motel room phone book. There wasn't a single *Dalton* listed, let alone an *Arnold* Dalton. I picked up the phone again and called directory assistance. I was told there was no listing for an Arnold Dalton.

And so now I am unsure what to do. I've certainly encountered a number of bizarre circumstances, but nothing quite like this. At first I thought that someone surely must be playing some trick. But then again, why? That doesn't make any sense. There's more to this than I know at this point. I'm positive. And I realize now, for sure, that I didn't take down the wrong address. I didn't take down the wrong phone number.

So, I've decided to stay—at least for tonight. I'll go back and check out the house again in the morning. I'll do some more checking on this 'Arnold Dalton' and see if I can find him. After all, people don't just disappear.

But now, as I lay back in my bed in the motel room, there's a gnawing in my gut that says everything is not quite right with the house at 2629 Woodland Street.

I've had this sensation—this *perception*—before. At the risk of being arrogant or overconfident, I must say that I am usually not wrong when my gut instinct has something to say about it.

TWO

Thursday Morning, October 27th.

It is six-thirty, and the sun has just poked its bald, yellow head over the treetops. I left the curtains open last night, and my whole room is bathed in a cool, lemony glow.

There's an in-room coffee pot on the counter in the small bathroom. It brews only two cups, but I am grateful for both. A shave and a hot shower are icing on the cake.

I call Karen, my ex-wife in Chicago. We have joint custody of Shana. The divorce makes the whole situation that much more difficult, with me being on the road and all that, but I've pretty much gotten used to it.

Karen tells me Shana's fine, she's still sleeping. I tell her not to wake her up; I'll talk to her later. We chat for a moment. My relationship with Karen has gotten better since the divorce, and now we get along fairly well. Platonic, is about the best you could say about it.

But strangely enough, Karen says that *I* had a phone call at *her* house last night. Someone called looking for *me*. Last night. It was from a man named Arnold Dalton.

"Arnold Dalton?" I ask.

"That's what he said," Karen replies. "Said he lived on Woodland Street. Wanted to know if you were here."

"What did you tell him?"

"I told him you were a scumbag."

"I know you better," I said with a smile. Karen would say no such thing. She's playful, and I like it. For a couple of years after the break-up, she hated me. The divorce had been pretty bitter. Now she was back to normal. Or as normal as you can be, after something like that. I suppose I miss her.

"You're right, Trevor," she said with a laugh. "I told him that we were divorced. I didn't know where you were."

"Did he say anything else? Leave a phone number, anything like that?"

"No. He said that you'd probably be at his house soon enough. He said he was expecting you."

And that was pretty much the extent of our conversation. I really wanted to talk with Shana, just to hear her voice and see how she was doing.

That would have to wait.

I hang up the phone with my anger simmering just below boiling point. Just who is this 'Arnold Dalton' and what does he want? Why did he call me at *Karen's* house? She's moved since our divorce. I've never lived at that residence. No one would have *any* reason to call me there. What kind of a game is he playing? I could be in the wrong *city,* for all I know. 'Arnold Dalton' could be in Egypt. I can't understand why someone would pull a joke like this, or why. The more I think about it, the angrier I get.

Suddenly the phone rings.

"Hello?" I say. There is only silence.

"Hellooo?" I hear nothing. "Hello?"

More silence.

"Look," I say. "I don't know *who* you are or *what* you're

up to. But my company has spent a lot of money to fly me up here and I don't think they're going to appreciate silly stunts and games."

I slam the phone to its cradle. I am going home, back to Chicago. This is a wasted trip. Whatever—*whoever* —Dalton is, or whatever he wants, I don't know. I don't care. I'm—

The phone rings again. I snap it up and place it to my ear.

This time, there *is* someone there. I recognize Dalton's voice instantly. In his deep hoarse voice, he speaks. His words are haunting. Chilling.

"The dead . . . will have their day . . . . "

I am at once confused. "What do you mean?" I ask.

Again, his hoarse voice repeats.

"The dead . . . will have their day."

The line goes dead. He is gone.

I remain in my room for a while, trying to piece together what I know. Sitting here, looking out the window, watching the sun rise, I decide two things. Number one, I will do a *little* more investigating. Investigating *what,* I don't know. But I will at least give it a shot. And two, I am going to leave—*tonight.* I will check out of the motel this morning, book a flight on the evening plane from Traverse City to O'Hare, and be home by ten o'clock.

I pack my bags, carry them down to the front desk, and tell the manager on duty that I am leaving before my scheduled checkout date.

She looks at me rather sheepishly, and seems embarrassed about something.

"I'm very sorry for the inconvenience," she says sincerely.

I mull this over a moment before I speak.

"Inconvenience?" I ask, trying to imagine what she

means. The room was fine. *Everything* was fine.

"Yes. It was rather . . . *unexpected.*"

"Actually, I'm leaving because I finished my work early.
There's been no inconvenience."

Her face brightens and she manages a smile.

"I thought you were leaving because of the phones."

"The phones? No, why?"

"The construction workers up the street accidentally cut
a major trunk of phone lines. The entire building, including
all of the rooms, have been without phone service since last
night."

THREE

I am accustomed to a lot of strange things in this
business. It's true that most 'ghost' stories turn out to
be just that—stories. Yet, I am fascinated with the
whole 'Ghosthunter' bit. I joined Paranormal Phenomena
Incorporated four years ago as an unpaid intern. What I
make now is certainly nothing to brag about, but I think it is
a good-sized paycheck nonetheless, especially when I
compare it to my overnight job at the convenience store,
which was where I was working before. And what I do now,
I must say, is a *lot* more than fascinating, and I think I make
a good researcher. A better researcher than a clerk, anyway.

Truth be told, I'm probably the most skeptical person
you could ever meet. I've never believed in ghosts or
hauntings, and, in *most* cases, I still don't. What most people
consider to be paranormal activity, after a thorough
investigation, turns out to be nothing. I've been on more
goose chases than ghost chases.

But not this time. I know that what is going on is
something completely different than any other case I've been
on. I've been in houses and actually watched paranormal
activity transpire. I've seen what some people would call

'ghosts'. Been there, done that, as the T-shirt says.

But the events of the past twenty-four hours have convinced me that what is going on here is more than just someone's idea of a prank. The whole phone thing threw me for a loop, for one. I had gone so far as to ask the motel manager if I could pick up the phone and try dialing out from the front desk. Nothing. No dial tone, nothing. I even went back up to my room. Nothing. No dial tone, nothing.

But I *had* spoken with Karen. I talked with her for five minutes this morning. I'd also received that strange phone call, with the voice of doom warning me about the dead.

Yet now the motel manager is telling me that the phones haven't worked since *yesterday*.

To the delight of the manager on duty, I tell her that I have changed my mind. I *would* stay a few days, after all.

FOUR

From a pay phone in town I call Karen again.

"Sorry to bother you again," I say.

"Again?" is her single-word response.

"Yeah."

She is confused, and doesn't know what I mean. Then she asks me why I didn't call her earlier in the morning, like I usually do when I'm traveling.

Truth was, I *had*. But I didn't tell her that. She gets worried easily. No sense in getting her all worked up. I simply ask her if anyone has called this morning. She says no, and wonders why I ask.

"Last night?" I ask. "After I left for O'Hare?"

Again, her answer is no, and she asks me why I think someone would call *her* looking for *me*.

The county clerk's office is about the only place to start when you have a situation like this. After a cup of coffee and a short drive, I arrive at the gray stone county building. It also houses the offices for the district and circuit court, the 'friend of the court' which is kind of an oxymoron if you ask me, and a host of other offices. The county clerk's office isn't busy at this time of the morning, and I have no trouble finding out the information I'm looking for.

The current owner of the property and house at 2629 Woodland street isn't Arnold Dalton after all . . . it's a woman by the name of Emily Mays. She lives in a small village about fifteen miles away called Wharton. Not too far from here. I decide that she would be the first person to start with, being that I can't find any Arnold Dalton.

Wharton is an interesting town. Being that I'm from Chicago, a small town (to me) is like, maybe, 25,000 people. Wharton might be lucky if there is 100. It is a quiet, sleepy berg with one gas station, a party-mart, and three bars. Finding Emily Mays' house isn't a difficult task.

She lives in a *mobile* home. Nothing wrong with that, mind you. My father lives in a mobile home in Ohio, and it's nicer than half the homes I've been in. I think some people think *mobile home* somehow means 'cheap' or undesirable. Not true.

But Emily Mays' home is the epitome of substandard mobile home living. Complete with cars on blocks outside, broken appliances strewn all over the yard, a clothesline that stretches from here to the edge of the Bonanza back forty. To cap off this array of displaced apparatus, a two-foot satellite dish is mounted just outside of the broken screen door. Emily Mays might not have quality transportation, but you can bet she's got 247 channels of the best programming satellites can beam down to her.

I have a hunch, as I pull into the driveway, that Emily Mays lives alone. Maybe her place is the gathering center for the kids, or at least a place to dump their garbage. But Emily Mays herself, I am sure, lives alone. Another one of those gut feelings.

As I get out of the car, I hear a dog barking from inside the trailer. A yipper. One of those little dogs that's no bigger than a football, and would travel about as far with a good drop-kick. Not that I would do such a thing, mind you. Relax.

I wade through the mass of debris that litters the yard and driveway and step up on a rickety redwood porch. I can hear activity inside. The dog keeps yipping and raising a stir, but no one comes to the door. Finally I reach out and knock.

A full minute goes by before the door slowly opens. A gray haired, bespectacled woman in her sixties peers back at me. She looks surprised . . . maybe even a bit angry. I don't think she gets too many visitors.

I ask her if she is Emily Mays and she nods and says she is. She opens the door a bit farther, just enough for me to see that she is carrying the dog, like it is some kind of warning that *if you're going to try anything, buster, you'll have to answer to Fluffy*. The dog stares back at me with bulging brown eyes, growling faintly. I frown. In five seconds I could have Fluffy in a mayonnaise jar.

When I ask her if she owns the house at 2629 Woodland, she immediately becomes defensive. For no reason, at least as far as I can tell. She draws her head back in a sort of rooster-like motion, as if surprised to hear the address. *Yes,* she tells me, she *does* own the house, and then demands to know why *I* want to know. She stares at me, her beady eyes bugging out from behind her pop bottle glasses. Fluffy continues to growl, and I'm mentally assessing where I might find a jar for the little fuzzy bugger.

At this point I usually pull out one of my business cards and hand it to the person that I'm speaking with. I don't this time. My business cards state that I am an investigator of

287

the paranormal. Some people become frightened at that, some laugh. Others don't know what a paranormal investigator is, which, I was sure, would be the case with Emily Mays.

I ignore her question about why I want to know, and when I ask her if she knows a man by the name of Arnold Dalton, another wave of surprise just about bowls her over, like a perfect strike right down the center of the lane. She looks like someone has just smashed her in the face with an aluminum baseball bat. An expression of stunned disbelief comes over her face, maybe disbelief mixed with fear. I can't tell.

Holy shit. Now she *is* angry. Through her pop-bottle googly-glasses she demands to know how *I* know of Arnold Dalton. Before I can answer she wants to know who I am, but before I can say anything she again demands to know how I know of Arnold Dalton. I tell her that he had called me at home. Fluffy is still snarling at me, and, so help me God, I am about to snare that little bastard with a treble hook and go pike fishing.

I have to read people's faces a lot in this business. More often than not, the face will tell you exactly the opposite of what the mouth is saying. In the case of Emily Mays, I can read her face like the *Chicago Tribune*.

Upon hearing that I had spoken with Arnold Dalton, her face goes completely bleach white. The blood runs from her face like water from a roof. I thought she was going to faint.

Then she slams the door in my face. I call out to her from the porch, asking if she is all right. From behind the closed door I hear her shout at me, telling me to go away. She tells me to leave and never come back. Fluffy growls, and the little dog sounds like a puking weasel.

As I pull out of her drive, I wonder why on earth she

acted that way. She seems completely horrified by the name Arnold Dalton. Does she know him? Does she know *of* him? Who is he? And why did he call me and want me to meet him at a house? A house that he told me was his? It is obvious that Emily Mays isn't going to be any help. Neither was Fluffy, for that matter.

I decide to pay another visit to the house at 2629 Woodland Street. I had been hoping that Emily Mays would give me permission to take a look around the property, and possibly even give me a key and allow me inside. I laugh. Fat chance of that now. But I can at least walk around outside the house and get some photographs. I have a digital camera that puts images right on to a regular 3 ½ inch computer diskette. I can load the pictures on to my lap top and store them there, and then re-use the disk.

In twenty minutes I am at the house. The day is bright. A bit cool, but beautiful nonetheless. The trees are beginning to change their colors and in the field behind the house a large maple tree is fading from a dark green to a smoldering, burnt orange. The overgrown grass in the yard and the meadow behind the house is a golden brown. Long, thin blades are tossed gently about by a light wind. I shut off the car, unpack my digital camera, and walk around the house.

It is really too bad that the home has been allowed to reach such a state of disrepair. It is far beyond the restoration point. The foundations appear to be crumbling, and the entire structure is sagging inwards. But in the bright sunshine, the home looks more appealing, as if it is crying out to be saved, to be loved once again. It truly is very sad. I'm sure that at one time it had been a very beautiful house.

I take several pictures of the structure from different angles, including close-ups of the boarded windows. Soon, the entire disk is filled, which is about forty pictures. I take the disk out and replace it with another one and take some more shots.

I don't notice the back door until I am peering into the camera's mini viewfinder. I am about to take a picture when I see it.

The back door is *open*.

Only about four inches or so, but it is open just the same. I hadn't noticed it yesterday evening, but then again, it had been getting dark. I could have easily missed it.

We have a standing rule at Paranormal Phenomena Incorporated: Absolutely, under *no* circumstances, is trespassing allowed. It would be grounds for termination if the agency found out. However . . . there are no signs posted anywhere that say 'do not trespass'. No 'private property' signs, nothing. In my mind I can't see it as trespassing if I don't *know* I'm trespassing. I mean, my logic might be a bit flawed, but that excuse has gotten me out of more than one situation in the past. Once I was even detained by the police. My standard response was that I was a photographer compiling pictures for an article. I was sorry, I meant no harm, blah, blah blah. Didn't see any signs (which I hadn't; there weren't any). It was easy for the police to figure out that I wasn't stealing or vandalizing anything, and I was released with a warning. But rarely had I ever been in trouble; never had I ever run into any serious problems . . . as long as I follow the rules.

And today, my curiosity is getting the best of me.

I walk toward the house and peer in through the open door, then turn around to make sure that there is no one watching. Which is extremely doubtful that there would be, given the remote location of the old house.

Satisfied, I push the door open and step inside.

FIVE

I glance at my watch as I step inside the old home. It is exactly two o'clock in the afternoon; the creaking door sounds like a bell tower ringing at the top of the hour.

I am in a small foyer. It smells dank and musky and reeks of filth. I am certain that I probably have been the only person in the house in years. And I am also certain that wherever Arnold Dalton placed the call from, it wasn't the home on 2629 Woodland Street.

The floor creaks beneath my feet. My first few steps are cautious; I don't want to fall through rotting floorboards and break my neck. After a few steps, I gain confidence and move with ease. Despite the condition of the outside of the home, the inside seems fairly intact.

I continue through the foyer and into a narrow hallway. There are old paintings hanging on the walls, which I find amazing. A house that has been vacant for this long would almost certainly be the target of vandals; it's incredible that most of the things in the house are intact.

I stop and take a look at a few of the paintings. They are old scenes; farms, mountains and the like. All of the paintings have been discolored and faded by time.

After a few moments, I continue walking. The floor continues to moan and cry out with every step I take. The old boards beneath my feet are warped and uneven, and my shoes seem to roll over the small waves.

Ahead of me the hall opens up into a large room. The living room, I presume. I continue walking, my presence announced by the creaking boards beneath my feet.

On my left is a small bedroom, and I stop at the doorway and look inside. Years of dust and debris are scattered about. Chips of yellow paint are falling off the walls. There's only one furnishing, an old table that has been upended. It is on its side with a broken leg, hopelessly hobbled. I take several pictures with the digital camera and move on.

The living room is, for the most part, empty. Empty and dark. All of the windows have been boarded up quite well, not allowing even the tiniest beam of sunlight to squeak through. Except for a layer of dust, the floor is barren, as are the walls and ceiling. There are no light fixtures, no fixtures on the walls here. Again, I take a few pictures with my digital camera. The flash illuminates the room, creating an eerie afterimage.

There is a staircase on the far wall that leads upstairs. I stand at the foot of it, looking up. It is brighter upstairs, probably because the windows on the second floor have not been boarded up. This is something that I find unusual, and I make a mental note of it. *Why would someone spend the time to board up the windows on the first floor, yet leave the windows on the second floor untouched?*

The stairs groan beneath my feet. The steps feel solid, but I am very cautious anyway. Last year in Iowa I broke my arm climbing an old staircase in an abandoned hotel. I don't want to go through that again.

I hear a noise upstairs, and I stop. It is a scraping, a

light scuffling. The sound does not alarm me, but I take note of it anyway and continue.

Upon reaching the top of the stairs it is as I suspected: A pigeon takes flight from one of the upstairs bedrooms, flying out the broken window in a flurry of beating wings. This is often the case with so-called 'haunted' houses. Noises are, in 99.9 percent of the cases I've investigated, caused by mice or bats or birds. It's just that most people don't take the time to investigate. They get freaked out, and would rather believe that the noise was the work of some spook rather than face their fears and find out the truth.

There are four bedrooms upstairs. To my surprise, all are furnished. Each room has a bed and a dresser, and two of the rooms have wooden chairs. The mattresses on all of the beds are falling apart and have been torn to shreds by animals. Mice and rats love to make nests in beds. The soft kapok provides a warm, comfortable shelter to burrow in during cold winter months.

Like the floors downstairs, the floorboards up here are warped, the walls are water-stained. Plaster is falling from the ceilings. There is little doubt that the home is in its final stages of deterioration. Despite the broken windows, the air is thick and damp. More so than it is downstairs.

I take a few pictures with my digital camera, replace the disk with yet another new one, then take a few more shots. The light upstairs here is better, and the automatic flash on my camera isn't needed.

If there is anything strange about the house, I don't sense it right away. The house is old, it is falling apart. It is the kind of house that children would hurry by on a dark night, looking the other way, not wanting to even *glance* at the house for fear of what they might see. The kind of house that they would tell stories about during slumber parties.

Yet, I'm still certain, beyond any doubt, that the house

at 2629 Woodland is not as it seems. I don't know why, for sure. It appears to be just another old home, decrepit and dying, waiting out its last, final years alone. This is the fate of millions of homes across the country. The house at 2629 Woodland Street had been a haven at one time, a place to eat and sleep and grow. Now, the only thing that remains of the past is a fragile old dying skeleton.

It is at the top of the stairs that I stop.

No, I do *more* than just stop.

I *freeze*.

A chill begins at the top of my neck and trickles down my spine. I am at once confused, and, I must admit, frightened.

Below me on the stairs, my shoes have left imprints in the fine layer of dust.

But—

Next to my footprints are *another* set of tracks. *Another* pair of shoes. They are a bit smaller than my feet, a bit smaller and thinner. I came up the steps once; there should only be one set of footprints. *My* footprints. Now there are *two* sets. Someone—*or something*—has followed me.

And now I can *feel* it. I can *feel* and *sense* a presence around me. The hairs on my arm are tingling, standing straight up on end. I remain motionless, scanning the stairs, the area around me. I hear nothing. I see nothing.

I slowly begin walking down the steps. Each creak of the stairs booms through the house. I try and step quieter.

At the landing at the bottom of the stairs, I stop. I click off a couple shots with the digital camera and slowly begin to turn. It takes me nearly half a minute to complete a semi-circle, and what I see as I gaze up the staircase paralyzes me.

Footsteps are forming in the dust.

I watch them slowly make their way down the final few steps. They, too, as I have done, stop at the landing.

Something is *right here, right now, in front of me.*

I can't move. I *won't* move. Even if I wanted to, and sometimes I *do* in this business, I *won't.* I stay put. I stand there, at the bottom of the stairs, for a full five minutes. The mysterious footsteps don't move, either.

Finally, after a few deep breaths, I take a step back, expecting the prints to form alongside my tracks in the chalky dust on the floor. They do not.

Slowly, I hold out my digital camera and take three successive images of the prints. Then I take a few more slow steps backward and take another three photos, all aimed at the area where I had just been standing.

Still, the footsteps don't follow me. I turn and walk down the dark hallway to the back door, and spin once again. It is brighter by the open door, and I can see my own footsteps in the gray dust.

Only my own.

I take one last look down the hall, step outside, and close the door behind me.

SIX

Back at the car, I stand staring up at the house for a long time.

My feelings about the house at 2629 Woodland Street are correct. It is *not* just an old building left to fend for itself, slowly giving in to the ravages of time.

There is something *in* the house.

Something *living,* something existing that is not of this world.   A level six, is what Paranormal Phenomena Incorporated refers to it as.   Level one is nothing but a report.   A report from a *possibly* reliable source that some type of activity is going on.   Level two is an active investigation of the premises; level three is an inconclusive study that leans toward non-activity, or, a 'non-haunting'. Level four is yet another inconclusive study that leans toward *some* type of activity, but not much.   Level five is *strong* conclusive evidence of phenomena occurring, and Level six is actual physical proof.

Surprisingly, PPI has investigated a number of level sixes over the years. I myself have been in on my share.

As I drive away, I can't help but turn my head and glance at the old home. I'm not sure what I expect to see, but curiosity is buzzing in my head like a bee caught in a coffee can. There is a lot going on at 2629 Woodland. I travel thousands of miles across the country every year, and I *do* find many homes to be what some people refer to as 'haunted'. I estimate that virtually every city, every town in America has a half dozen of these 'haunted' houses. Typically, the evidence is much more subtle. Doors that close by themselves. Noises in the night. Sudden smells or stenches that seem to drift through a room. In this business, I do not find that all uncommon in the least. Many people that call us are shocked when we say that we're not interested in investigating they're home. *Sure*, we tell them. *It probably is haunted*. But we're not interested in things that go bump in the night. What we are looking for is the actual, physical evidence: concrete proof. We look—and hope—for *contact*. That's what we search for. We look for incidents like this one: the house at 2629 Woodland Street.

Still, I am not yet ready to file a report. Procedure would be to call the main offices immediately. Especially in a situation such as this. Doing so would bring a half dozen staff members—which is about half the company—flying in by tomorrow morning. They'd be scurrying around like silly squirrels gathering nuts for winter. I not sure if I'm ready to bring in the troops just yet. I'd like to find out a little bit more about the house: the history, the basics.

And Arnold Dalton. He just seemed to disappear—if he ever existed at all.

But of *course* he does. *Someone* does. *Someone* called me on the phone. His voice was as real as anyone's, as alive as you or me.

And why did Emily Mays refuse to speak to me? What does she know about Dalton? What does she know about the house?

I decide to make one more effort to speak with her.

Perhaps if she knows I am going to be persistent, that I'm not going away, maybe she will talk to me.

I stop at a small cafe near my motel to grab lunch. I haven't eaten since breakfast, and the hamburger is filling and needed. I eat hungrily and quickly, my mind still churning with questions. I don't even wait for the waitress to bring me my bill; I just drop two fives on the counter and leave.

In twenty minutes I am rounding the final corner before reaching Emily Mays' house. I take my foot off the accelerator and coast through the turn, waiting for her trailer to come in to view.

But first, I see police cars.

There are three of them. Two brown and white sheriff cruisers, one dark blue Michigan State Police Suburban.

And an ambulance.

The ambulance is parked in Emily Mays' driveway, next to the state police vehicle. The sheriff's cars are parked on the shoulder of the road. There are a few people standing by, rubbernecking neighbors, no doubt, watching the goings-on. As I drive by, I see a Gurney being wheeled out of the house. On it is a very unconscious and unmoving Emily Mays, I can see that much. She is wearing an oxygen mask. Something serious has happened . . . but *what?*

I decide not to stop to find out. Something tells me that whatever has happened to Emily Mays was sparked by my visit earlier in the day.

SEVEN

I won't return to the house at 2629 Woodland this afternoon, and I'm debating on whether or not to call Holly at PPI and fill her in on what is going on. I'm supposed to call when an instance of paranormal activity exposes itself like it had at the house earlier, but right now that seems like it would be nothing but an intrusion to bring in so many other people. There would be no harm in doing some of my *own* ground work, some of my *own* research, before calling in Howdy Doody's National Guard, as I have come to call them. The team usually succeeds in screwing more things up than nailing things down. Holly, however, is as good as gold: when I tell her something is between her and I alone, it stays that way. It's good to have someone on the inside like Holly.

The day is wearing on, and so I return to the county clerk's office to request a listing of who has owned the property at Woodland before Emily Mays. The woman at the office is quite displeased that I am taking up her time. She does a lot of eye rolling and heavy sighs that indicate to me that I am being a burden. Tough luck. That's what she is here for.

Evidently, the house had remained in the family. The owner before Emily Mays was listed as Theodore Charles Mays, and the home had been willed to Emily in 1971. Theodore Charles Mays had purchased the home in 1920 from Frederick J. Mays, so I assume that Theodore was probably Emily's father. Emily must not have married, or if she had, she had kept her maiden name. There were no records beyond the 1920 purchase; the house was probably built by Frederick.

At the exact stroke of five, the woman at the clerk's office abruptly announces that it is time to close and that I have to go. She looks at me warily, like she's wondering if I'm the type that's going to give her any trouble about leaving, like I'm here for last call or something. I thank her for her time, scribble some notes down on a pad of paper, and walk out the door.

Back at the Lakeshore Inn, I shower and consider my options for dinner. Wickerton is by no means a large town, and there aren't many dining choices. Fifteen miles or so north is Mackinaw City, which looks a bit larger than Wickerton. On the map it does, anyway. The city of Petoskey is to the southwest, about thirty miles away. It's quite a bit bigger and no doubt there are more restaurants, but I decide that I've done enough driving today and I settle once again upon the small cafe down the street. Lunch had been good; I have no reason to believe that dinner would be any different. Besides, the cafe is only a quarter mile from the motel I am staying at. I can walk there, so I do.

October in northern Michigan is a beautiful time of year. The colors of the trees—brilliant reds and oranges and yellows and purples—have faded this late in the fall season, but a hint of their autumn bloom still remains. Within a few weeks most of the leaves will have been torn from their branches by the fall winds. Soon, snow would fall on the north country, a blanket of pristine white that would cover miles upon miles of fields and forests. We get snow in Chicago, but nothing like Michigan does.

The air is chilly, and large gray clouds tumble in the sky overhead. As I walk along the gravel shoulder of the road, a frigid wind tosses my hair about. I zip my wool pullover up to my neck. The trees hiss as the breeze shakes the dying leaves.

The small cafe is completely empty. For a minute I think it is closed, then I see a flash of a face from behind a kitchen window. A female voice tells me to have a seat anywhere, and someone will be with me in a minute.

The 'someone' is a beautiful woman that looks to be twenty-eight, maybe thirty. Smooth, honey-colored skin still holds a hint of a summer tan. Brown hair hangs to the middle of her back. She's wearing blue jeans and a white blouse with the cafe's logo embroidered just above her right breast. *Cafe Wickerton,* it says. She's rather attractive, and she glides with a certain confidence, an assured, purposeful stride.

The woman smiles, places a glass of water and a place mat on the table, and hands me a menu. Gentle brown eyes meet mine. She tells me that the fried chicken is the special, along with potatoes and corn. Soup of the day is vegetable beef or chicken gumbo. Without looking at the menu I tell her that the special will be fine, along with the gumbo. She smiles, again, wider this time, nods, says thank you, and skirts away, returns momentarily with the soup, then scurries off again.

I begin retracing my steps of the day, trying to piece together what I know so far. I am *very* curious about the episode at Emily Mays, and now I am dismayed at myself for not investigating further. Perhaps the event—whatever happened—is just a coincidence, and had nothing at all to do with my visit with her earlier. Perhaps she's a hypochondriac that calls for an ambulance every time she blows her nose.

Perhaps.

The waitress brings me a plate of the most delicious-looking fried chicken I have ever seen, a real artery-choker. Mom would be jealous. She refills my water.

"Is there anything else I can bring you?" she asks.

"No, thank you."

She begins to walk away.

"Um, actually, there is," I say. She stops and turns. "I wonder if you might know someone. Someone by the name of Arnold Dalton."

She walks back to my table, frowning as she looks up into space. Her face is beautiful, and I don't know if I'm staring at her in anticipation of an answer to my question, or whether I am staring at her simply because I find her so attractive. Maybe it's a little of both. Maybe it's a little of one and a lot of the other.

After a moment of pondering, she shakes her head. "No, I don't recall anyone by that name. I've lived in Wickerton all my life. I'm sure I'd recognize the name if he was from around here."

"How about Emily Mays?"

By the look on her face there is no doubt that she knows who Emily Mays is. She frowns and nods. I sense from her nonverbal answer that Emily Mays probably isn't the most highly-regarded person in the community.

"Yes, I know Emily Mays."

And before I know it, the waitress—Andrea is her name—is seated at my table, sipping coffee, telling me about Emily Mays and her strange family. I listen intently, and I can't take my eyes off of her. She has a smooth, delicate smile and a soft voice.

"For as long as I can remember," she says, "none of the

Mays' family members could ever get along. There were fights, disputes, quarrels. I don't know why. I know that the entire Mays family lives apart, in their own little t. I don't think they associate with one another very much."

"What about a house? On Woodland Street? 2629 Woodland Street. Do you know anything about that place?"

She frowns in thought, then shakes her head.

"I'm familiar with the street, yes," she replies. "It's kind of an out-of-the-way place. But as far as the house, there's not much I can tell you."

By the time I get up to leave it has grown dark. I thank Andrea for speaking with me, and bid her good night. She smiles, and it kills me.

I am not here to flirt with the locals, I remind myself as I step outside into the chilly night. *I am here to work. I am here to find out what is going on at 2629 Woodland Street.*

EIGHT

At the Lakeshore Inn I lay back on the bed with my laptop computer balanced on my thighs. I've retrieved the diskettes that contain the photos I shot earlier in the day. I am anxious to take a look.

The first image flashes onto the screen. It is a picture of the outside of the house. The photo is clear and the color is good.

The next photo is almost identical, and the following one is of the west side of the house. But these aren't the pictures I want to see. I want to see the ones from *inside,* the ones that will show the extra set of footsteps on the stairs.

I place another diskette in the drive and another picture appears. This is a shot of one of the upstairs rooms. Nothing unusual. Nothing really unusual about the next half dozen pictures.

Finally, the first picture of the footprints flashes on the screen, and I'm relieved. I had feared that maybe the photos wouldn't turn out, or if they did, the prints in the dust would be gone. I am glad that this isn't the case. I *hadn't* imagined anything earlier in the day; here was proof.

I press the space bar to bring up the next picture. The

diskette drive whirs and the image rolls onto the screen, and my mouth falls open in disbelief. I lean toward the monitor, my face frozen.

It is . . . *something*. *Something* is there.

A hazy, white image. There is a form at the foot of the stairs on the landing. It has a very human-like quality, although it is difficult to make out much. I can see what I believe is legs and arms, however, the area above the shoulders is distorted and fuzzy like warm breath on a cold window. The shape—the 'body' if that is what you could call it—is facing toward me. It is a chilling, bizarre scene. Why it has shown up in the photo is beyond me; I certainly didn't see anything like this when I was taking the picture. And the digital camera I have is nothing special. It doesn't capture electromagnetic activity or auras or anything like that.

Until now, anyway.

I zoom in to get a closer look but the magnification doesn't reveal anything beyond what I've already seen. I normalize the size of the still, and I just stare.

The image is very disturbing. Certainly I've seen things of this nature before, but events seem to be happening so fast. I haven't been here forty-eight hours, but it feels more like a week. Often I might remain in a place for weeks on end before discovering or witnessing any supernatural activity—if there is any at all to see. Yet here, in Wickerton, the show seems to have already begun—or perhaps I joined it already in progress.

I stare at the picture on the screen for a long time before shutting down the laptop and drifting off to sleep.

NINE

The nightmare is horrible. I am laying on my back, engulfed in darkness. I am confined in some sort of box, like a coffin. It is dark and I cannot move. I try pounding on the wood above my head, screaming to be let out.

And I am not alone.

There is something in the box with me, an evil, dark presence that I can't see. I can feel it mocking me, telling me that I won't get out, that I can't get out, that I'll never get out. The wave of terror swells inside of me and I begin scratching at the wood above me, kicking and clawing, trying to escape. It is no use. I can feel the presence all around me, getting under my skin, crawling into my brain. It is laughing at me, shrieking with delight. No words are spoken, but I can hear a voice. It is in my head, as clear and real as my own.

You can't escape. You can't escape. You will die here, and you will remain here. Forever.

The nightmare ends as I snap up in bed. It is dark, and I am disoriented. My body is covered with sweat. My heart is thumping madly and I am gasping for breath. I look around, and reality drifts back. I am in a motel. The Lakeview Inn. Wickerton. I am safe.

I lay back down in bed, but it takes a long time to return to sleep.

Seven am, October 28th. Friday. I awake to a howling wind that seems to shake the entire building. Outside, leaves are ripped from their branches and tossed into the air, traveling horizontally in the gale. The sky is gray and dark, and I think that it's a good possibility that snow may come early this year. I, for one, hope not.

Breakfast at the Cafe Wickerton. I walk there again, the wind whipping through me with every step. By the time I arrive, I am shivering. I'll buy a heavier coat later today.

To my disappointment, Andrea is not at the restaurant this morning. The place is filled with a dozen patrons, in contrast to its quaint emptiness last night. I sit alone in a booth and the waitress—a large, bespectacled woman—brings me a cup of coffee and a menu. She smiles, says good morning, and is on her way again, returning after a moment to take my order of an omelet and toast.

As I look around the tiny diner, my best guess is that the small cafe is filled with locals. There are a lot of casual nods as people meet each others' eyes . . . a bit more friendly than you would expect from mere strangers. Or maybe that's just the nature of the people.

There are five college-aged kids seated in the booth in front of me. They are quiet and look pallid and hung over. One of the kids has a silver stud in his nose and another one in his eyebrow. I've seen this type of ornamentation quite a bit as of late. I guess it's some kind of jewelry that is supposed to make you attractive to the opposite sex or something. Maybe it is, I don't know. Maybe that's what's hip these days. I personally tend to shy away from fashion accessories that are applied with a nail gun.

At the booth next to me two people get up to leave. There is a newspaper on their table; after the man and woman are gone I stand, lean over, and snatch it up. It is today's edition of the Marchfield County Reporter, the local daily paper. I scan the headlines, the world news, the national news. Not much going on. Page two, same ol' same ol'. Page *three* . . . .

The name Emily Ruth Mays hits me between the eyes. Above her name is a single, stark word:

Obituaries.

Emily Mays is dead.

I stare at the article, my mind a flurry of confused thoughts. What had happened? The obituary gave no clue or no explanation. It just stated that she had died suddenly. It didn't give the date of a funeral or where flowers could be sent. Emily Mays, age 63, was dead. It was a simple, nondescript death notice. There was nothing about her life, what she did, where she might have worked. No laudable testimonies about volunteering for the thrift shop, the ladies auxiliary, or anything like that. I kind of got the impression that the editor of the paper probably didn't want to waste too much advertising space, and had printed the obituary using the shortest sentences possible, to save room for marketing dollars.

The obituary did, however, give the names of surviving relatives. Now I am getting somewhere. There are *three* surviving relatives of Emily Mays. Now I have a list of *three* people that I might be able to speak with to find out more about the house at 2629 Woodland Street. Maybe one of them would have some information about Arnold Dalton.

TEN

After breakfast I return to the motel. The red light on the phone is blinking; I pick up the receiver and dial 4, the number to retrieve recorded phone messages at the motel. Holly from office had called. Just checking in with me, letting me know not much was going on there. No messages to report, nothing. I expected her to say that Arnold Dalton had called, but she doesn't, so apparently he hadn't. If he had, I don't think it would have surprised me.

I call Holly back and tell her that there's not much to report. It's a bit of a lie, a fib of convenience, you might say. But if a bunch of people got involved now, it would only confuse matters. I've already decided to investigate the house at 2629 Woodland myself—alone—before sounding the alarm and calling in the boogeyman brigade from Chicago.

I had written down the names of the surviving members of Emily Mays' on a notepad, and I plop it down on the night stand and pick up the phone book. Of the three names listed as surviving members of Emily Mays, not *one* name was listed. *Anywhere.* I call directory assistance; no listing for any of the three names.

Of course, there is always the possibility that they live out of town; perhaps even out of state. That would complicate things. But, if they *were* from far away, living in another state, it was probably doubtful that any of them were familiar with Arnold Dalton. They probably wouldn't be able to provide much help.

Still, the names are the only solid leads I have, so I'll have to pursue them somehow. I'll try looking them up in public records at the county building. If I'm unsuccessful, I'll put Holly on it. She's pretty good at finding people.

But one thing is for absolute certain: the sudden death of Emily Mays has only magnified my suspicion. I sit on the side of the bed, thinking about the old home on Woodland Street, and the footprints in the dust that materialized before my eyes. And the strange, white aura that showed up on the digital image. Honestly, I didn't come here and expect to find a situation like this. I consider myself a hardened skeptic—you have to be in this business. Dozens of people call every day from all over the country. All over the *world,* for that matter. Their attic is haunted by their long-dead Aunt Grace, they say. Or their dog growls at the toilet bowl. Like I've already said . . . most calls are a lot of bunk. So you have to take all phone calls with the old proverbial grain of salt, with more than a hint of suspicion thrown in. You *have* to be cynical. In this business you're either a hardened skeptic or a fool. I do not want to be the latter.

The woman at the county clerk's office is not happy to see me, and she makes no effort to hide her dismay. There are a number of people in the office this morning, and as I walk through the glass door she frowns, glances at the clock, and makes it known to all that it is just about noon and the office is closing for lunch. I do an immediate about face and leave. She'd be gone for an hour; there's no sense in waiting. Besides . . . there's that little twinge inside of me that is telling me to go back.

Again.

I climb back into my rental car and head for the house at 2629 Woodland Street.

If there is ever a day to visit a 'haunted' house, today is the day. Dark clouds swarm menacingly above the treetops. The wind blows with a fervent intensity that bends the trees and tears the dying autumn leaves from their branches. Steven Spielberg himself, I imagine, couldn't create more ominous conditions. The mood is dark and foreboding, just like you'd expect if you were to visit a strange old house.

But today I don't plan on going inside. Today I am going to explore the outer grounds for a while. There's a large field behind the building, and I remember seeing the remains of an old rusted car poking up through the tall grass. That seems to be a trait in Wickerton: Everyone has a car up on blocks in the front yard, or a stripped, rusted skeleton of a car out back. Maybe it's a requirement for living in the community, or maybe a status symbol of sorts. Where I live in Chicago, we have laws about that kind of stuff. A car in my back yard in Chicago would net me a one-hundred dollar-a-week fine. Here in Wickerton it's probably a tax deduction.

I slow the car as I approach the house. The structure is dark, silhouetted against a bruised, slate-colored sky. The swollen storm clouds are purple and black. It feels like it might rain at any moment.

I close the car door and stare up at the house for a moment. For the first time in my career with Paranormal Phenomena, Incorporated, I feel a real twinge of fear. Not mere discomfort, not simple uneasiness, but *fear*.

But why? What is it that I'm afraid of? A building? Rotting boards and beams and foundations? I have encountered many strange things, but the chill I now feel in the mere presence of this house pierces my skin and digs straight to the bone. I know it is premature, but I feel that there is something far more than a simple 'haunting' going on at 2629 Woodland Street. Hauntings, for the most part, usually present no more than a nuisance in most cases. Noises at night, ghostly images in a window. I see things like that all the time. It's almost become boring. What PPI is looking for, exclusively, is *intelligent contact.* Dialogue. A conversation with the dead, or whatever you want to call it. Actual, physical *proof* of another realm. Oh sure, we have enough proof to show, beyond any shadow of a doubt, that another realm *does* exist. But *where* does it exist? Why? Who inhabits this realm?

I have a few answers, but they aren't the answers that most people want to hear. They are answers that are too unbelievable for most to believe. Unless, of course, you've been in my shoes. Then you would know that the realms and dimensions that are here now, all around us, are always changing, always turning and twisting. Nothing is as it seems, and when it is, it changes again. The laws that are applied to our earthly, natural world are not binding in the world of the beyond. This unearthly realm—or whatever you want to call it—has rules and laws all its own. And when it needs to change them, for whatever purpose, it does. The realm beyond is as unpredictable and erratic as the weather. The last forty-eight hours have proven that to me once again.

I skirt the east side of the structure and continue into the field behind the house. Here, the grass is very tall and cowers to the gusts of wind that swoop down from the sky. I envision this field as a cornfield at one time. Or sunflowers or pumpkins. Who knows. But it's far too big to be simply a back yard.

And I am correct about the car. It appears to be an old

Ford Model A. This is one car that *won't* be restored. It's been stripped and mutilated beyond repair, and there is absolutely nothing salvageable.

Without warning, a ruffed grouse explodes from the grass near the decaying vehicle and my heart is sent into near arrest. Grouse are noisy; its wings hammer the air as it takes flight, and the loud clamor startles me. As the bird disappears into the sky I relax, the sudden burst of adrenalin already starting to fade. I watch the dark shadow of the fleeing grouse as it vanishes into the forest.

Suddenly, another bird bursts from the grass, this one just a few feet from me. Again I jump, shaken by the abrupt explosion of drumming wings. I can do nothing but shake my head and smile. Got me twice, they did.

I continue through the field. The grass licks at my legs as I stride on. Soon, a raindrop hits my forehead. Then I feel one on my arm, then another. I turn around and start back toward the car.

Something hard cracks me in the head. I duck and cower sideways, wincing in pain. The small white stone bounces off my shoulder and disappears into the grass. Suddenly another round ball hits me, and in seconds the air is filled with them. Marble-sized hail is falling. The icy balls strike me in the back, the neck, the arms and head.

My walk instantly turns into a run. The hail falls harder, and the sound of it pummeling the grass and ground is deafening. Thunder cracks. The hail falls even harder, and I am still quite a distance from the car. It will be faster if I run to the back of the house and duck inside. I can see the back door, still open just a crack, like I had left it yesterday. I head for it.

The hail balls have grown larger, and each one that strikes me feels like the sting of a hornet. I can see the white nuggets hitting the roof of the house, my rental car, the dirt road. The ground is already covered, and it's only been a few seconds.

I leap over the back stairs and hit the door full-force. It explodes open with a crash, slamming into the wall and shuddering. Chest heaving, I stop in the foyer and turn around to watch the raging storm. The hail is coming down violently, and the sound of it hitting the house is like a freight train passing by. It echoes through the rooms and reverberates in my head. I stand watching the hail for a moment, watching it bounce in the field and accumulate. In some areas it is so thick it looks like snow has fallen. If this is what fall is like in Michigan, I don't want any part of it.

Behind me, the dark hallway leads into the living room. Without much more thought, I slowly begin to walk down the hall. The hailstorm drowns out the echoing of my footsteps. I walk carefully, looking at the years of dust on the floor. I can see my footprints from yesterday, just barely. That is all. Here, in the hall, there are no other footsteps but my own.

I stop where the hall ends and the living room opens up. It is dark; far too dark to make anything out. I don't have a light with me, and I'm not about to go to the car and get the small penlight that I have in my bag. Not at least until the hail stops, anyway. My eyes are becoming accustomed to the dark, but it is still too gloomy to see much of anything.

I turn back around, open the bedroom door, and stop. Not for any particular reason; I just stop and peer inside the empty room. There is a crack in the boards that cover the window, and a thin stream of misty gray light is filtering through.

Then I notice the door at the far wall. At least, it *looks* like a door. A door . . . that has been boarded up.

ELEVEN

I didn't see it on my first inspection, but I hadn't paid too much attention to these lower bedrooms. Besides, the door could have easily been missed in the darkness. Even now it is difficult to see. But I am sure that there is a door behind those boards. Whereas all of the windows of the house have been boarded up from the outside, this door—and I must assume it is a door—has been boarded up from the inside. Plus, it's on an inner wall. I'm sure that the door doesn't lead outside, but rather to another room, or a perhaps a basement.

I walk toward the boarded up door, and I am correct in my first assumption. Behind the boards *is* a door. Someone had hastily nailed ten wood beams horizontally over top of it, leaving a space for the rusty metal doorknob.

I stand a few feet away, staring. Why would someone board up a door on the inside, yet be so careless as to leave the back door literally unprotected? I found no evidence of the back door being boarded up or even locked.

I reach out and grasp one of the boards, placing my fingers around the edge and gently prying the wood away. It comes off the wall very easily, as does another, then another. Now all of the boards have been torn off. They lay in a pile off to the side.

Before me is a dark, wooden door. I am a bit apprehensive, but not afraid. I've been doing this long enough to know that the biggest danger to myself is usually *caused* by myself. Overreaction due to fright has caused more injuries than any paranormal phenomena ever has.

Yet again, the strange footprints in the dust, and the bizarre white aura in the digital image are enough to make my nerves dance like live wires. I feel that I am getting into something that is far weirder than anything else I've ever encountered.

I'm about to reach forward to open the door, then I decide to return to my vehicle and retrieve my penlight. It's small, but it has a very bright beam. I don't want to be walking through a dark room or basement and knocking into things.

I return to my car—and get a surprise. The windows are shattered. The hail has smashed the front and rear windshields. The passenger and drivers' side windows are okay, but the mirrors are spider-webbed. There are dozens of dimples all over the hood and the roof. An inch of hail covers the floors, the seats, the dashboard. Hail mixed with sharp beads of glass. I have always thought that windshields were made out of safety glass that doesn't break apart, but the sheer force of the hail was apparently too much even for the tempered windshield.

I use last week's *U.S. News & World Report* magazine and sweep as much of the hail and glass from the seats and floor. The rest will have to wait. I open up my carry bag, dig for my penlight, find it, and head toward the back of the house. The thick grass is wet, and dark watermarks stain the pant legs of my jeans. The sky is still gray and cloudy. Light sprinkles continue to fall, but for the most part, the worst of the storm appears to be over. I hastily jump onto the back porch and slip back inside the dark house.

The flashlight is a big help. The beam is surprisingly bright and intense, and I shine it upon the floor as I walk, expecting to see footprints other than my own in the dust. There aren't any . . . only mine.

I stop where the hall ends and opens up to the living room, swishing the beam over the staircase and up the bannister. I see nothing new. I turn and enter the bedroom and walk to the door I have uncovered.

I concentrate the beam of light on the doorknob. It is old and rusty and weathered, and as I grip it, it feels strangely cold. Much colder than the temperature of the air in the room. It turns easily in my hand, and the door, closed for many, many years, chugs slowly open.

The creaking noise is almost unbearable. It is the sound of old metal on metal, a long, aching squeal that echoes through the room. I can feel a cool rush of air sweep past, and I realize that it must be a basement.

Sure enough, as I train the light into the opening, I see wooden steps descending into an inky darkness. Cobwebs hang from the walls and the wooden ceiling, and a dozen spiders scurry away from the intruding light. The house seems to whisper to me, speaking the language of long ago, a language that only it can understand.

I don't think twice about the stairs. I am too intrigued, too curious not to explore more. I want to know what is so important down these steps that someone had felt the need, long ago, to board up the door. *To keep someone out? To keep someone from finding something? Or, perhaps . . . to keep something in?*

My first step, the very first moment my foot touches wood, is the only step I take. The stair collapses beneath my weight and I fall, plunging into darkness.

TWELVE

Everything is black, my head hurts, my shoulder is screaming in pain. I can see a faint beam of a light nearby, shining upward like a tiny searchlight. I am disoriented.

Slowly, a kind of murky consciousness returns. I have fallen down the stairs. Down into the basement. The basement of the house at 2629 Woodland Street.

I sit up, and my shoulder eases. I don't think I am seriously injured; my shoulder was in pain because most of my body weight was laying on it. What probably helped spare serious injury was that the floor of the basement is dirt, not cement or stone or wood. The sand has broken my fall, softening the blow.

I reach for my penlight and sweep the beam around the dark, dusty room. The walls are large fieldstones held into place by a dirty, pink-colored mortar. Spider webs, no doubt home to dozens of species of arachnids, are caked across the ceiling, the walls, and the corners. They are as thick as wool in some places.

But the basement is empty. There are no boxes, no crates, no shelves. Only soft sand beneath my feet. The air

I breathe is dry, and dusty. And that's it. There is nothing down here except me and a lot of sand. I am a bit disappointed, having thought that there must be some kind of dark secret, some mysterious cavern or room. It's not that at all.

I shine the beam over my feet and along the ground. There is nothing here but sand and small stones. Not even any footprints, except for my own. Any memory of any yesterdays has long since been erased by time.

I move about slowly, ducking beneath the staircase and shining the light up the stairs. Shadows cringe and fall away. Upon inspection, it appears that the very first step gave way and I simply fell straight through the stairs. My problem now is how to get out. If the stairs won't support me, I could be stuck down here for a long time. A *long* time.

I place a cautious foot on the first stair, slowly putting more and more weight upon it. The step seems to be strong enough, so I bring the other foot up. I do this again and again, until I am nearly at the top of the stairs. I take a long, single stride and step over the final stair, and over the hole that I had fallen through when the step collapsed beneath my weight. I am safe.

I turn and shine the penlight down the steps, again thankful that I haven't hurt myself more seriously.

Suddenly I sense a presence. I can literally *feel* a presence—something—coming toward me. It is coming up the stairs, but I see nothing. Yet, I can *feel* it, coming closer and closer. The air around me is charged with energy, and I am frozen, staring down into the dark basement.

I want to run. I want to turn and flee as fast as I can, but I don't. My eyes dart about the room, looking for evidence of any movement. There is none. But the feeling of something here with me now is *strong*. The air in the room has grown thick and heavy.

And the smell. It's faint at first, but it grows stronger. Now it is a putrid stench, an odor so revolting that I bring my hand up to cover my face. I feel like I'm swimming in an invisible cesspool. The stench is that of raw sewage and putrid chemicals.

Then, without warning, I can feel it pass *through* me. It takes only an instant, but the unseen entity passes directly through my very being. It slides through my internal organs, searing through my flesh, through my skin, through my soul. It is a terrifying experience, and for an instant the feeling of total horror and evil and wickedness is frozen inside of me.

Then it is gone.

The sensation passes, the smell dwindles, the awful feeling seeps away. It lingers on for a few moments, and then it diminishes completely. I waste no time in vacating the room, fleeing down the hall, and outside to safety.

THIRTEEN

I sat in the car, hands on the wheel. My mind spins, and my chest is heaving. I take several long, deliberate breaths, exhaling slowly, calming myself down. I close my eyes, only to open them a moment later and stare back at the house. It is dark and uninviting. My eyes dart from the front door to a broken window, then back to the front door.

Driving my rental car in its present condition isn't what you'd call a pleasant afternoon drive. The wind rushes through the open windshield. It is cold and clammy, and my hands are numb—but at least it's not raining or hailing. I had planned to drive back to the motel and call the rental car place from there, but as I come across a small convenience store I pull into the parking lot. This is far enough; I can go no further.

I call the rental car facility from the pay phone, and they insist that I'll have to bring the car back to Traverse City. Fat chance, I tell them. I give directions to the man on the phone on how to pick it up where it sits. It is no longer my problem. It was an accident, or an act of God or whatever you want to call it. Amid his protests I hang up. The clerk at the convenience store is just finished with his shift; he is nice enough to give me a lift to a local rental car business in town.

Getting another vehicle takes most of the afternoon. The only vehicle they have available is a 1996 Chevrolet minivan, and it is being serviced and wouldn't be ready until sometime after five.

I use the time to wander the small town. I bought a heavier jacket . . . a thick, gray, pullover that I'm sure will do the trick. And I bought my daughter a small trinket from a jewelry store. It is a necklace with a stone pendant that's been cut to the shape of Michigan.

Throughout the afternoon I am continually reminded of the bizarre presence that I felt earlier in the day at the house. Every time a wind brushes against me I can feel the chill of terror that engulfed my whole body while I stood in the bedroom near the basement door. My mind is still reeling in a hundred different directions. I have no answers, only questions. Dozens of them.

The hailstorm has set me back a day, but time is one thing that I *can* spare. PPI doesn't keep close tabs on what I am doing or even where I *am* in most cases. As long as I check in and tell them that I'm doing 'something'. Our management principles are rather loose. PPI is owned by Elliot Hughey, the rather eccentric millionaire (there's speculation at the office that he's a billionaire) who considers his search for paranormal entities a 'hobby'. A rather expensive hobby, I would presume. But if you've got that much money, I guess it wouldn't matter. Maybe Paranormal Phenomena, Incorporated is one big tax deduction for him. It makes no difference to me. My paycheck always clears the bank, and having a corporate American Express card is just one of the perks, along with an excellent insurance plan.

The minivan is ready at five-thirty. Too late to return to the county clerk's office. Besides, I am hungry, and the thought of a juicy burger or steak at the Wickerton Cafe is too enticing to pass up.

And on top of that, Andrea might be there. I know what you're thinking, but trust me. I don't hop around the country collecting women in every town I visit. Truth is, I haven't been with anyone since my divorce over a year ago. I'm usually not in any one place long enough to build much of a relationship with anyone.

Andrea is indeed at the cafe this evening. I can see her slender body through the plate glass windows as I get out of the minivan. She sees me and smiles, and gives me a quick wave with her hand before disappearing behind the kitchen doors.

Once again, the cafe is empty except for me. The restaurant seems to be much busier earlier in the day than it is in the evening, and I sit down at the same booth I had sat in earlier this morning.

Andrea emerges from the kitchen and approaches me at the table. She smiles and says hello, asks what I'd like. I order a burger platter with everything.

In a few minutes she brings out the order, and, to my delight, she sits down to talk for a moment, then gets up and turns the black and orange sign on the front door so now it reads *'closed'* from the outside. I tell her I'm sorry to arrive so late and begin hurrying my meal, but she waves it off, tells me to take my time. She disappears, returning a moment later with a pot of coffee in one hand, and two mugs in the other. She sits at my table. We are alone . . . and about to have a very interesting conversation.

FOURTEEN

When the conversation turns to occupations, I am hesitant. I am always a little apprehensive to tell people what I do. I never know how they're going to take it. Some just smile and say something like *'oh, that's interesting'*. Others think it's fascinating, and still others think it is a complete waste of time and how could anyone ever make any money pursuing such idiotic things as spooks and ghosts.

Andrea, to my delight, seems spellbound. I have her full attention as I tell her about what it is that I do, why I'm here. She listens, her mouth open and her eyes wide, as I tell her about the footprints and the mysterious image captured by my digital camera.

However, I don't tell her about the experience I had today. Not because it would seem unbelievable, but it was simply a terrifying episode. I'm not sure if even *I* want to discuss it. At least not with Andrea.

But there is something that I *do* want to discuss with Andrea, and that is the death of Emily Mays. Or, more importantly, the three surviving relatives. I know she knows of them, she's already said so. When I ask her, I feel like I've just struck gold.

All three *do* live in the area, and she is able to provide exact directions to each of their homes. I hastily scribble while she talks, then I re-read her directions to make sure I have them correct. My spirits are high; I'm spending the evening in the company of a beautiful woman, and I have concrete addresses to the relatives of Emily Mays . . . three people that might possibly know something about what happened at the house at 2629 Woodland Street.

FIFTEEN

That night, it is the nightmare that wakens me from a very troubled sleep. I had gone to bed early, before midnight. I have been awakened by the same nightmare that I had just the other night. It was identical.

I am trapped, on my back, in some sort of box. A coffin is what it must be, although it seems bigger. It is completely dark. I can't see anything, and the ensuing claustrophobia is maddening. I pound at the wall above me, screaming, screaming at the top of my lungs to be let out. It is hard to breathe, and I begin choking and gasping as I continue pounding at the wood. I scrape with my nails, pawing above and around me, trying to find some way out, some hole or means for escape. There is none. I am trapped, and my feeling of complete dysphoria only grows.

And the voice speaks again.

You can't escape. You can't escape. You will die here, and you will remain here. Forever.

The whole episode is so real, so intense that I awake crying, my face streaked with tears. I am sweaty and my breathing is heavy, my heart pumping furiously. I sit up in bed and take several long, deep breaths. Gradually, my breathing and heart rate begins to slow. But the nightmare is still fresh, still burning in my mind. I finally drift back to sleep after about an hour.

Six-thirty, Saturday morning, October 29th. Another windy, gray day. Just *looking* outside makes me shiver. The sky is dark and dreary, and dry leaves swirl like small Tazmanian devils through the mostly empty parking lot. There are only a few cars parked, including mine. October, despite its autumnal beauty, must not be a big tourist month for Wickerton.

I brew coffee, shower, shave. The usual morning routine. A copy of today's *Detroit Free Press* has been left laying just outside my motel room door. I sip coffee while perusing the paper.

Yet my mind is somewhere else. I have names and addresses to the relatives of Emily Mays, and I am anxious to begin the day. All three surviving relatives live near Wickerton, no more than five miles from the motel where I am staying. But it is still early—or at least a bit too early to go around knocking on doors.

To kill time, I go for a walk along the beach which isn't too far away. The waters of Lake Huron are churning and boiling beneath the ashen sky, and the wind bites at my face. I am glad that I thought to pick up a heavier coat yesterday.

At nine o'clock, I decide that it is time to begin knocking on doors. I load my gear (which doesn't consist of much. My digital camera, my laptop computer, and a cassette recorder) into the minivan and head for my first destination: The home of Randy R. Mays. The obituary stated that Randy is Emily's brother. He lives on Kinley Drive, which is only about a mile or so out of the Wickerton village limits. In five minutes I am there, pulling into a narrow, two-track driveway.

In contrast to his sister's home, Randy Mays' house—at least the outside—is well kept. The lawn has been recently mowed, and the yard doesn't look like it's a dumping ground for household appliances. There's a metal shed set right next to the west side of the house. It is shiny and new, and probably has yet to see its first winter.

But there doesn't appear to be anyone home. The garage door is open, but there is no vehicle parked inside. As my rented minivan stops in the driveway, no one peers out the window in curiosity.

After knocking on the door several times it is apparent that no one *is* home. I step down off the porch, and I'm almost in the van when I hear someone call out. The voice is distant, and I stop and turn.

There is a man coming toward me from the house next door. I close the door of the van and walk toward him. Even before he reaches me, he asks if I am looking for Randy. I tell him yes, I am. Now the man stops just a few feet from me. He tells me that Randy and his wife packed up both cars yesterday, loaded up a bunch of clothes and their dog, and left. The neighbor told me that he'd gone over to see what was going on, but Randy wouldn't tell him. He just said that he was leaving. He was leaving and he wouldn't be back. He left his home, his property, and a good portion of his belongings.

I thank the man for the information, take another look at the empty home of Randy Mays, then leave. Now I am more puzzled than I have ever been. More questions. More questions, still no answers. I have a handful of facts, but nothing seems to click. I am still no closer to finding out anything more about Arnold Dalton.

Next on the list is Linda Mays Cantor, the sister of Emily Mays. Andrea told me that Linda had married and divorced, and the news was the talk of the town. Linda's husband was on the Wickerton city council, and he had struck up a relationship with another woman on the board. When Linda found out that he was being a bit less than faithful, she lost her marbles. Attacked him with a knife, almost burned the house down. No jail time, just probation. She's never remarried, has no children, and, like Emily, lives alone.

I got turned around and couldn't find her house, so I drove back into town and retraced my tracks. I have better luck this time. Her driveway is so hidden by a clump of trees that it is nearly impossible to see. And there is no mailbox, either, which I find strange. Every other house along the road has a mailbox except for Linda Mays Cantor.

Before I even stop the van, I can feel it. I can feel the apprehension welling up inside me, the slight twinge of uneasiness even before the van comes to a stop. Without knowing anything, I can sense that something here is very, very wrong. The feeling is so strong that I debate as to whether I should even leave the van.

But I do. I take a deep breath, open the door, and get out.

The feeling of impending danger seems to grow with every step I take toward the house. I reach my hand out to ring the doorbell, but I pause with my hand in the air. I can see through the living room window, and I am certain that ringing the doorbell will not be necessary.

On the floor is the body of a woman. Ms. Cantor, I presume. Her eyes are bulging, a look of absolute terror on her face. She is, quite obviously, dead.

SIXTEEN

I am in no hurry to investigate the body. I stand before the window, staring into the living room.

The body of Linda Mays Cantor is on the floor. She is on her back. All of the color has drained from her skin, and her dry, stiff tongue is hanging out of her gaping mouth. She has been dead for some time. At least a day, I am guessing.

Using my shirt sleeve, I turn the doorknob. No sense in leaving my fingerprints, or destroying anyone else's, should foul play be suspected. But I sense that foul play isn't going to factor in this particular situation. Before I even step into the house, I know that the death of Linda Mays Cantor was brought upon by sheer terror. Sure, it might be ruled as a heart attack or an aneurism, but one look at the expression on her face tells me that this woman died of fright. She had been scared to death, in a tragically literal sense.

Inside, there is nothing really out of the ordinary. The house is well kept, and, except for a newspaper that is open on the floor, there certainly isn't any sign of a struggle. It looks like she died standing right there in the living room. Her body is already beginning to smell, and I bury my mouth and nose into my coat.

I pick up the newspaper. It is yesterday's issue, and it is no surprise to me that it is open to page 4, to the obituary of Emily Mays. But again, this brings only more questions. More questions, still no answers.

After much hesitation and internal wrangling, I decide *not* to call the police. Linda Mays Cantor's body will be found soon enough, I suspect. I don't want to draw any attention towards me or what I'm doing here. The police would ask questions, why was I at her home, why did I go inside if I knew she was dead, et cetera. It would be too much attention in a small town. The fact is, the woman is dead; nothing is going to change that. Besides . . . I have already begun to worry about the last person on my list.

His name is David A. Mays. The obituary column says that he's the cousin of Emily. He lives in a house in the village of Courville. It's a small, sleepy community on Mullett Lake . . . about a twenty-minute drive south of here.

As I get closer to the town, I realize that I've been driving fast; nearly 70 in a 55 miles per hour zone. I slow down. I'll be there soon enough. Question is: what will I find this time?

The directions Andrea have given me are exact, and I have no trouble finding David Mays' house. You can't miss it, really. There are big bold letters—*huge* letters—on top of the mailbox that simply state *Mays*. As I pull into the driveway there's a sign on the grass with hand painted letters that says 'Private Property . . . no solicitation . . . this means *YOU.*' Friendly character, this David Mays.

He is standing in the doorway before I even stop the van, giving me the good once over, like perhaps I am familiar to him. He is an older man, in his seventies, I guess. He opens the screen door a crack as I approach, and is about to say something, but I speak first.

"Mr. Mays, my name is Trevor Harris. I'd like to ask you—"

He immediately interrupts and tells me that he had nothing to do with the death of his cousin Emily, and he doesn't have anything else to offer. I'm surprised at his sudden defensiveness, but then again, Andrea had said that the whole bunch was a little off their rockers. Lots of toys in the attic, these folks.

I raise my hands in a gesture of innocent petition and I am quick to tell him that I'm not here to investigate the death of his cousin. I'm here, I tell him, because I'd like to know more about the house at 2629 Woodland Street.

If I thought he was on the defensive before, it is nothing like the show he displays now. He throws open the door and takes a step forward, toward me. I am a bit taken aback by his sudden movement, and I flinch a bit. He glares at me with wide eyes. His face has two days of gray growth, and his chin and cheeks look like gray sandpaper.

He is about to say something else, but I interrupt. I tell him that I want to know, specifically, why the house at 2629 Woodland Street is haunted. A bit blunt, perhaps. It's not a tactic that I would normally use. But I know that the home is haunted, and I'm certain *he* knows, too.

His eyes are suddenly afire. His cheeks sprout red roses and he starts to tremble and shake.

But I'm not through. I ask him who is Arnold Dalton.

When he hears the name 'Arnold Dalton' I think he's going to have a heart attack right here and now. He doesn't, not yet anyway, but I am almost sure I will be looking at my second corpse of the day. A personal record.

He says nothing, and after a few moments he regains his composure. "Mr. Mays," I begin, a little softer tone in my voice. "I need to know what is going on at that house. I'm asking you to help me."

His eyes shift to the ground, and he is silent for a long time. He looks back at me, looks away, then back. To my surprise, he invites me inside.

David Mays lives alone, and his home furnishings are meager. There are a few paintings on the walls, a reclining chair, and a small TV. The place looks to be more like an efficiency apartment than a home.

We are seated at a small kitchen table. He is uneasy and does not look me in the eyes very much. He offers a glass of water and I accept, and he returns from the kitchen, places two glasses on the table, and begins.

He talks for three hours; I don't even attempt to get a word in edgewise. I am too dumbfounded, too amazed by what I am hearing to interrupt. It is nearly six o'clock when I leave, and I feel mentally and physically exhausted, reeling in shock at what David Mays has told me.

SEVENTEEN

Things have begun to come together and make sense. For the first time since I have arrived here, I think I have some answers, some insight to what is happening at the house at 2629 Woodland Street. And certainly a better insight of what had happened, years ago, at the home.

David Mays had told me everything, which, he had sworn to himself years ago, he would never do. He was determined long ago to put the memories of the old house behind him and never speak of the events that occurred within. I saw incredible fear in his face as he relived the horror of the past.

He said it all started about 1935. David was a boy of ten or so, and his parents had both died while he was still young. He went to live with his cousins—his father's brother's family—at the house at 2629 Woodland Street. This included his Uncle Ted, his Aunt Agatha, Linda, Emily, Randy, himself, and the eldest Mays boy, Joseph. It was because of Joseph, David said, that everything happened the way it did.

Apparently Joseph was an oddball right from the cradle.

From the day he was born, David said. He was the kind of kid that was always getting in to trouble of some sort, always wrapped in the bindings of mischief. Which wasn't necessarily alarming, but as he grew older he became eccentric. Weirder. Living in the house with his family at 2629 Woodland Street, he didn't have many friends. The house was quite a ways from town, and he wasn't allowed by his parents to go many places. He played alone most of the time, and shunned family activities, resenting his sisters for some odd reason or another.

It was about the time that he was twenty-five when a car broke down only a few yards from the house on Woodland. A man and a woman came to the door and asked for assistance. Joseph was totally enraptured with the woman. He hardly noticed her husband. Before him was the most beautiful woman he had ever seen in his life. The thought of the woman—the fact that he couldn't have her—literally drove him out of his mind. He knew that if circumstances were different, she would be his. If she only got to know him, he thought, maybe she would *learn* to love him. She *could* be his.

And so, he decided he would change the circumstances. He would make her his own.

Joseph returned to the vehicle with the man and woman, explaining that he knew a bit about engines and maybe there was something that he could do. This was a lie, of course, but he needed time to lay his plan.

After telling the couple that he probably could fix it, he asked the man to come with him back to the house to help him with a tool kit. It was heavy, he said, and it was downstairs in the basement. Joseph said that he'd hurt his back and couldn't carry heavy things very well, especially up or down the stairs.

It was there that Joseph murdered the man. He killed

him and quickly dragged his body into the field before arousing the suspicion of the woman, who was waiting in the broken-down car.

Joseph made no attempt to lure the woman into the house, but rather approached the crippled vehicle, pulled a knife, and forced her to go with him. He told her that he loved her and that he wanted to be with her forever. She'd learn to love him, he told her, and she could have everything she wanted. Affectionate fellow, this Joseph Mays.

When she began to scream for help he grabbed her and dragged her, kicking and screaming, into the house, down the stairs, and into the basement. When she saw the blood on the sandy basement floor and on the steps, she became hysterical. Joseph tied her up and gagged her, and locked her in the cellar in the darkness.

Determined to go through with his plan, he dug a hole in the meadow and buried the man's body. Then he used his father's car to tow the broken-down vehicle into the field. He left the vehicle on top of where the man was buried, like some crude metal gravestone. The murdered man's name, according to David, was Arnold Dalton.

Using scrap lumber stacked behind the house, Joseph fashioned a large wooden box. Bigger than a coffin (I shuddered when David told me this, remembering my nightmares) and about twice as wide. It must have been a chore getting the huge box from the outside of the house all the way to the basement, but he had managed.

Then he began digging. He dug a hole in the basement deep enough to fit the box. Deep enough to rest three feet below the surface when he buried it. The woman probably went insane with fear when she saw what was going to happen. But Joseph told her that everything was going to be fine, everything was going to be okay. He placed two bottles of water in the box, some jerky, and an apple, then forced

Dalton's wife inside. He removed the wad of clothing from her mouth and she began screaming as he forced her, legs and hands still bound, into the box. Joseph talked to her the entire time, telling her how everything was going to be okay, that she was sure to see his way soon. Very soon, he had said.

Against her pleas and cries and screams, he nailed the lid of the box shut, and filled in the hole. Gradually, as more and more dirt fell over the box, her cries grew fainter and fainter. When it was completely buried, the screams of the woman could not be heard. He returned to his bedroom and wrote in his journal that he'd met a woman, and was soon to be married. He had described in sickening detail how he came to know his new bride-to-be. This was how David —and the rest of the family—had discovered what had transpired.

His plan apparently had been to keep Dalton's wife in the box for a day, then dig her back up to see if she'd had a change of mind.

There was, of course, a terrible flaw in his logic. In his hurried state he hadn't thought his plan through, and had not provided a way for her to get sufficient oxygen. The next day when he returned to the basement and dug up the box, the woman was dead—a victim of asphyxiation. Joseph became so distraught over what had happened that he blew his head off with an old shotgun his father had stored in the cellar.

When the Mays family returned a week later, they discovered his decaying corpse in the basement. The house reeked of rotting flesh, a stench that was so repulsive that every single member of the family had vomited. For whatever reasons, they decided not to go to the police. David said that he didn't know why, that it had been the elder Mays' decision. The best guess David had made was that his father was a proud man, and he knew that when it got out that one of his sons was a murderer, it would tarnish the family reputation forever. If anyone asked, Joseph Mays had headed west, to California, and they didn't know how to contact him.

They took Joseph's body and buried him in the forest, far beyond the field behind the house. All evidence of the woman was placed into the box and re-buried in the basement . . . where it still is, David claims, to this day. The family swore to never speak of the incident again, and, David is adamant that no one did.

Not until now.

But that was not the end. The story David Mays told me was gruesome and bizarre, and even a tad unbelievable. But it was what David told me next that gave me a chill like I had never felt before in my life.

EIGHTEEN

I had asked David Mays what he thought had made Joseph so strange, why he had acted the way he did throughout his life. Without hesitation, David replied that there was something in the house, something that had *always* been in the house. He couldn't explain it, no one in the family could, but they all *knew* it was there. It was an evil presence of some kind. I had asked David if he believed the house was haunted, and he shook his head.

Yes, he had said. *The house is haunted, but it's more than that. That there house . . . that house is possessed. That house is just plain evil.* Mays insisted that there was an entity, a spirit of some kind, that dwelled in the house. Long before the murders, David said that they could feel the strong presence of something, accompanied by a terrible smell. The entity began inhabiting the bodies of *them*. Members of the family. David said that it had happened to all of them at one time or another, including himself. He said it was like watching a movie unfold before his very eyes. One minute you'd be chatting away or reading a book, the next, you'd be out of control on the floor, shaking in a fit of terror. He remembered feeling so powerless, unable to control his actions. He could feel a tremendous presence of evil inside of him, a presence that made him sick to his stomach. He twisted and thrashed uncontrollably on the floor while everyone looked on, terrified.

Then, as quickly as it had entered, the 'entity' would leave. He said that they knew when it was gone because you could actually hear it moving about in the house.

And it seemed to grow in power, stealing its strength from members of the family that it systematically possessed from time to time. After one particular episode when Emily had been 'invaded' they could hear the entity walk across the floor and down into the basement.

Emily's father had had enough. Thinking that he might be able to trap the entity downstairs, he boarded up the basement door, packed up the family, and moved that very night. They moved to another house several miles away, on the other side of Wickerton. No one in the family ever spoke of the incident again. Emily Mays had been willed the home and property, but she had never again set foot in the house at 2629 Woodland. None of them had.

Now, as I drive the van farther away from the house of David Mays, I wonder if I should have told him. I wonder if I should have told him that I opened up the basement door. That I, too, had felt the overwhelming presence of evil. That whatever had been there, for however many years, had gotten out.

NINETEEN

At six-thirty as I pass by the Wickerton Cafe, I notice that the lights are still on, despite the fact that the restaurant is closed. Then I catch a glimpse of Andrea inside. I slow, and turn the minivan around.

She has just finished sweeping the floor when she sees the headlights swing into the driveway. She meets me at the glass door, unbolts it, and welcomes me inside, closing the door and locking it behind me. I tell her that I don't want to intrude, but I saw her and I just wanted to say hello. She says that it's no trouble, and she asks if I'd like to stay for coffee.

It is at her request that I tell her about the events of the day. I go into great detail about my visit at Randy Mays' home. The gruesome scene at Linda Mays Cantor's house, and my unbelievable visit with David. She listens, eyes wide, as I tell her about the strange entity that David claims inhabited or 'possessed' the house at 2629 Woodland Street. She is captivated, and I ask her if she believes in such evil spirits or entities or whatever you'd want to call them. Her answer surprises me.

She says that the local Native Americans believe that a

terrible spirit inhabits the northern region of Michigan. The legend states that this invisible 'creature' or whatever it is, wanders about, looking for the newly dead, to take their souls. To *steal* their souls, is how she puts it. The souls are then reportedly taken to a mystical forest that is supposed to exist near Black Lake, about fifteen miles east of Wickerton. Andrea says that such a forest exists . . . it is a swamp that is so thick with alders and brush that it is nearly impenetrable. However, whether or not any souls reside there is simply up to whether you believe the legend.

I ask her if she herself believes. She is hesitant here, and she becomes very silent. And sad. I can see the emotion welling up in her cheeks. She looks as if she is about to cry. She apologizes, dabs her eyes with a napkin, and says that she's not sure if she believes that or not. But she tells me that if it is true, how sad it must be for a soul to have to linger on forever in some strange place, imprisoned and forgotten, not allowed to rest or to be with loved ones.

I too, think of this now. But there's something else that is on my mind that troubles me much more than wayward souls.

At ten o'clock, I say good night to Andrea. She walks me to the door and there is a moment of hesitation, a millisecond of uneasiness while I say good night. I wanted to reach out and take her in my arms, to feel her closeness next to me. I sense, perhaps, that she feels the same. But the moment goes on for too long, becomes awkward, and the opportunity, if it existed, is lost. I smile and say good night, she does the same, locking the door and turning off the lights of the cafe as I climb into the minivan.

TWENTY

My thoughts are still churning as I pull into the motel parking lot. Were circumstances different, I'd go right back over to the house at 2629 Woodland Street. But not tonight. It's too dark, too risky. I'll go in the morning.

I call the office and leave a message for Holly, just giving her a quick update. Not too much to report, I tell her. I'll know more tomorrow.

And I will, I'm sure.

I lay back in bed, but I'm not tired. I keep wondering if the nightmare will come back. It doesn't bother me now, knowing exactly where it came from. The 'box' that I felt I was trapped in is, I'm sure, the box that's buried in the basement of the house. I think of that poor woman being trapped in the box years ago, and how she must have struggled to stay alive. The feeling of being trapped, the darkness, the helplessness. Tomorrow I will see for myself. I'm going back to the house at 2629 Woodland. I'm going back, and I'll dig up that box.

Sunday Morning, October 30th. Eight o'clock. I've slept a bit later than I wanted to, but I feel well-rested nonetheless. I'm anxious to get started, so I take a quick shower and leave the coffee pot untouched. I won't be in the motel room long enough to drink a cup.

In contrast to the previous days, today is sunny and bright. Fall's chill is still evident, and the air is crisp and cold, garnished with the musky smell of autumn leaves. I load up the minivan with my laptop, my digital camera, and the minicassette recorder.

There's a hardware store on the other side of the street that has just opened up. I buy a flourescent lantern—one of those heavy-duty, super-bright lights. It's a bit expensive, but it will do the trick.

And I buy a shovel.

The Wickerton Cafe is filled with customers this morning, and Andrea is not there. I stop to get a cup of coffee and a bagel to go.

The house at 2629 Woodland Street looks less ominous in the light of the morning sun. It has, however, taken on a different aspect now that I know its bizarre history. A number of my questions have been answered, but those answers have brought more questions as well. I hope to know more shortly.

I carry a large bag over my shoulder, and the shovel as well. Just before I reach the house I pull out the lantern and click it on. It's extremely bright, even during the day. It should serve me well in the darkness of the cellar.

I am slow and cautious as I walk through the house, taking note of the walls and ceilings in the rooms. I am getting a much better look at the inside of the house; the lantern lights up the rooms like daylight.

I am overly cautious—for good reason—as I walk down

the stairs and into the cellar. The top step is gone, broken away from the fall I took the day before yesterday. And so far, there is no evidence of any other 'unearthly' presence. The house at 2629 Woodland seems quiet, almost peaceful.

In the cellar, I set the bag down and place the lantern on it and waste no time getting started. I don't know exactly where to begin, but the cellar isn't that big. I'm sure that if I just start digging I'll come across the wooden box soon enough.

The blade of the shovel breathes a short whisper every time I sink it into the earth. The ground is settled and much harder than I expected. I work up a sweat lifting the heavy dirt out of the hole and tossing it on to a small mountain that is getting higher and higher with every shovelful.

Suddenly my blade strikes something hard and hollow sounding. I carefully scrape the dirt away and kneel down next to the small pit.

The blade has struck wood.

I tap it again with the shovel and hear the same, hollow, dull thud.

I have reached the box.

I never doubted that it would be here. The excitement of finding it is overwhelming. I dig faster now, tossing the dirt up over my shoulder, not caring where it falls.

Soon, the entire top of the makeshift coffin is exposed. I dig along side of it, making a small space for me to step without having to stand on the box itself.

The lid has been carefully nailed down. I can't get the shovel blade in between the box and the top itself, and I spend almost an hour going along the edge with my pocketknife, slowly prying the lid farther and farther open. Finally, I am all the way around.

I use the shovel blade to give the lid—the top of this crude coffin—a final pry. There is an audible groan, a squeal of dry wood, and the lid suddenly pops. I place the shovel next to the bag, reach down and grasp the edge of the top of the box with my hands, and lift.

TWENTY ONE

I guess no matter how you prepare yourself, I don't think you can ever get properly composed to view a dead body. Or in this case, the skeletal remains of one. Beyond a deep breath, a sigh, and an *okay, here we go* moment, there's not much else you can do but just get on with it.

The woman is there, all right. The ivory-colored skeleton lay on its back, or, rather, the *woman* lay on *her* back. Her clothing is decayed and rotting, covering portions of the bones. Ropes are still wrapped around her legs and hands, although her body has shrunk away from her bindings, leaving nothing but rotting, brown bracelets. Dust has seeped through the box, covering the corpse and clothing with a glaze of gritty frost.

And as I gaze down at her, I am swept with sadness. I can almost see the overwhelming terror, the panic and fear. It's all there, I'm sure, still present in the decaying, lifeless bones. I can sense the anguish, the trauma, the hopelessness that this woman went through, crying out from this box, trying to struggle free, screaming at the top of her lungs. No one could hear her, no one had come to her rescue.

And now I am certain that she is responsible for the

strange footprints that appeared on the stairs, the milky white aura in the digital photo. Her soul has been here, trapped within this house, unable to leave. She's been a prisoner; a prisoner in both life, and death, with no possibility for escape.

As I stare down at the deteriorating bones, there is no victory in my discovery, only sadness. A senseless death—two senseless deaths, actually.

And so I decide, without a second thought, that the remains of the woman do not belong in the house—they belong next to her husband. Her husband, buried in the field beneath the old shell of the car.

There really is no dignified way to carry her remains outside and into the field, so I empty my bag of its contents, placing the digital camera on the steps along with the laptop and the minicassette recorder. The rest of the bag is filled with simple odds and ends—a flannel shirt, a small toolkit, an extra lantern battery. I dump all of the items into a pile in the sand. Then, almost in hindsight, I pick up the digital camera and take several pictures of the woman's remains before I disturb them. You might find this disrespectful, taking pictures of the dead; I for one, do not. The pictures will serve no profit to me, but only as necessary research. I do not, nor does the company I work for, sell or distribute pictures of this nature, either for publication or any other reason. You will not see these pictures plastered across the seedy pages of trashy tabloids or being traded via the speeding lines of the internet.

Piece by piece, bone by bone, I begin placing the remains of the woman into the bag. It is a gruesome task, but I do it with seriousness and reverence. I've encountered a few similar situations in the past. Houses that were haunted by the souls of the dead, souls that hadn't been allowed to rest. It is, in a word, sorrowful.

Soon the task is complete. All of her bones are in my bag, as well as the fragments of her clothing. I carry the shovel and the bag up the stairs, down the hall and out the back door.

The sun is high in the sky, and I glance at my watch. It is already past noon. The temperature has risen, too, and I am bathed in a perfect, Indian summer afternoon. There is no breeze, and the perimeter of the field is encompassed by large trees, mostly devoid of their leaves. They watch me like giant, spiny statues as I walk down the old wooden planks of the porch and into the field.

Digging a hole in the field next to the car is no easy task. The ground is filled with rocks, some of them the size of bowling balls, making the digging all that much more difficult. Many times I have to stop and drop the shovel and use both hands to pull out a heavy stone that I can't get out with the blade.

Three hours later, I am standing at the foot of a grave next to the old car. The grave is about four feet wide and nearly five feet deep. I regret that these specifications wouldn't be up to normal standards for a proper burial, but I don't think the woman—I've begun to refer to as a person, not just a cold pile of bones—will mind.

I pick up the bag and climb down into the hole. I regret that I don't have anything I can bury the bones in. No box, no coffin, nothing.

So I begin, ever so carefully, placing the bones in a neat pile at the bottom of the hole. I come across the old ropes that had bound her hands and feet, and toss them aside, up and out of the hole. She won't be needing them.

When the bag is emptied I take one long look at the pile at my feet. I whisper a quiet prayer. Then I climb out, pick up the shovel, and begin the arduous task of filling in the hole.

An hour later it is finished. It was much easier filling in the hole than it was to dig it in the first place. I rest, leaning on the shovel. Then I look around the field.

It is a circle that I see. Not a physical circle, not at all. I see a circle as I stare up at the large trees, their branches devoid of much of their leaves. Soon, the cloak of winter will be upon them and the trees will remain lifeless and dormant. The spring will arrive and the trees will emerge, continuing on their circular trek along the wheel of life.

I see the circle in the clouds of the sky, a raven that swoops low over the field. The circle the sun makes as it treks across the sky.

And the circle of my own life. The circle of life, of many lives. It is an endless circle, an ever-continuing cycle. And, although our circumnavigation must end, as the travels of all living things must, the wheel itself churns on. I have heard the phrase that life is a vicious cycle. Or, as my college roommate Clay Hattenburg put it years ago, *life's a bitch, then you die.*

For a number of reasons, I disagree with Clay's pessimistic wit.

My gaze returns to the disheveled earth at my feet. I stare at the torn ground for only a moment before gathering up the bag and walking back to the house.

I n the basement I gather up the rest of my equipment. I am a bit uneasy now, and I don't know why. Perhaps it is the memory of that awful sensation of—

Of what?

Whatever I had encountered that had passed through my very being. I can almost smell that terrible odor, that awful stench from a few days ago when I opened the basement door for the first time. But my sense of foreboding passes, and I pack up everything and leave the house without incident.

I take a few more digital pictures from the front of the house. In the sunshine it looks so much warmer, so much more comfortable and inviting than it had the past few days. I glance in the field out back; from here, on the road, it is impossible to tell that a hole has been dug. The grass is too high, too thick. Hopefully, the woman can get the long, peaceful rest she deserves.

TWENTY TWO

Six o'clock. I am back at the motel room. The second shower of the day feels wonderful, and I brew up a pot of coffee and sit down on the bed, my laptop computer open before me. I remove the diskette from the digital camera and slide it into the computer drive.

I click open the first photo file and the drive whirrs. At the bottom of the screen a red status bar indicates the progress of the image processing. The screen is then filled with the first image on the disk.

Suddenly, I cannot breathe. I cannot speak. The air from my lungs has been caught up in the vortex of some supernatural vacuum, and the room about me spins in a twisting vertigo. My chest feels hollow; I feel as if I am drowning.

I sit up straight, spilling coffee all over the bed. The stain seeps into the blanket, darkening the fabric. What I am seeing is impossible. It is . . . it is . . . *just not possible.*

The picture is one of the ones that I took of the woman's remains in the basement. Only, the picture does not show remains . . . but rather, a *woman.* An actual *woman.* She is staring back at me, a gentle smile on her face.

And I know beyond any shadow of a doubt who the woman is. Her cheeks, her hair, her eyes. The face staring back at me from the image on the computer screen is—

Andrea.

I bolt up from the bed, grab the keys from the desk and race out the door, running down the hall and out of the motel. The minivan roars to life and I speed the entire two blocks to the Wickerton Cafe. I pull into the gravel parking lot so fast that I almost strike another car that is pulling out.

I leap out of the vehicle, not even taking time to kill the engine. There are a few patrons here tonight, they all stare at me as I burst through the door. The cook leans back and sticks his head out the kitchen window, tells me he'll be there in a moment. I don't wait. I walk through the kitchen door and ask him where Andrea is.

He doesn't say anything. He has a puzzled, inquisitive look on his face. Then he asks me who I am looking for.

Andrea, I tell him. *The woman who works here.*

I describe her to him, yet all the while he is shaking his head. He tells me that there is no 'Andrea' that works at the Wickerton Cafe, never has been. In fact, he says, the only 'Andrea' he has ever heard of is the Andrea that disappeared years ago along with her husband—Arnold and Andrea *Dalton.*

TWENTY THREE

There are some things we are never meant to understand. Some answers remain elusive for years, some just refuse to surface. Quite often, the quest to understand the unknown —the realm beyond—is very dissatisfying. In the case of Arnold and Andrea Dalton, the questions that remain are ones that I will probably never be able to answer. How Arnold Dalton, if that is who he was, called me on the telephone and actually *spoke* with me. And why *me?*

And *Andrea.* I had spent hours with her. She was as alive as any living, breathing person I have ever met. Yet now there was no trace of her.

But perhaps most disturbing of all is something else altogether.

That presence I felt when I opened the cellar door. It was something so inherently evil, so horrifying that I don't even care to think about it. This 'entity'—or whatever it is—isn't merely some displaced, wandering spirit. Whatever it is, it is now out there somewhere. I know this because I felt it in the house. I smelled it, I sensed its wicked presence pass within me.

And tonight, as I scan the rest of the digital images on my laptop computer, I *see* it.

In the very last picture of the house. The one where I was outside, standing next to the minivan. The very last picture I had taken of the house.

There is something in the picture.

It is a form. A shape of some sort. There is something—*something*—standing in the yard next to the old house. I can see it in the digital image staring back at me. It has a face that is half-human, half-beast. Scarred and twisted flesh frame two red, glowing, malevolent eyes that burn into my soul and sear their image into my brain.

I am shaking as I stare at the image on my laptop. My mind is a blur and I feel like I'm going to vomit.

Andrea Dalton, the poor imprisoned soul whose life was stolen from her, can finally rest.

But this thing . . . *whatever it is* . . . is out there. It is still out there—

Somewhere.

CALL

FOR

HELP

P atricia's shift began at midnight. She would man the phone for eight hours, just like she did the night before, and the night before that. There were several others that worked the night shift at the 911 emergency dispatch, but, for the most part, things were pretty quiet in such a small town. They might receive one or two *serious* calls; the rest were pretty much the run of the mill car/deer accidents, someone trying to locate such-and-such a street in one of the many small towns that dotted the northern region of Michigan's lower peninsula, or someone who had accidentally speed dialed the number from their cell phones. Occasionally, a drunk would call to order pizza.

She had learned that, as an operator, she was responsible not only for assisting in emergencies, dispatching the proper authorities and the like, but pinch-hitting as a part-time mom and moonlighting as a psychologist. Some people just needed someone to talk to, to let them know that everything was going to be fine. They just needed someone to hear them, someone who would listen and sympathize. Jesus loves you and all that.

Patricia had just finished her first cup of coffee when the call came through.

"Nine One One." Her voice was professional, matter-of-fact.

"You've . . . you've got to help," a male voice cracked. It was the sound of desperation, the sound of hopelessness. Patricia heard a sniffle.

"I'll do what I can. What is your name, sir?"

"I just killed my best friend." Sobs.

Okay, thought Patricia. *Here we go.* It wasn't often that a call such as this came through.

"Okay, sir, may I have your name, please?"

"An . . . Andrew. Andrew Baxter."

"Your address, Mr. Baxter?"

"My what?" More sobs.

"Your address, Mr. Baxter?"

"My address? Oh yes. It's 434 Blossom Lane."

"Thank you. Now, what happened, Andrew?" Her voice was pleasant, but concerned. The caller was distraught, and she needed to connect with him quickly. He'd told her that he'd killed someone; perhaps he hadn't. Perhaps the victim was still alive. She needed more information, but her fingers were already tapping the computer keyboard, sending a note to central dispatch.

"I . . . I just couldn't take it anymore," Baxter said. "I mean . . . we've known each other for years. Worked together. But things changed, and we started fighting."

"Mr. Baxter, you said you killed him?"

"That's right, I . . . I—"

He choked back another sob and didn't finish his sentence.

"Mr. Baxter?"

"—I really . . . I killed him," he finished. He let out a loud wail, then began weeping uncontrollably. Patricia used the brief moment to finish her note to central dispatch, who would, in turn, send out a car. And an ambulance.

"Mr. Baxter, it's okay. You need to talk to me. Can you

explain what happened?"

"What *happened?!?!?* I *killed* him! And he was my best friend! He was my best friend . . . but he . . . he just kept getting worse and worse."

"Mr. Baxter, everything is going to be okay. Now . . . what do you mean, 'worse and worse'?"

"You know," he replied in frustrated exasperation. "We just got into arguments. A lot of arguments. But lately, it seemed like that was all we did. Fight. We fought about everything. *Everything.* But mostly, he just kept trying to run my life. I did everything for him, too."

The picture was getting clearer. This was obviously some type of spat between two gay men. For whatever reason, Andrew Baxter had killed his partner.

"Mr. Baxter, has anyone in the home been drinking?"

"Huh?"

"Alcohol?"

"Oh. No, we don't drink. No drugs, either, so don't bother asking."

Good, good, Patricia thought. One or the other—or both—usually made these situations worse than they already are.

"Is there anyone else in the house?"

"No. It was just him and me. Now it's just me."

"Do . . . do you live together?" Patricia asked.

"Yes. For years. And it was great at first. We got along great."

"Mr. Baxter, maybe your friend isn't dead. Perhaps you could help him."

Baxter choked out a sob. "No, no. It's too late for that."

"How do you know?"

"Because I slammed his head into the kitchen table!" he shrieked. "I grabbed the side of his head and smashed and smashed and *smashed!* I didn't . . . I couldn't stop! I didn't stop until his skull splintered. I heard it crack, you know."

Patricia winced. "How long ago was that?"

"I . . . I don't know. An hour, maybe."

"Is he there now, in the home?"

"Yes."

"Mr. Baxter, can you see if he's still breathing?"

"He's not. He's not."

"Can you check, please? It's very important. Do you know how to check for a pulse?" Any information she could provide to the medical response team would be a help.

"Yes?"

"Could you do that, Mr. Baxter? I'll wait right here."

"O . . . okay."

Patricia heard shuffling on the other end. "Got a real live one, here," she said quietly to Ben Mulford, the night supervisor. Mulford nodded, immersed in a call of his own that was certainly much less distressing than the call Patricia had taken.

There was a noise on the other end, and Baxter's voice cracked.

"No . . . he's . . . he's not breathing. No heartbeat. He's dead. He's *dead!* And I did it!"

"Okay, Mr. Baxter," she replied as smoothly as she could, slipping into her mother mode. "Help is on the way. Someone will be there to help in just a few minutes. The police will be there soon. Will you let them in?"

"Y . . . yes," he replied. "I'm in a lot of trouble, aren't I?"

"The important thing, Mr. Baxter, is to get you the help that you need."

There was a pause, then a sniffle on the other end of the line.

"He deserved it, you know."

Here was a twist. Baxter had all along expressed remorse for what he had done, but now he was insinuating that the death of his friend was justifiable.

"How so?" Patricia replied.

"He's a manipulator. Always has been. But now—" He let out a sob, but immediately choked it back. "—he just got so damned *greedy!*"

"Mr. Baxter, I—"

"He's greedy! He's greedy . . . and . . . and *mean.* He was the one getting all of the attention. Him, him, *him!* It was *me* who started everything. If it wasn't for me, he wouldn't even have a job! And he pays me back by trying to be the star. He . . . he became a hog. A greedy attention hog."

"What do you mean by 'attention'?" Patricia asked, wondering how long it would take for the police to arrive. Baxter had lost it, and if he was capable of doing something like killing his partner, he was certainly capable of hurting someone else—or himself, for that matter.

At least he had the sense to call 911, Patricia thought.

"You know. We work together. *Worked* together. We got along great for years. Now it's over. It's over . . . and I . . . I'm *glad.* I really am. Oh, I know it was wrong to do what I did. But I'm free now. I'm free from his domineering attitude and his ordering me around. *'Do this Andy,'* and *'do that.'* He wanted me to do things that I just couldn't do! It was maddening!"

Okay, Patricia thought. *We won't go there.*

"Okay, Mr. Baxter, it's all right. Tell me . . . are the police there yet?"

"I . . . I don't see them."

"Okay. Just take it easy, and they'll be there soon to help you."

"Am . . . am I going to jail?" Baxter asked meekly.

Well, if you bashed in the skull of your friend, that's usually what happens, Baxter-Buddy, Patricia thought. But of course, that wasn't what she said.

"The important thing right now is that we want to help you, Mr. Baxter. Will you let us help you?"

"Y . . . yes," Baxter squeaked.

That was good. At least Baxter didn't appear like he would be confrontational when the police arrived.

"Okay," Patricia said. "They'll be there any minute."

Baxter let out a deep sigh. "It's over, I guess. We sure had our fifteen minutes of fame."

"Mr. Baxter?"

"You know. Our time at the top. Andy Warhol said that we all get fifteen minutes of fame. Or is it seconds? I don't know. We were the best, you know." His voice gloated with the glory of days gone by. "People laughed and laughed. They loved us. It was supposed to be an act, you know. Just an act."

"What do you mean, 'act'? Is that what you did? You're an actor?"

"Y . . . well, no. Kind of, sort of."

"What is it that you do?"

"Ventriloquism."

"You're a vent—"

A breeze of realization came over her as the man interrupted.

"It was an *act!*" he screamed. "That's all it was. That's all it *ever* was!" Anger steamed in his voice. "But he took it so *serious.* Some of those things that he said were just plain mean. *Hurtful.* He was just a dummy to begin with, and now, that's all he is. A dead dummy!"

"*Hel-lo,*" Patricia said quietly, covering up the mouthpiece so the caller wouldn't hear. She waved to Ben. She mouthed the words *pick up* to him, and he nodded and pressed a button that allowed Patricia's conversation to be heard through his earpiece.

This guy's lost it, she thought. Baxter is insane.

She looked at Ben, shook her head slowly, and twirled her index finger around her ear. Ben nodded.

"Mr. Baxter, if I'm hearing you correctly, you are a ventriloquist, and you—"

"Yes," Baxter said, interrupting. "I killed him. His head splintered like a board. I know. I heard it. Cracked just like a big hunk of wood."

Patricia raised her eyebrows and glanced at Ben. Ben shook his head and removed his earpiece, then stood up. He looked at Patricia and raised an invisible coffee mug to his lips. Patricia responded with several quick nods.

"Okay, Mr. Baxter. If you—"

"They're here, I think," Baxter interrupted.

There was a brief moment of silence, and then Patricia could hear knocking.

Thank God, she thought. *This looney-toon is gonna be locked up in Portsmouth for a long time.*

Portsmouth Wellness Facility was an old sanitarium in Michigan's upper peninsula that now served as a half-prison, half-psychiatric ward. It had been the focus of a lot of media attention, being that it housed one of the most notorious killers in recent memory. Patricia presumed that they'd have a place ready and waiting for Andrew Baxter.

"I've . . . I've got to go now," he said.

"Take care, Mr. Baxter."

There was a click on the line. Baxter had hung up.

Michigan State Trooper Allen Fidyorek and his partner were the first to arrive at the small apartment. At first, he had been informed that they would be investigating a possible homicide. But the last transmission from dispatch moments ago now said that it was probably a false alarm. They were required to investigate, regardless.

He knocked again. Moments before he'd heard a voice from behind the door, but now there was nothing.

"Mr. Baxter?" he said, knocking again. "Police, Mr. Baxter. Open the door, please."

Several silent moments went by. Fidyorek tried the knob. It turned in his hand, and the door swung open.

"Mr. Baxter?"

He remained just outside the door, peering in.

Nothing moved.

However, from where he stood, he could see a smear of blood on the wall near the kitchen, and splotches of blood on the carpet.

He removed his gun as he silently alerted his partner, who withdrew his own firearm.

"Mr. Baxter?" His voice was stronger, commanding.

There was no answer. Slowly, ever so slowly, he pushed the door open. His gun was ready, and he slowly swept it across the room, prepared for whatever would come.

Suddenly, he stopped. The door continued to swing open slowly, like the curtain at a movie theater.

"What in the hell—"

He lowered his gun and stared.

On the couch was a ventriloquist's dummy, staring blankly back at the two troopers. A telephone receiver sat on its lap, beeping that insane, rapid *beep-beep-beep-beep* when it's been left off the hook too long.

THE EXECUTION OF STEVEN MINARD

Truth be known, I found it strange to be the one not only covering the string of murders that plagued Michigan for the past several years, but also the only reporter allowed to interview Steven Minard on what would be his last night alive.

There were perhaps hundreds of newspaper reporters who wanted to be in my shoes, and, in fact, I'd been dogged by all of the major news networks, asking if I'd appear live, on camera, to discuss my interview with Minard. There was a carnival-like fascination around the rapidly approaching execution of the man convicted of what most certainly were the bloodiest, most violent murders in recent history.

The slayings began with Jacob Miller on September 7th, 1995. Miller, a prominent attorney in Grand Rapids, owned a summer home in Harbor Springs. His mutilated body was discovered there by his wife. He'd been sliced by a razor repeatedly; his skin bore long, thin lines where the razor had serrated his epidermis with the precision of a surgeon. They were straight, meticulous wounds, never crisscrossing over one another, not zig-zagging in jagged doglegs or sloppy slashes—which would have been the case if a victim was squirming and thrashing and all that. It was widely believed that the killer subdued his victims in such a manner that would render them immovable, unable to defend or fight back, not allowing them to struggle enough to shake the razor blade from its perfect, unerring course.

But the most appalling element of this brutal crime was the fact that his head had been completely severed, removed from his body, and placed in the commode like a wad of paper in the trash. The white porcelain bowl was stained with splatters of blood, flesh, and matted, gooey hair.

What puzzled authorities (among many other things) was the manner in which the victim had been decapitated. The cut was clean, and whatever had been used to slice through the neck region had been extremely sharp. All tissue and bone had been cut cleanly, as if done with great ease.

And there was a note from the killer, explaining why he had done what he had done, and that the death of Jacob Miller would only be the first of many. His reason for the murder, and those that would follow, was to call to attention the 'viciousness of our present humanity.' The killer explained that those who he deemed the most 'inhumane', the real 'savages' of this world, would be the ones he selected as victims. His reasons were often fantastic; one victim was a doctor at a children's hospital. A note was left saying that the victim made too much money, and should have shown his concern for children by donating a large portion of his salary . . . or by not accepting such a ludicrous figure in the first place.

And the murders *did* continue, just as the killer had warned. Always with the same brutality, always utilizing a razor to the skin, always placing the victim's head in the commode. Sort of the killer's way of saying that the world was going down the toilet, I guess.

My interest in the matter was heightened by the fact that I had covered the stories in the past, plus the coincidental fact that the man convicted of the murders (after he was finally apprehended) hailed from Indian River, Michigan . . . the same small town that I am from. That was years ago; I've worked for a small newspaper in Michigan's upper peninsula for nearly ten years now. I never knew Steven Minard, hadn't seen or heard of him. Still, I (and others at my office) found this coincidence a bit bizarre.

For several years the murders had a stranglehold on the entire state of Michigan. He struck at random, at places hundreds of miles from each other. Sometimes two weeks would go by between killings, sometimes several months would pass before another murder.

And there were always letters. The killer played with the police, toyed with the special investigators. The FBI had a task force set up exclusively for the capture of the perpetrator, and profilers from around the country had been at work to create a description of just who could possibly be behind the barbaric murders.

In the end, of course, they were all wrong.

The convicted killer didn't have any of the features or qualities that the profilers said he would. This, the 'experts' claimed, was due to his 'superior intelligence', his 'meticulous planning', and was the reason that he had remained elusive for so long. When they finally made an arrest, they realized how far off the profilers had been. The guy didn't come close in physical sketch or mental aptitude.

The string of terror came to an end in November, 2001. Steven Minard was arrested on an unrelated assault/rape charge when he confessed to the murders—all of them—and was sentenced to be the first to die under Michigan's newly-instituted death penalty. Minard was arrogant and haughty, claiming that the only reason he had been caught was because he had *allowed* it, that he was too smart for the authorities, that he'd made his point. He'd even twisted around his motive to include the death penalty itself, likening his own looming death to—and I quote here—"the continuing pit of filth that the inhabitants of the world were falling into." Whatever that meant.

There was no doubt in anyone's mind that Steven Minard was completely insane, and a danger not only to others, but to himself as well. He was ordered to be held in a special cell at Portsmouth Wellness Facility in Michigan's upper peninsula, about a two-hours' drive from the newspaper offices where I worked.

The Portsmouth Wellness Facility, in essence, has nothing to do with 'wellness' of any kind. Years ago, it had been merely a place where crazy people had been housed. The facility had originally been built not to hold dangerous criminals, but harmless individuals who had succumbed to the ravages of mental illness. Today, however, it is a holding tank for psychotics and crazies. Most are very violent criminals, all are in some way disturbed, and considered beyond rehabilitation. Minard would be right at home.

At least until his execution by lethal injection, which was scheduled for Wednesday, December 20th, 2002.

Tomorrow morning.

I had requested the interview; I never expected to get it. When the call from Portsmouth came through, and my editor said that it had been approved, that Minard himself had agreed, I was flabbergasted. Excited, of course. Every reporter in Michigan—and around the country—had wanted an interview with Minard. Portsmouth authorities normally didn't allow any, of course, but they had finally bowed under pressure at the last minute. Perhaps Minard had something to say to the families of his victims, maybe he got religion and wanted to repent. Kind of a final 'come to Jesus' epitaph. Regardless, I think that the Portsmouth folks thought that it would be good publicity to allow one interview, the last that Minard would ever give. Especially since Minard was to be Michigan's first person executed under its new (and very hotly contested) death penalty law.

For several reasons (which will I will explain shortly) I was more than *thrilled* to be the appointed interviewer.

I was told to be at the front gate of Portsmouth at seven o'clock that evening, not a minute before or a minute after. Have proper ID, prepare to be searched. The usual drill. But most important: don't be late. One minute after seven, and I wouldn't be allowed through. Prompt fellows, those folks at Portsmouth.

The day was unusually cold and windy. Snow blew in from Lake Superior, and the temperature struggled to reach five degrees. I wore my long underwear beneath my jeans and chamois shirt, and I packed an extra hat, a spare pair of gloves, and a snow shovel—just in case. The snow was late this year and there was only a foot or so on the ground, which was odd. Usually by the middle of December we have several feet of the damned stuff.

The drive from my office was uneventful, except for a rather large black bear that lumbered across M-28 late in the afternoon. I damned near hit the thing, which would have really screwed things up.

I arrived early and wound up putzing around the tiny town for twenty minutes to burn up the clock. Portsmouth is a small town with one main street boasting a dozen or so stores. There are two gas stations at both ends of town, several bars and restaurants, and a curious old building that looked like it could have been a theater at one time. No doubt the town's largest employer was the sprawling 'hospital' that lay a half-mile from the outskirts of the village.

At six fifty-eight, I pulled into the long, spiraling drive that wound through the woods. The enormous iron bars that circled the facility came into view, and I could make out the newly-affixed razorwire that was wound along the top. There had been a few embarrassments several years ago; the razorwire had been added to alleviate further problems and calm the townsfolk.

I stopped at a place where the large iron gate cut across the blacktop. Two brick buildings sat on both sides of the road, and I could see shadows moving behind barred windows. Seconds later, a portly man with a gray uniform came over to my car and asked for some identification, which I had ready. He looked over my driver's license a moment, then handed it back to me. Then he asked me to shut off the car, and to *please exit the vehicle, sir.* It all seemed much too official, much too structured. A simple *can ya get outta the car?* would have sufficed.

For the next ten minutes, he went over every inch of my car, searching for whatever people like him search for. Weapons, keys, files in cakes, whoopie cushions in my back pocket . . . I don't know. He didn't find anything, of course, and finally ordered me back into my car. Then he walked back to the building.

On the other side of the fence, a brown and white Crown Victoria with the words *Portsmouth Safety* emblazoned on the doors approached. The driver got out, walked over to one of the buildings, chatted with someone, then returned to his car. He then turned the car around and stopped. This, apparently, was going to be my escort.

The huge iron gates swung open, and I was waved through. A man on my left motioned that I was to pull forward, and I followed the Victoria as it made a painstakingly slow trek along the winding blacktop. I glanced into my mirror and was surprised to see yet another cruiser right behind me. Apparently, no one was taking any chance with the reporter. I thought that this precaution was because both Minard and I were from the same town, that maybe they thought we were old pals and that I would try and pull something. But, then again, I figured if they would have had any doubts about my intentions they never would have allowed the interview in the first place.

Why had I been chosen to conduct the final interview of Steven Minard? I'm not sure. I think that it was simply because I had been fortunate enough to scoop all of the stories. I've always had a knack for being at the right place at the right time. And with this particular string of murders, I'd been successful in learning a lot of 'inside' info that the press wanted (not to mention the public, who devoured my stories, gaped in horror . . . and wanted more) and I became the 'expert' reporter, kind of the Bob Woodward of the case.

I followed the cruiser to yet another large, iron fence topped with razorwire serpents. Sort of a fortress within a fortress. A gate opened up, and all three of us—my Grand Prix and the two cruisers—entered slowly. The gate closed behind us, and I remembered thinking that there was no way someone was going to get in or out of this place if the Portsmouth authorities didn't want them to.

Which was precisely the reason Steven Minard was kept here. Not only did they not want him to escape, but there were also several people who had threatened to get in and sort of 'take care' of Mr. Minard before his scheduled execution date. He sure picked the wrong victims, that was for sure. A lot of people wanted to see Minard die, and *now*. Even folks who were vehemently opposed to the death penalty agreed that Steven Minard should probably be the exception.

I parked and locked my car in a sparsely-filled lot. One of the men got out of his cruiser and led me across the blacktop and up the steps of an enormous old, brick building. The door was new; it was gun-metal gray and probably weighed a thousand pounds. He pressed a keypad and a buzzer sounded. After a few moments there was another buzz and a heavy *click* that said the door was now unlocked.

The uniformed man opened the door and ushered me inside.

Thirty minutes later, after I had been briefed regarding the do's and don'ts, I was led from the small room in which I had been confined, to a long corridor. Doors with tiny rectangular windows lined either side of the hallway, and I deduced that this was where the violent offenders, the worst of the worst, were held.

Not so for Steven Minard, however.

Portsmouth had considered him an at-risk individual from day one, placing him in his own cell in a small, dusty-blue brick building that was detached from the main structure. This kept other prisoners from contact with him, and it kept Minard in a place where he could be of no danger to others. He was, I had been informed, allowed to go outside (under heavy guard) for twenty minutes a day. These brief excursions required the shackling of his arms and legs. Steven Minard, I was told, was *not* leaving Portsmouth for any reason—not until tomorrow morning, anyway, when he would be sent on a one-way trip to the Great Beyond.

We exited the long corridor through a series of doors that were opened by guards behind glass panels. None of the guards seemed to pay particular attention to us, but I did see one man grinning and shaking his head as he looked away.

After passing through the last door, we were outside in an area that was the size of a basketball court. There was quite a bit of snow here; more so than we had farther north. A shoveled walk tunneled to a barren-looking building, and a plowed track wound around the white arena in a large circle. Gray walls grew around the perimeter. Once again, the familiar cyclones of razorwire coiled above the wall like steel grapevines. This was where the prisoners go for exercise, but today I think most of them opted to remain in their cells.

Upon entering the small building, my escort stopped at the door. I was instructed to go inside, where yet another uniformed officer waited. He sat behind a drab, off-white desk. Above and behind him, television monitors that must have been at least thirty years old displayed black and white images of the outside perimeter of the small brick building. One screen showed a small hallway that seemed to go nowhere. Upon a closer look, I could see that there was actually a door at the end of the corridor. This, I would soon find out, was where Portsmouth's most infamous houseguest was lodged.

The guard behind the desk came around and asked me a series of questions. Whether I'd ever met the prisoner before, if I was related to him in any way, do I have any relatives that are related to Minard, has anyone I've known had contact with him, to the best of my knowledge. The man asked me to take off my shoes (this was actually the *second* time for this, the first being upon my entry into the main building) which I did without protest. He poked and prodded at them like he just may, in fact, find an Uzi between the sole and the heel.

He asked that I untuck my shirt, and, upon doing so, he discovered my long underwear.

"Cold out, eh?" he said.

"Yeah."

"Shirt off. Pants off, too. You can leave on the skivvies."

I complied without complaint, knowing that it would be useless to do so. This was the big house . . . you do what the housekeepers ask. Or else.

He fingered through my pants and shirt, found my *BIC*

pen, and placed it on the counter. Then he patted me down. Satisfied that I didn't have a kilo of heroin in my crotch, he nodded toward my discarded jeans and shirt. I put them back on.

He picked up my pen. "Against the rules," he said, in a tone that I thought was a bit puffed up, like this guy didn't get to give orders to anybody from the 'outside' very often, and he was going to exercise his power, you betcha.

I frowned. "I'm here to interview him. How am I going to write if I don't have a pen?"

"You should have thought about that."

"I never think twice about taking a pen anywhere."

He held the pen and eyed it like a scientist inspecting a rare microbe. "Aw, hell." He handed it back to me. "He's shackled to the wall. As long as you don't get too close to him. In the hands of someone like him a pen would be a pretty dangerous weapon."

I took the pen and looked at it. "Yeah, I guess you're right," I said, placing the clear plastic *BIC* into my front pocket. "I'll make sure he doesn't get his hands on it."

"You know what he wants?" the guard asked.

I gave him a puzzled look, but I didn't say anything.

"You know. For his last meal in the morning. You know what the som' bitch wants?"

I shrugged.

"Chuckie Cheese. Chuckie *fuckin'* Cheese. Like we got a Chuckie Cheese within a hundred miles." He rolled his eyes. "Warden says he's gettin' a biscuit, hash browns and a fried egg. One cup of coffee, one glass of orange juice. That's it. Chuckie *fucking* Cheese. Can you believe that, eh?"

I shook my head and made one of those laughs through my nose that wasn't quite a snort.

"Come on. Time to meet the dishonored guest."

And with that, he pulled a set of keys from his pocket

and started down the short hall. I followed until he stopped. Then he peered through a thin viewing window, leaned back, and inserted the key. There was a loud *clunk* as the tumblers disengaged. He grasped a silvery knob the size of a grapefruit, and the huge iron beast slowly swung open.

"Minard. Company's here. Hope you dressed for the occasion."

"Oh, that's great," a pleasant voice replied. "Send him in, send him in."

The guard took a step back and leaned close to me. I still couldn't see Minard yet, and I think that's what the guard wanted.

"Remember. Sit down on the bench on the far wall. Don't get up until you're ready to come out. When you're finished, close this door behind you. I'll hear it. And Christ . . . be on your guard. His legs are shackled, and both hands are shackled to the wall."

"Both hands?" I asked.

"Warden thinks that he might try and do himself in before we get a chance to. You know . . . spoil all the fun."

"Yeah, sure."

"I'm waiting," I heard the pleasant voice say.

"While you're in here, you're pretty much on your own. State don't allow cameras in this room with all that invasion of privacy shit. Just use your head. I'm fifteen steps away, but a lot can happen before I get here."

I nodded. "Has he ever hurt anyone? I mean . . . during his time here?"

"Nope. But we don't let him get near anybody, neither. Just because he hasn't, doesn't mean he won't. 'Member . . . he ain't got nothin' to lose. He's toast in the morning."

The guard walked past me and stepped into the hall. I took a deep breath, turned, and went into the small room to face the man that the Los Angeles Times called *the most sadistic killer of the decade.*

What shocked me most about Steven Minard was his appearance of absolute innocence. The guy didn't look like he would rip off a Cub Scout, let alone torture and murder some twenty people. His hair was blonde, thinning along the upper sides. I'm sure he had one of those hurricane holes at the rear top of his head, the kind that seem to swirl the hair counter-clockwise around a thinning patch of skin. I've got one, but I'm able to cover it up if I comb around it just right.

His face and arms were a pale, sickly yellow; wax and smoke. Childhood acne remained present in the numerous craters that scarred his cheeks. His teeth were yellowed, not quite so much as his skin, but yellow nonetheless. He had a thin, caterpillar-like growth beneath his nose that *might* have been a mustache.

And he was *tiny*. The man that sat on the cot on the opposite side of the room had a small frame. I was sure that, if he were to stand, (which he couldn't) he would barely hit the five-foot mark. Quite frankly, Steven Minard didn't look like he had the makings of a flag football player, let alone a psychopathic killer. And it was perhaps even harder to believe (at least from my point of view) that this very innocent-looking man would be strapped to a table twelve hours from now and given a shot of life-ending juice.

"Hi," he said. "You must be the guy."

"Tom Caldwell," I said, nodding.

"Hi," he repeated. "I'm Steven."

I sat down on a thin bench opposite the sparse cot.

"So you're the guy that gets to interview the infamous killer," he said, grinning like an eight-year-old on Christmas morning. "Pretty good for your career, I bet."

I managed a smile, but it was forced. I've always thought I had a knack for instantaneous character discernment; rarely are my first instincts incorrect. And as

I tried to assess the individual six feet away with his smarmy, boyish face, I was pretty certain of one thing: Minard was an asshole.

"Thanks for your permission," I said.

He nodded and raised his eyebrows. "Hey, no problem. Hope you get what you want."

These words would hang in the air and buzz in my ears until I would exit the building an hour later.

"Mr. Minard, I—"

"Steve," he interrupted. "Call me Steve."

"Yes. Steve."

"Better. Less formal, you know."

"Yes. I have a few questions prepared, but I'd like to begin with—"

"First, let me say something," he interrupted again. "Then you can take it from there."

I nodded. "Okay," I replied, pen in hand. "Go ahead."

His smile widened, drawing his eyes to a thin squint. He shook his head. There was an odd sort of superiority to his face, some kind of haughty confidence, like he had been holding a trump card. I could almost see him extending his hand and placing the card on an imaginary table as he said:

"I didn't do none of'em."

I was a bit surprised to hear this, but I really had no interest in the fact. I pretended to write the phrase down, word for word. Then I looked up at him. He was still grinning, and it made me want to slap that stupid expression right off his face.

Then I *did* hit him . . . with two words he did *not* expect to hear:

"I know."

I spoke the words with a gentle, assuring nod. I was very matter-of-fact, and my face remained expressionless and cold. The truth is, as most know, often very cold. Frigid, in fact.

His grin began to fade, and he looked puzzled. Suddenly, aware that his expression was betraying his own confidence, he laughed.

"Of course you do," he said.

"I do," I reaffirmed with two short nods. "I believe you."

He blinked. I had caught him off guard.

"You . . . you *do?*"

"Yes, I do." I didn't tell him that, five seconds after meeting him, I *knew* there was no way he could be responsible for the heinous crimes he had supposedly perpetrated. I certainly didn't know where he was going with his statement, but I was going to let him roll with it. I undeniably wanted to hear why he had confessed to crimes that he hadn't committed. And one thing was assured: the next hour was going to be pretty interesting—for *both* of us.

"So . . . *why?*" I asked. "Why would you admit to doing something that you didn't do—especially when you knew of the possibility of a death sentence?"

Minard grinned. I had given him what he wanted: my attention. One of the most powerful drugs in the world.

"I did it," he began, "for the same reason anyone does anything. I did it for the fame. For the publicity. I got to *be* somebody."

He held his grin, searching my eyes for a reaction that I was not going to give him. I would, however, follow along the conversational path that he wanted me to walk. So I bit into him a bit more.

"That's a bit excessive, don't you think?" I asked.

"Not in the least. I was already going to prison before I confessed to the murders, and I decided that if I was going to be locked away, then I was going to at least make it worth everybody's while."

"Who's 'everybody'?"

"You know. People. The media. The cops. I was all over the news. Now they're talking about making a movie about me." He said this with such boyish enthusiasm that I *did* manage a bemused smile, which pleased him immensely.

"Just imagine! A *movie!* About what I did!"

"But you just said that you didn't commit the crimes."

"Oh, I did a few. I did them two rapes that I got busted for. There were a few other things that they threw out. But everybody *thinks* I did them other murders! I'm famous, you know."

"You're famous, but you're also going to die very soon, Mr.—Steven. That seems like an unbelievable price for fame."

"Does it?"

"Yes. To me it does."

"Then why do suicide bombers blow themselves up on busy streetcorners in the middle east? What makes a bunch of crazies fly jets into buildings?"

"Religion had nothing to do with the murders of those people," I stated. "You can't compare the two."

"Sure you can."

He paused and looked at me. Clearly, he wanted me to dig. He had no intention of simply offering information; he wanted me to play an interactive, attentive part of the conversation. I had no choice but to prod.

"How?"

"Suicide bombers want the same thing I want," he said. "Attention. Publicity. Fame. To make their mark in the world. They want to be remembered. One man's terrorist is another man's patriot."

"Is that what you are? A terrorist?"

I was allowing him to lead me, and he relished the

position I had granted him.

He shrugged. "I'm whatever. That's not really important. What's important is the fact I'll be remembered. I'm infamous."

"And, all the while, the person responsible for the murders has eluded captivity. He's free to continue killing."

"But he hasn't."

Minard was correct. Since his arrest, the killer hadn't struck again . . . which, of course, would have made Minard's confession inadmissable.

"So, there have been no more murders since your arrest. What if the killings begin again? Don't you feel the least bit responsible?"

At this, Minard's smile grew, and wrinkles formed around his cheeks. I had most certainly hit upon something; I could almost hear the hammer smack the anvil.

"That's exactly what I want," he replied, his voice dripping with arrogance. "I want to die letting people know that the real killer is still out there. That he hasn't been caught.

"And you know . . . it's been *perfect*. Not one murder has been committed since I was caught. The real killer could have screwed things up for me if he'd done someone else, but he hasn't."

"Why do you think he hasn't?" I asked.

Minard frowned, looked at the yellow ceiling, then looked at me. "I dunno. Maybe he was tired with the routine. When someone like me came along, he probably couldn't believe his luck. Maybe he thought that they were getting to close to him, and, now that the cops thought they had their man, the heat would be off him. He could relax."

"But over a year has gone by. Don't you think the killer would have struck again?"

Minard nodded. "I think he will. I *know* he will. He'll

wait for me to be juiced, then *whamo!* He'll grate his next victim into cheddar cheese and slam dunk their noggin in the ol' bowl. It'll scare the shit right out of everyone. When they thought they had their man, they'll realize that they'd been played with all along. And the killer will still be out there. Don't you see?"

I nodded assuredly, but, in truth, I hadn't a *clue* what Minard was talking about. I'm no shrink, but even I could see that this guy's head was more than simply screwed up.

"Yeah, I see," I lied.

"It's a great story," Minard said. "You'll go back and write your article and tell everyone that I said I didn't commit the killings. No one will believe me, of course. But I'm willing to bet that the killer is going to strike, and soon. *You'll* be famous, too!"

I managed a slight grin, just enough to allow him to think that this pleased me. In reality, I was becoming more and more repulsed by Minard with every passing minute. Plus, I couldn't see how the authorities had convicted such a mindless idiot for crimes that had taken a lot of thought and planning. I doubted Minard could plan a trip to the market, let alone a murder like the ones he had been convicted of.

"I must say that I feel very little remorse for you," I said coldly.

"That's fine," he said with a careless shrug. "I'm sure a lot of people feel the same way."

"I'd even go as far as to say that I'm going to be happy to see you die."

He smiled, but he picked up a flicker in my eyes that made him uneasy. His grin faded entirely. Perhaps, in that moment, he came to grips with his mortality. He had an expression that was both fearful and confused, like he was trying to pry into my soul but couldn't. A ray of sunlight speared through a dark cloud; Minard had never been so blinded, yet so fully seeing. At that moment, he realized that I hadn't been truthful to him at all, that I had simply commiserated with him to lead him on, to get him talking. All the while he had thought that he was leading me, that I was hanging on each word he spoke. Perhaps he realized he had been duped; I don't know.

I *do* know, however, that it was the last time I saw Steven Minard alive.

I walked out of the cell and closed the heavy door behind me. The guard was already on his way to escort me out, and he locked the door.

"Get your story?" he asked as we walked to the front room.

"Yeah."

"He's a nutcase, huh?"

"Yeah, he sure was," I said, shaking my head. "Thank you for your help."

"Sure."

He said nothing more as I exited the building. Outside, another guard escorted me to the main complex. The process of getting out was much quicker than getting in, and within five minutes I was on the highway, wondering what people would think when the story finally hit the morning papers.

EPILOGUE

Tom Caldwell had just pulled out of the gas station in Mackinaw City and merged back onto southbound I-75. He turned on the radio. A live news conference was in progress, and he fiddled with the dial, then turned the volume up. He recognized the voice as that of Sheriff L. Herb Brinley of the Mackinaw County Sheriff's Department.

"The mutilated body of convicted mass murderer Steven Minard was discovered in his cell last night, less than twelve hours prior to his own execution."

Cameras clicked and tiny motors whirred. A murmur rolled through a small crowd.

Tom smiled.

"A guard from the Portsmouth Wellness Facility found the remains of Minard in his cell. He had been decapitated, and his head placed in the commode. We found a tiny razorblade concealed within a ballpoint pen. Also discovered was a two-foot wire with thumb rings on each end, constructed of what is believed to be surgical steel. Other items discovered were a pair of bloodied long underwear, found in Minard's cell. This pair of long underwear did not belong to Mr. Minard. A typewritten note was left by the killer, found on the floor

next to the body. Because of certain clues left in the note, we now believe that Steven Minard had nothing to do with the murders he had been previously convicted of, and we are focusing on newspaper reporter Tom Caldwell, who had interviewed Minard only twenty minutes before he was found dead. Caldwell has since been missing, and we have instituted a statewide manhunt."

More cameras clicked, and several raised voices blended like soup. Tom reached out and turned the radio station to the Cheboygan AM band. Frank Sinatra sang *Witchcraft.*

It had been easier than he expected. There had been a tense moment when the guard had threatened to take away his pen, which concealed the tiny, inch-long razorblade. The deadly surgical steel wire had been carefully concealed in his leather belt, and the guard had only given the item a casual once-over. It had taken him less than two minutes total to stuff a sock in Minard's mouth, where he lost consciousness after only a half-minute. Caldwell then removed his own shirt and pants, uncapped the pen, and went to work.

In less that a minute he was finished with his special brand of art. He had removed the steel wire from his belt, placed his thumbs in the rings, wrapped the silvery thread around Minard's neck, and pulled. The fine steel cut through flesh and muscle like warm cheese. Tom's long underwear had been bloodied; these he stripped off and pushed beneath the cot. Then he slipped quickly into his jeans and chamois shirt, snaked his belt through the loops, took one last look around the bloody cell, and left.

Actually, it had been so damned *easy.*

Tom turned the radio up and drove on, smiling as the sun faded in the western sky, wondering where the killer might strike next. Even *he* didn't know just yet.

But it'll be soon, he thought, as he whistled along to the Sinatra tune.

It'll be soon.

About the Author

Christopher Knight's first book, *ST. HELENA*, first published in 1998 exclusively as an audiobook, was an instant regional bestseller. Written and performed by himself, the 3-hour epic included dramatic music and stunning sound effects. The following year it was made available as a trade paperback, along with his second novel, *FEROCITY*. The first printing of both books sold out in a record three months. *THE LAURENTIAN CHANNEL*, along with the psychological thriller *BESTSELLER*, have fared equally as well. *SEASON OF THE WITCH* is his first compilation of short stories. Read excerpts of selected Christopher Knight books at:

www.audiocraftpublishing.com